T0067091

My Mother's Secrets II:

A Second Chance

Tina Trumble

AuthorHouse™
1663 Liberty Drive
Bloomington, IN 47403
www.authorhouse.com
Phone: 1 (800) 839-8640

© 2015 Tina Trumble. All rights reserved.

No part of this book may be reproduced, stored in a retrieval system, or
transmitted by any means without the written permission of the author.

Published by AuthorHouse   03/12/2015

ISBN: 978-1-5049-0078-2 (sc)
ISBN: 978-1-5049-0077-5 (e)

Print information available on the last page.

Any people depicted in stock imagery provided by Thinkstock are models,
and such images are being used for illustrative purposes only.
Certain stock imagery © Thinkstock.

This book is printed on acid-free paper.

Because of the dynamic nature of the Internet, any web addresses or
links contained in this book may have changed since publication and
may no longer be valid. The views expressed in this work are solely those
of the author and do not necessarily reflect the views of the publisher,
and the publisher hereby disclaims any responsibility for them.

1

Awakening

Spinning, dizzy, the darkness within me and all around me. I search for the field where I had just seen my mother, but it is gone. I hear nothing, I see nothing, I feel nothing. I do not know how long I have been here, where here is or how long I will remain. I feel as if I am floating, above or below where I need to be. Suddenly there is a tiny dot, I can see it I rush toward the dot, its tiny circle growing and growing. The pain, I can feel the pain now. In the pain there is awareness and an awakening. I stay with the pain. The pain is more comforting than the nothing. I was afraid of the nothing, the darkness. It reminds me of my nightmares that once plagued me faceless and unknown. I hear Jimmie, and he is talking to someone. His words are soft and calm. I am OK. Jimmie is here and I am OK. I try to wake, but my eyelids are heavy. I try harder willing myself to stay awake.

I hear another voice. A woman's voice, "We're going to get you up now" she says. A strange smell wakes me, my eyes wide. I look around at my surroundings. The hospital, I knew that. My mind becomes aware, my babies. My boys, Jimmie sits in a chair on the other side of the room. There are two little hospital beds on wheels in front of him. He is holding one of the babies. I look at the woman who is holding my arm.

"You awake?" she says. I nod or think I do. I want to see my babies. I sit up, the woman helping me. She wraps my arm around her; another woman takes my other arm and pulls the IV pole. They assist me walking into the bathroom. "How are you feeling?" The nurse asks. "Fine" I almost cough out. Then the coughing begins. "It's from the anesthesia, here hold this pillow over your belly, so you don't rip your incision" the nurse hands me a pillow while I am sitting on the toilet. The nurse hands me a new pad to replace the blood soaked one. Then the women help me walk back and set me on the bed. "Hey" I say to Jimmie. He rises, bringing the baby with him. "Can I see him?" I ask him. He holds the baby so I can see. I want to hold him, but I am very weak. He is so beautiful, pink and new, sleeping and peaceful. Jimmie sets him in the tiny cart, returning immediately to my bedside. He brushes my hair out of my face and pulls a hair tie out of his pocket. He pulls my hair up for me. "We're back in the hospital again" I say. I am so tired. I want to see my babies. "How are you feeling?" he asks. I force a smile. His eyes search mine, they read something almost painful, but I can't be sure. The nurse comes in and puts some medicine into the IV line. "This may be a bit cold, but trust me you'll thank me later" she says. "I don't want any more medicine." I protest. I can feel the medicine run through my veins. "Lay down" she says "Remember, hold this over your belly, if you get up again. You'll have to get up and walk in a while, but you should rest for a while." I nod. I take Jimmie's hand. He holds my hand, his eyes still looking sad, I'm sure he's just tired. He squeezes my hand and sits in the chair next to my bed. I can feel the pain subside. "So, how are they?" I ask. "They're perfect, just like you. eight pounds six ounces and eight pounds three ounces. Shawn Edward and Ryan James." He whispers. "Twenty-one inches and twenty and one half inches, most women would have had a rough time having one baby that size and you had two!" Jimmie smiles, "How long was I out?" I ask. "A while about ten hours, everyone's been here and gone, I won't leave." Jimmie says kissing my hand. "Good" I say and hold the pillow over my belly as I cough. "You had some trouble" he says "You bled quite a bit, they had me scared for a while, but you're fine now. Thank God. I was so scared. I'm so glad you're awake.". I nod acknowledging his words, but sleep is taking me back out to its sea of darkness. I feel him kiss my head. I wake up and the nurses are going to make me walk. Jimmie is sleeping in a chair by the two babies. I lean on the nurses as they pull me from my bed. My legs feel light, the huge belly that inhibited my steps before has shrunk considerably. I find my strength and start walking, leaning on the nurses at first then less. We walk down the hall and back to the room. I walk pulling my IV to the babies. I don't dare try to pick them up yet. I just stare at them.

"You OK?" the nurse asks and I nod. She leaves the room. I stare at my sleeping boys. I touch ones soft pink cheek. They are perfect. I touch their tiny little fingers and their soft heads. They have a lot of black hair covering their heads. "Hi there" I say as one opens their eyes. "I'm your mom" I whisper, the baby looks at me, as if there is recognition in his eyes. The nurse comes back in. "You are going to try to breast feed?", She asks. I nod. She hands me a bunch of paperwork to look over. "Do you want to try? This one's awake" she says picking up the baby. Jimmie stirs at the movement. "What's up?" he asks the nurse. "We're going to feed this one" she says. I open my arms, taking the tiny baby. I stare into his blue gray eyes for a moment. He starts to wriggle and cry, I open my gown and attach him to my breast. He attaches and starts sucking. My breasts feel so heavy and almost painful. Jimmie sits next to me, watching our baby. I nursed Ashley and it really isn't something you forget how to do. The baby fed, I burp him and then the nurse hands us a tiny little diaper. I can't get over how small they are. The nurse is satisfied she nods "You got it" she leaves the room again. The baby changed, I hold him on my legs so I can stare at him. "What do you think? You ready Daddy?" I ask Jimmie. "They're great, tiny though, it's amazing" he says. He seems tired. "Which one are you?" I ask the baby. Jimmie says "This is Shawn, see I marked his foot" he pulls his tiny foot out of the blanket and shows me the red marker streaking the letter S. He tucks the tiny foot back inside the blanket. He walks over bringing little Ryan, pulling his tiny foot out and showing me the letter R he has written. I laugh.

The babies do look exactly alike. They have Jimmie's cute little nose. Their chins are exactly the same. Unless we pull out a measuring tape and find the one that is a half an inch shorter, there really isn't any way to tell them apart. Jimmie lays little Ryan next to Shawn. They are identical. I study their faces looking for something, anything to tell them apart, but I can't. What kind of mother can't tell their own children apart? Jimmie must read my thoughts. "They are identical; I stared at them for hours. That is why I wrote on their feet. I couldn't tell them apart, please tell me you can't either, I feel like a horrible father." He says. I shake my head. "I can't either. You're not a horrible father."

Jimmie smiles at my words and lets out a relieved sigh. "I'm glad you wrote on their feet, at least that way we know who's who" I say maybe with an air of sarcasm. "Let me lay them back down. You need your rest." He takes Shawn and then Ryan laying them in their little carts. He sits on the side of my bed stroking my forehead with his finger. "I love you" he whispers and kisses me. "I love you too," I reply.

We sit in the silent room, him just content to sit on the side of my bed while I rest. Suddenly and almost frighteningly one of the babies begins to cry, and then the other cries out too. I get up and pull my IV pole, Jimmie shakes his head. "I'll get them" he pulls both carts next to the bed. He hands me Ryan and I feed him, he fusses at first not wanting to attach, but finally he does. He holds Shawn soothing his cries. Soon both babies are back to sleep. The nurse comes in again "Did you feed the other one?" she asks, I nod. She writes it down on her clipboard. "You need to walk again" she says. Jimmie looks confused "She needs to rest, she's been through a lot. Leave her alone." He says his voice angry. "She needs to walk, walking helps get the anesthesia out of her system, gets her blood flowing." She explains to him. I get up with no assistance needed and pull my IV pole behind me as I walk to the end of the hall and back to my room. "She's tough" the nurse says as I sit on my bed again. I hold the pillow over my belly and lay back down. Jimmie nods to her and says "You have no idea." I smile and lay in the bed ready to sleep. Jimmie lays his head on my lap and I brush his hair with my hand. "They look just like you" I say to him. He smiles sleepy eyed "My mother said the same thing." We both sleep.

My stomach wakes me up, not the pain, or a crying baby, but hunger. I am starving. It is almost dawn. I can see the sunlight starting to peek through the blinds on the window. I pet Jimmie's sleeping head. He stirs "Good morning beautiful. How's my girl?" He says. "Hungry' I say. "How are you? You should get some rest, go home, and come back later.", He shakes his head at me. "I'm fine, you're the one that just had twins, you rest.". He is so sweet to me. However, I think that it will be a bit hard for him to nurse the babies. Besides, I won't be here too much longer, will I? Maybe one more day? The nurse comes in bringing my breakfast, she suggests we feed the boys soon, which is fine with me, I can feel that my milk has come in.

The day passes feeding the babies, the doctors and nurses coming and going. They remove my IV. The pediatrician comes and gives the babies the once over confirming what we already knew. That they are perfect and healthy. They will be circumcised later this afternoon. Liz comes in with Donna bearing balloons and flowers. Ashley and Heather come in with oohs and aahs and fussing over the boys. Ryan and Arthur come to visit, my father too. I am surprised to see that Ryan is the more emotional one this time. He is touched that Jimmie and I chose to name one of our boys after him. Many more visitors come: Ronnie from the bar, a few of Jimmie's friends from work, I even receive a bouquet of flowers from Tony Capella Sr. We take many photos and the boys are held and beloved by everyone. Jimmie is so proud. He hasn't stopped smiling. I am starving, I feel like I could eat a horse. After our guests leave, Jimmie and I sit waiting for our babies to come back from their minor surgery. "Are you going to stay again tonight?" I ask him. He nods "Yeah, I think I should don't you?" I really don't see the need for both of us to be here. He should go home, but I don't push it. "If that's what you want to do" I say almost too passively. He furrows his brow, "I want to be here, with you" he says adamantly. I nod. He's so weird. I don't even want to be here. I feel fine, I just want to take my babies and go home.

My bandage is off; my incision is just below my belly button. The doctor used glue and stitches instead of staples. I am happy about that. I had seen some pictures when I was researching what would happen during the cesarean. Some women have some terrible scars. He sees me eyeing my incision "Does it hurt?" he asks. I shrug "Only when I move........or breathe....or cough.....or laugh." "Why don't you take the pain meds?" he asks curiously. "I hate them, they make me sleep, they make me feel nothing, I don't know, I guess I would rather feel pain than feel nothing" I try to explain. "You are so........" he starts and stops himself, he takes my hand. I smile at him, "What? I'm so what?" He kisses my hand and stares at me a while. Then he smiles his little crooked smile, "You're so you." The nurse wheels our babies back in, they are both fast asleep. I get out of bed finding my bag. I find my thank you cards that I had stuck in when I packed and begin filling them out to our friends and family that came to visit. Jimmie nods off sleeping in the chair. The boys begin to cry and I change them both. Then I hold Shawn and feed him, laying Ryan across my legs. Then I feed Ryan then hold them both one on each shoulder until they are sleeping again. See, I can do it. Jimmie didn't even wake up, but now I can't get up either. I can't carry them like this and hold my pillow on my belly while I stand, so I just sit. I softly hum to my babies, rubbing their tiny little backs.

I am startled when I look up to see Jimmie staring at me. "Hey, sleep well?" I ask. He rubs his face, "They woke up?" he asks, I nod "I changed them both, and fed them, they are sleeping now.". He smiles "Are you ever going to need me for anything?". I shrug, "I do need you.". I don't know why he would feel any other way. He does so much all the time, what am supposed to do, tell him I can't handle my own babies? He picks up little Ryan and holds him to his chest. He sits beside my bed. "They are great, aren't they?" I say more than ask. He nods. "Yup. Just like their Momma." He smiles. I shake my head at him. "Just like their Daddy." I say and smile. He leans in and kisses my head again. My heart is so full of love for my babies and Jimmie. My eyes begin to tear. I blink them back. Hormones! We sit silently in the precious moment until our exhaustion overcomes us both and we fall asleep.

2

Finally home

Jimmie brings the truck around to the front of the hospital. The nurse wheels me down to the entrance in a wheel chair. Holding a baby in each arm, I let her push me through the halls. It's procedure or so they tell me. I am thrilled to be going home. We fumble adjusting the infant carriers to fit correctly, but we get it. Today is March second, I was supposed to have the boys today. Jimmie still opening my door, I get out of the wheelchair and grab one of the carriers throwing the blanket over the top to keep the cold air off the baby's face. He grabs the other one and inside the truck we go. Jessie greets us at the door. Ashley immediately removes little Ryan from his carrier. Heather removes Shawn and they retreat with the boys to the living room. I don't even get a greeting, not a smile, or a wave. "Hi there! Nice to see you too!" I say sarcastically getting a "Hi Mom" reply from Ashley. I put my things into the laundry and unpack my bag. I notice the dishes aren't done and begin to run the sink to wash them. Trysten comes into the kitchen, hugging me. "I'm so glad your back! I thought I was going to die of starvation." I giggle "your Mom hasn't been cooking for you?" he nods "she does, but you're way better at it." I mess up his hair and he runs up the stairs returning to whatever he was doing. Jimmie comes in his face red

"Really? You're going to do the dishes?" He says sounding angry. "They were here, the boys are fine, I was just..." I defend my actions but he cuts me off. "You are not the maid! Or the cook! Seriously Sara..." he yells at me and I am shocked. My eyes fill with tears, I am not usually this fragile, but I am tired, and I am sure my hormones are all out of whack. I throw the sponge into the sink and shut the faucet off. I walk hurriedly into the living room sitting next to Ashley on the couch.

Jimmie goes outside. I push the episode away and out of my mind. I watch Ashley looking into the face of her brother. She loves them so much. I take him from her, knowing I need to nurse soon. I take him into the nursery, changing his diaper and cleaning him up. He wakes and I feed him sitting in my rocking chair. After burping him I lay him in the crib turning on his mobile. Ashley brings little Shawn in and I do the same for him. I turn on the monitor and go into my bedroom to lie down. Ashley joins me on my bed and we watch TV for a while until I fall asleep.

I wake up hearing one of the boys crying, Ashley gets up and brings little Ryan in to me. I get up and change his tiny little diaper. He eats again and sleeps. "They don't stay awake much do they?" Ashley asks. I shake my head "They grow while they are sleeping." My mother always said that. These are the easy days. They cry, I change them, feed them and they sleep. Things are going to get much more complicated in the months ahead. So, for now I will enjoy that they sleep. Heather appears in the doorway to the hall "Dinner is ready" she whispers. Great I am starving. Ashley and I go into the dining room to see Jimmie setting mashed potatoes, chicken and stuffing casserole, and corn on the table. He even made dinner rolls. Aww, how sweet is he? "No one likes my cooking" Heather says grudgingly. "Come on Aunt Heather, we can't eat out every night" Ashley jokes. I raise my eyebrows at her she explains "Aunt Heather thinks cooking is either ordering out, going out, or macaroni and cheese.". "I made sandwiches!" Heather defends herself. Trysten and Tyler giggle. Jimmie nods his head. I don't let our eyes meet. I know he is trying to help, but he yelled at me for something as stupid as doing the dishes. "This looks delicious and I am starving, so let's eat!" I say.

We enjoy our dinner talking about the kids' school projects and Heather's job. Jimmie says "I have to go back to work on Monday, but I'm off until then, I might work a bit more on the upstairs rooms." I don't answer him. I just nod. I hear the babies down the hall and get up to go to them. I am changing Shawn when Jimmie comes into the nursery. "You've got bionic hearing, I didn't even hear them until you got up." I finish changing the baby and then feed him, Ryan wakes while Shawn is still feeding. "I'll get him" Jimmie says and changes him then takes Shawn from me, while handing Ryan to my other arm. With both boys back in their cribs we return to our dinner.

Heather cleans up, obviously taking notice that Jimmie isn't pleased with her lack of ambition. He's not as sympathetic to her as I am I guess. I return to my room, shower being very careful of my stitches. I crawl into bed and realize, I need to pump before I can sleep. I do. I use my electronic pump filling several bottles. Finally empty I can sleep; I rinse everything carefully and return to my room. Jimmie is lying in bed. I lift the sheets and climb in resting. He rolls to face me, but I am facing the wall. He puts his arm around me and kisses my cheek. "I love you, you know right?" He says. I nod. "Are you mad at me?

Don't be mad at me please." His voice high. I think we are both just tired and trying to adjust. I roll over shaking my head. "I'm not mad, thank you for dinner" I say and kiss him. He starts kissing me harder, I know where he wants this to go, but it can't. I pull away. "Eight weeks mister," I say and roll back over. He snuggles into me. "I know, but you are so damn sexy" he whispers. How? How in the world can he find me attractive right now? I am a complete mess! "Whatever!" I say poking his ribs. "What? You are. You're so beautiful. You don't see it.", He says. I fall asleep with him rubbing my shoulders.

I feel him get out of bed, and then I hear the babies crying. We go into the nursery each picking one and change them; he grabs one of my prepared bottles and warms it feeding Ryan while I nurse Shawn. Ryan rejects the bottle at first, but eventually takes it. Jimmie and I lay the boys down and return to bed, just to do it all over again, and again, and again. About every two to three hours the routine continues. At our 6am feeding I decide to stay awake while Jimmie goes back to bed. I start laundry and begin to cook breakfast for everyone. I eat a bunch of toast and eggs, I can't believe how hungry I am, I just can't seem to get enough to eat. Jessie comes out, begging to go outside, I let her out after punching the code on the door. I notice the amount of snowfall we had the night before. Everything is buried in a blanket of white. I would guess close to 2 feet of snow has fallen overnight. The porch is piled high. The steps are covered. Jessie barrels her gigantic body through the snow. Even she doesn't like being cold she goes as far as the ground and does her business turning back to the warmth of the house. Well, good thing no one has to go anywhere today.

Heather joins me for coffee at the counter. She seems so depressed; I cannot imagine that things are easy for her. "So, how have you been?" I ask. She sips her coffee and sighs "I'm alright, I have no energy. I don't know, guess it's the weather." We watch the sky as it drops even more snow onto the piles out the window. "You seem down" I say regretting it the moment the words cross my lips. She nods "I am I guess, I don't have to pretend I'm happy anymore, and it's good, you know not having to put on the act all the time, but I guess I just don't know how I am supposed to act now." I take her hand "Just be yourself, if you're down, be down. It's OK, just don't forget you've got a lot of people who love you." I hear one of the babies cry down the hall, I hurry to get him, before Jimmie wakes up.

The rest of the Saturday is spent mostly the same, taking turns with the babies, diapers, feedings, and the endless work that having a home with three older children and two infants brings. Jimmie works on the upstairs, plows the snow from the driveway, shovels the steps, and helps with the babies when he can. At dinner he asks "Do you mind if I go down to the bar?" I shrug my shoulders and reply "No, go ahead, have fun, drive safe." I never expected him to stay out until after 2am, and then come stumbling into the house waking up not only the babies, but the kids as well. I am not angry, just surprised. I wonder what brought this on, stress I am sure. I feel myself slipping into thinking he doesn't want all this responsibility. That he is going to abandon me like Paul, I push the thought out of my mind. I have to shoo him from the nursery when he comes stumbling in, leaning on the doorway. "Sorry I'm late" he says apologetically. "Shh" I whisper, "I just got them down again." He stumbles to the bed falling across it, his shoes still on. I take his shoes off for him and get his shirt off. He starts trying to maul me, I push him off "Stop it, you're wasted." He sighs heavily and rolls over and soon is asleep or passes out. I lay awake pushing the negative thoughts out of my mind. Why is he acting like this? Is he overwhelmed? Am I doing something wrong? Should I be more attentive? I don't have much time to think because Jessie starts barking, waking the babies again.

Sunday morning I wake Jimmie, I had promised Liz that I would bring the babies to the Sunday service, and also talk to the minister about their baptism and performing our wedding service this summer. I make Jimmie breakfast in bed, eggs, toast, bacon, and orange juice. I am sure that he will be hung over so I bring two aspirins as well. He sits up as I enter "Good morning, sorry about last night, I just got to talking and time ran away from me." I smile "It's fine, you're entitled. I made you some breakfast; don't forget we're going to church with your mother today." He smiles "I remember, are you sure you want to?" I nod and change into a nice pair of black pants and a button down shirt. The pants are a bit snug, but at least I can get into my pre-pregnancy clothes again. I don't tuck the shirt in, so my overhanging belly doesn't show through the shirt. "You are bouncing back pretty quickly there momma," Jimmie says smiling his little crooked sexy smile at me. "I guess" I say fussing with my shirt. "The babies aren't even a week old yet, give yourself some time" he mumbles through his half full mouth. I nod. I wake Ashley and prepare the diaper bag for our trip to church and then lunch at Liz's. Jimmie comes out when Ashley and I are just about ready.

The service is nice and light and pleasant. Everyone fusses over our little boys. Ashley proudly shows off her brothers to some friends from school. After the service the pastor gives me his card to call him to set up a good time to talk about the baptism and couples counseling for Jimmie and me. It's standard to go through a bit of counseling before a pastor will perform a service, or so Liz tells me. Lunch at Liz's is much of the same, everyone fussing over the babies. The Aunts and Donna fuss over me, "You've lost so much weight. I'm still trying to lose my baby weight, and my baby's about to graduate!" one of the Aunt's laughs. Shawn and Jimmie take to the back deck drinking their beer. Donna says "Shawn is so proud; he shows everyone his little nephews pictures on his phone." She holds little Michael so he doesn't fall on the babies sleeping in their infant carriers. I rock them both with my feet. "Jimmie's proud too, that's all he talks about, you, the boys, Ashley, the house. I'm glad he's happy." Liz shouts from the kitchen. "When's the wedding?" the other Aunt asks. I feel bad not being able to remember their names, I will have to listen very carefully until I figure it out. "Sometime this summer." I respond. "No date yet? Summer's only a few months away." She adds. I shrug "Well. I've been a little busy." Everyone laughs. I wasn't trying to be funny. Seriously, the wedding is something I have even really thought about. I make a mental note to discuss planning it with Jimmie later. Maybe this will be just what Heather needs. She loves all that stuff; I'll let her help me. That is if Jimmie still wants to go through with it.

3

Making the Plan

That evening as I snuggle up to a sleeping Jimmie I summon the courage to just ask. I will never know if I don't ask. "Hey, babe?" I whisper. He rolls putting his arm under his pillow. "Hmm?" he asks sleepily. "Do you still want to get married?" I whisper. "Of course I do" he whispers, but is now awake. "OK, it's just we haven't talked about it in a while, and you seem so different, I just wanted to make sure." I say and pull the sheets up to my neck. "Sara, I just" he sighs. "I'm an idiot" he says. "No, you're not, you're fine, I just wanted to ask. I shouldn't have said anything at all.", I say sighing and rolling over to face the wall. "No, I wasn't there for you when you were stuck at your Dad's during the hardest part of your pregnancy. I scream at you minutes after you come home from the hospital, I take off to the bar until closing, I'm sorry. I'm a jerk and I'm sorry.". He rants on "I don't know what I'm doing, I love you, I know that. Everything just happened so fast." I understand, everything did happen fast, but it didn't just happen fast to him, it happened fast to me too. I'm not denying that. "Maybe we should wait then" I say into my pillow. "Why? Do you want to? You don't want to...marry me now?" his voice almost breaking. "No, I'm not saying that." I roll to face him, his face is reddening and his eyes look glossy. "I'm saying everything happened so fast, us, me moving here, getting pregnant, you moving in, the fire, the house, we just had twins! We haven't even been together a year and I don't know I just think maybe you're a bit overwhelmed with everything" I say trying to comfort him, but instead I think I've made him angry. "You're right" he says his voice trimmed in anger. "I'm too overwhelmed to deal with it all" he stomps out of the bedroom. I guess I said the wrong thing. I don't get up to go after him, I don't have the energy to fight with him and besides the boys will be up soon for their 10 o'clock feeding. Jessie jumps on my legs just as I hear the monitor. I go into the nursery and change Shawn, then Ryan. I feed Shawn and hold him on my legs while I feed Ryan. This is going to get complicated as they get bigger. I might have to figure out a new system. I lay Shawn in his crib, with Ryan on my shoulder. Jimmie comes in and takes Ryan and lays him down. We stand over them watching silently as they sleep, then he takes my hand leading me back into our bedroom. "Sara, I'm not overwhelmed" he says and hugs me. "I am fine, you are my life, and nothing would make me happier than for us to run off and get married right now. You're mine, and I won't be happy until the world knows it." I squeeze him a little, "OK" I say. "So, are you overwhelmed with everything?" He asks I shake my head "Stupid question, you can handle anything, but you don't have to do it alone! I want you to tell me what you want me to do, you don't ever ask me to do stuff anymore. Why? I feel like my Sara is disappearing", he says. I'm not disappearing. "I just know that you're busy, with the house and working. I can handle it." I explain. He leans down and kisses my forehead "I know, but you shouldn't have to."

I decide to move on with the conversation turning back to if he wants to help with the wedding or if Heather and I should do it "So, when do you want to do it?" I ask. He pulls me away from him looking into my eyes "Right now? I thought the doctor said you couldn't?" Men! I shake my head "Get married. When do you want to get married?" I ask. He smiles "I don't know August I guess, the weather's good then." OK so we'll get married in August. We get back into bed and he snuggles up next to me. I've got a good two possibly three hours before the boys wake up and I intend on sleeping.

I wake when Jessie growls, signaling to me that she hears something, then I hear one of the babies fussing. I slide out trying not to wake Jimmie, but he stirs anyway. I walk into the nursery change Ryan and lay him back in his crib, then change Shawn. Jimmie comes in with a warmed bottle. He takes Ryan and I take Shawn. It is definitely easier doing this together. I smile at him from my rocking chair. He is cooing making inaudible noises to Ryan as he feeds him. He's so funny with the babies. He's like a really big kid himself. "So, August?" he whispers to me. I nod. "Big or small?" he asks. I shrug "What do you want?" I ask. "Big" he says. I nod. "A big church wedding, the whole deal, flowers, reception, where do you want to do that?" he asks. "What about doing it at the Waterfront? I'm sure they would have enough room? I'm not sure, I've been away for a while, you have any ideas?" I whisper. Shawn is still nursing, almost asleep. "Well, what about Lakeshore Golf Course? It's pretty there, you'd like it we could do some really nice pictures on the water and they have a big reception hall" he suggests. I've driven by it, but never really paid attention to it. "That would be nice," I smile. He places Ryan on his shoulder to burp him. He spits up all over him. Yuck. I don't think I'll ever get used to that. Jimmie doesn't even flinch. He wipes it up with a cloth and tosses it into the hamper. Then he continues rubbing little Ryan's back until he is sleeping again. Shawn is finished, I move him up to my shoulder and start to try to get him to burp. "So, band or DJ?" Jimmie asks. I'm not sure. "DJ that way we can play whatever" I say and he nods. He opens his hands for me to hand him the baby. I do. He continues to rub his back and then he gets him to burp and he lays him down. I button up my night gown and he holds his hand out to help me out of the chair. Two days ago I would have needed help, but I am really fine now. I take his hand anyway. "So...about the wedding, how many are we going to be standing up with us? I need to know whom you are thinking so we can get dresses and all that stuff, it takes time" I ask as we tiptoe back into our bedroom. "Well, there's Shawn. He'll be my best man of course, then Ryan, Arthur, my friend Mike from school, Trysten, Tyler and Owen. You'll have to have Britney be a flower girl or something and maybe Donna but that's up to you." He tells me. I think about it. I don't have many friends, just Deb. Heather will definitely be my maid of honor, then Ashley; I guess I'll have to ask Donna and Deb to keep the ushers and bridesmaids equal. "I'll ask her and I guess Deb too, I don't have any other friends" I laugh. He hits me with a pillow. "You've been a little detained lately." He laughs. I hit him with a pillow just to counterattack; soon we are having a pillow fight and laughing at one another. Finally we both agree we need to stop, mostly because we don't want to wake up anyone and Jessie is pacing the floor nervously. He grabs me and pulls me down to the bed. He pins me down with all his weight on me. "I love you",he says and kisses me. He runs his finger across my head and down the side of my face. "I love you" I say and push him off me before he crushes me. "Sorry, did I hurt you?" he asks. "No, I think I popped a stitch laughing though",I say inspecting my belly. He kisses my stitches one by one. I think there must be at least thirty. "I can't wait, until you're all better" Jimmie whispers lying next to me putting his arms around me. "Just think, we almost down to seven weeks left, maybe I'll make you wait until the wedding" I say joking. "Um.... it's a bit late for that. You're not serious?" he asks I don't say anything, I am just kidding but he obviously doesn't see that "I'll die! I'll kidnap you and take you to Vegas, I'll never make it..." he is being overly dramatic. "Oh my gosh! I'm kidding, you dork!" I laugh in the dark. He kisses my cheek "Not funny! When I am going to get my "I'm sorry I was mean to you card?", He asks mocking my voice. "I can be mean to you. You like it!" I say and he squeezes me "You're right, you can be as mean to me as you want."

The next morning, Jimmie's alarm wakes me, and I push on him to wake him up. "Noooooooo!" he moans, I know he's exhausted. He insists on getting up with me to help with the boys at night. "Good morning, sunshine! Time for work" I say. I go make him some coffee while he showers. He comes into the kitchen, "Good morning beautiful, how's my girl?" he says smiling. I hand him his cup and give him a smile. He kisses my cheek and takes his lunch. "Have a great day" I say as he leaves.

I wake up Trysten and Ashley for school. The babies wake up, I feed and change them, I bring them out in their pack and play setting them in the living room. "I could have helped you with that" Heather says coming down the stairs. "It wasn't heavy" I defend. "Still, you're still healing, don't push yourself" she scolds me. I make her a cup of coffee and we visit with the kids before their bus pulls up. "Love you have a great day" I say to Ashley she hugs me quick before grabbing her lunch from the counter. Heather waves at Trysten "Love you," she says, but he doesn't look back, just waves as he runs to get on the bus. Tyler is eating his cereal at the counter. She looks at him, "Love you buddy." He looks up at her "Love you momma" and continues to eat. I think she feels like Trysten is pulling away from her, it happens he's at a funny age. I went through it with Ashley a couple years ago. He'll come around. She has been so depressed lately, but I think I have just the thing that will cheer her up and pull her out of her funk.

"Hey, What do you think about helping me plan the wedding?" I ask her and her eyes light up.

"Really, I'd love to! Did you guys decide on a date?" she asks enthusiastically. I nod.

"August, no date yet, but I guess we need to pick one soon" I explain.

"OK, that's not a ton of time, less than six months, I can do it though. Where's the wedding?" she asks.

"The church probably, his mother wants it there" I say. She frowns.

"It's not his mother's wedding. It's yours." She says with an attitude.

I shrug. "It doesn't matter to me, wherever, I'm sure the church will be fine." I explain. She nods. "Reception?" she asks

"I don't know." I answer

"How many in the party? Have you planned nothing?" she asks.

"Well, I want you to be my maid of honor, Jimmie's got his guys all picked, I'm basically having every woman I know be a bridesmaid." I laugh "Shawn, Ryan, Arthur, his friend Mike, so I'll have you, Ashley, Donna, and Deb if she'll do it. He wants the boys too, Trysten and Tyler, and his little niece Britney. Oh and probably Dad will have to give me away." I rant on. She looks at me and shakes her head. "You and I have a lot of work to do." We spend the morning searching for invitations on line. I call the pastor to schedule the baptism for next month and the following week an appointment for couples counseling, pick the date of August eighteenth for the wedding. Heather allows me to peruse the web looking for the invites while she calls the golf course. She books the date and an appointment to do a walk through of the hall in April. I pick out a couple of the invitations and look to her for approval; of course she doesn't like either of them. I will ask Jimmie later. It's his wedding too.

"What colors are you using?" Heather asks. Who cares? Really, is this an important detail?

"I don't know" I answer. She shakes her head again. "Sara, you can't plan the wedding without picking out colors, the colors make everything the invites, the flowers, the decorations, the dresses, everything!" she whines. I nod. The phone rings

"Hello" I say.

"Hey, just calling to see how you're doing." Jimmie voice says.

"I'm great. Heather and I are talking about the wedding. Hey, what's your favorite color?" I ask him. Silence.

"Orange" He chuckles. I know he is referring to the coral shirt I wore on our first date, and the coral bikini that I wore last summer.

"You mean coral?" I snicker into the phone.

"Whatever! I'm glad you're doing OK, I love you see you tonight." He says.

"Love you too." I say and hang up. I can handle coral. It's pretty pinkish orange. It'll be great for a summer wedding. I tell Heather we are using coral for the color. She nods approvingly. "I can work with that." She says. She clicks away at the keyboard while I put laundry in the washer. I start washing the dishes and she summons me to look at the screen.

She has designed a gorgeous wedding invitation. It's white with a coral ribbon around, a gold script

James Edward Goodwin and Sara Elizabeth McCann would like to request your presence as they exchange their vows Saturday, August 18th at the Greenville Methodist Church at 11 a.m.. Reception to follow at Lakeshore Gold Course 1pm-7pm. Please R.S.V.P. with your enclosed card by July 20th.

It's nice and simple. I like it. I hear the boys and rush to take care of them. I'm getting married. I have three kids, and I'm almost thirty, but I am getting married. I cannot help but feel a bit excited.

4

The Rhythm

The month of March is spent taking care of babies, going to the pediatrician, feedings, diaper changes, laundry, meals, and dishes. I am so thankful I asked Heather for help with the wedding. She loves working out the details. She spends hours staring at floral arrangements and looking at dresses on the computer. She even is making my invitation list out for me. April is upon us in no time at all. We have a big family party after the boys' baptism at church. My father didn't attend, but that didn't surprise me. My birthday is this week. I haven't really had time to think about it, the only reason I remember it at all, is because my appointment with the ob. gyn. is the same day. The boys are now seven weeks old. They are getting so big. The anniversary of my mother's death was last week, I am not sure if anyone else thought of it. I did. I went to the cemetery and laid daisies on her grave. I know that is not where she is, in a graveyard. I feel her all the time, whenever I have a moment of peace. I can sense that she is with me, watching out for me and all of us. I love spring. I enjoy being home too. I am not sure if I am ready to go back to work, but that's something I will need to discuss with Jimmie. I love being home with the boys and Ashley. I enjoy working in the yard, being sure to bring the monitor outside with me, while the babies are sleeping. I love this house, and taking care of my family. I know I have plenty of money to get me through at least a few years. The wedding is a bit pricey for my taste, but Heather knows what she's doing and she is trying to keep the prices down. I have started going for walks with the boys in the double stroller, the air is getting warmer and it's good for them to get fresh air. Jimmie didn't like the idea at all. I promised him I would take my cell phone. I text him when I leave and when I get back. I am just about down to the size that I was pre-pregnancy. I have not gone down much in my top though. I had to buy all new bras. I was 34A before the babies and now I'm a C cup. I had to switch to formula feeding the boys. I just couldn't keep up with them. That's OK. The doctor assured me that it was fine. Now, Jimmie, Heather, and Ashley can help with the feedings, it makes things a bit easier.

The morning of my birthday Jimmie wakes me as he is getting out of bed. He whispers "Good morning beautiful" into my ear and kisses my cheek. "Morning" I mumble, barely awake. I look at the clock. It's 6am. The boys have slept almost five hours. It's the longest they've slept yet. I feel a bit of panic, I sit up fast and rush into their room. They are fine, both fast asleep. Jimmie comes in "Everything OK?" he asks concerned, probably because I practically ran in here. I nod "Yes, they just have slept a long time, I was a little worried.". He hugs me "They're getting older, they will sleep through the night eventually.". I sigh knowing he's right, then I go out to make him coffee. I open the can and see something shiny in the grounds. What is that? I reach my hand in a pull out a bracelet, its silver with all kinds of little charms on it. It's very pretty, two little baby shoes, a red gem heart, a little silver fish, a silver daisy charm, and a silver soccer ball. I turn on the light so I can see it better, I don't think I've ever seen Heather wear it and I know it isn't Ashley's. "Happy Birthday!" Jimmie says coming in from the living room. I look at him and realize, it's a gift, for me. I smile and walk over to him. I hug him and step up on my toes to kiss his cheek. "Thank you. You're so sweet." I say he helps me open the clasp and fastens it around my wrist. Then I make his coffee and start packing his lunch as he showers. I wake the kids and get their breakfast. I show Ashley my bracelet. "I already saw it" she says "Jimmie had me help him find a place to hide it." She giggles. Jimmie comes out and I hand him his coffee cup and lunch. I kiss him goodbye, but he hesitates before leaving. "Hey, the doctor's today right?" he asks. I nod "This afternoon" I say in response. He nods and then motions for me to follow him into the living room, I do. When we are at the door he says "So, as long as you're OK, maybe you and I can be alone for a little bit later?". I smile and kiss him again "It's my birthday, not yours!" I laugh "Yeah, as long as everything is alright, maybe you can run me a bath." I say flirtatiously to him smiling coyly. He smiles and turns to go. "Have a good day." I say as he leaves. He turns facing me "It's going to be a great day!". I laugh and return to the kids.

That afternoon I load the boys in their infant carriers and carry them out to my car. I enter the doctor's office parking lot, a carrier on each arm and fumble with the door. Someone else who is waiting opens it from inside for me. "Thanks" I tell the woman. She is a young girl, maybe eighteen with a big round basketball belly. She nods and assists me as I make my way in. "How old are they?" the girl asks. I respond "Seven almost eight weeks." She smiles at my little babies. Trying to be polite and mostly because I am curious I ask "How far along are you?". She rubs her belly, "Eight months, I'm due May twenty-third." I smile at her, she's so young, and she's here alone, I remember those days when I was pregnant with Ashley. The nurse calls "Kayla?" and the girl gets up to go in. I rock my babies with my feet until the nurse calls for me. I carry the carriers and set them down when the nurse motions for me to step on the scale. "109" she says. I follow her in, fumbling carrying the carriers down the hall. I sit on the bed and she hands me a gown to put on. She exits, and I change, waiting for the doctor to come in, Shawn wakes up, fusses a bit and then sleeps again. The doctor comes in, "Good afternoon, Sara.". He says entering. "Let's get a look at your incision." He opens my gown and begins clipping the stitches pulling them out. "Looks really good. How are you feeling?" he asks. "I'm great, we're doing fine." I say. He nods. He feels my abdomen and checks me all over. "Well, you appear to be healthy, and everything is healing fine. I can release you back to work. Have you thought about contraception?" he asks. I shrug. He tells me about some choices the pill, an IUD, this new product called a ring. He goes over side effects of each, and I choose the ring. He exits bringing me back a box, with the product. "I can insert this one; it just goes over your cervix. You replace it every 21 days. Here, take this box. It's got a few months' supply in it. I'll write you a script for a refill." He explains. I take the box, looking it over while he does what he needs to do. I can handle that, the last thing I need is to get pregnant again right away. He exits. I dress and carry my babies to the receptionist.

I hear Kayla down the hall crying. From what I overhear she's all alone, no one to help her, her baby is breech and she needs to have a cesarean. I stop walking. I walk to the doorway from where I hear her talking to the doctor. I set my babies down and go to the crying girl.

"You're OK" I say to her, soothing her.

"You don't understand, my Mom kicked me out, my boyfriend ditched me when I told him I was pregnant. I'm all by myself, I'm staying with friends right now, I have a job, but once the babies born, I don't know what I'm going to do. I've got no one." She cries into my shoulder. The nurse looks at me like I am crazy, obviously I don't even know this poor girl.

"That's not true." I tell her. "You've got your baby." I say to comfort her. I pull out a pen from my purse. "Do you have some paper?" I ask the nurse. She rips a piece from a pad on the counter. I write my phone number down for the crying girl. "Here, call me. I've been where you are. It's scary, but you can do it." I hand her the paper and I see that she appreciates my gesture in her eyes. I go back out and pay the receptionist for my visit. I smile and carry my babies out the door. I hope she calls.

My father is at the house when I get home. He is waiting on the porch. He comes to meet me as I park the car. "Hey Dad!" I smile and greet him. "Hi there kiddo. I wanted to stop by, tell you Happy Birthday!" He says taking Ryan's carrier from the car. I carry Shawn and enter the code to unlock the house. "This thing is crazy" he says referring to the security system. "Yeah, but Arthur insisted it was necessary." I explain. I untie Jessie from her fenced in dog area and she runs to greet my father. "He's probably right. Nice guy Arthur. How are you? The doctor's today right?", Dad asks. I nod. "I'm healthy as a horse. The doctor says I can go back to work, but I don't think I am ready yet. I don't want to leave the boys.",I explain and then one of them begins to cry. I warm two bottles and go in to change them. Dad picks up little Shawn and I change Ryan. Then we exchange babies and I grab the bottles. He actually assists me in feeding Shawn. I am surprised, but don't say anything. He looks so funny, his giant body holding my tiny infant. He even burps him after he has finished half the bottle. "Can I get you some lunch?" I ask. He shakes his head. "No, I'm fine. I just wanted to stop by, see you for a bit. Jimmie says you guys set a date for the wedding August 18th right?" My father asks. I nod. "Yeah, I wanted to talk to you about that.", I say pausing; I know how my father feels about people. He avoids crowds and hates attention. I continue anyway, the worst he can do is say no. "I was wondering, if you would give me away? I mean its tradition, and we're having a big church wedding." I say. He sets little Shawn down in the play pen. He sighs deeply and I sit waiting for him to respond. He stares at the picture of my mother on the wall; I give him his moment to think. I knew I shouldn't have even asked. "If you don't want to, I'm sure Ryan will do it. It's fine." I say. He turns to me; I'm not sure what he's thinking. "I'd be honored to." He says and hugs me. He releases me "Thanks Dad. It means a lot to me." I say. He nods "It means a lot to me that you would ask.". He leaves. I lay the boys down and continue on with my day. I make one of my mother's banana split cakes for my birthday cake. I am making Jimmie's mother's creamy Parmesan pasta dish for dinner. I text Heather and ask her to pick me up a bottle of vodka. Now that the boys aren't nursing, I can drink again and besides it's my birthday. The kids come home from school and we do homework. Soon Heather and Jimmie come home from work. Heather pulls a large liquor bottle from a paper bag.

"Happy Birthday" she says handing me the bottle. She searches the cupboards for a glass and something to mix with it. She makes two drinks one for each of us, Jimmie joins us after he checks on the boys. We sit and talk about the appointment with the doctor and how their days were. Soon it is time for dinner. I pull my casserole from the oven and call the kids to the dining room. We just get started serving the kids' plates, when the doorbell rings. I go to the door and am surprised to see Ryan and my Dad. Ryan has a store-bought cake. "Happy Birthday!" he says handing me the cake I open the door wide and motion for them to come inside. "Aww you shouldn't have, I made banana split cake." I say "but thank you so much. Are you hungry? We are just sitting down for dinner?". They go into the dining room and I get two more plates and silverware from the kitchen. I set them on the table in front of them and take my seat. "Mmm, this is great Mom.", Ashley says. Ryan scoops a big serving for himself and says, "I knew you were making this. It's well worth the drive." He smiles at me. "Thanks for the cake." I tell him.

"Well, I'm sure yours will be better, but you shouldn't have to bake your own birthday cake." Ryan says. Heather and Jimmie's faces look shameful as they continue eating. I smile and say "See what Jimmie got me? I found it in the coffee this morning." I show everyone my bracelet. This seems to brighten Jimmie's expression a bit. Everyone admires my bracelet. Dad says "Nice. I like the fish." I nod, "It's sweet, I like all the little charms." I say. Jimmie smiles at me. My casserole devoured, I go get the cake and hear the boys crying. I set the cake down on the table and hurry to the playpen. Heather helps me change and carry the boys into the dining room. Retrieving the warmed bottles, she and I begin to feed the boys. "Here let me." Ryan says taking little Ryan from my arms. They all sing "Happy Birthday" to me and I slice and serve the cake to everyone.

"This is different, I've never had it before, it's delicious." Jimmie says to me.

"Mom used to make it, I haven't had it in years." Ryan explains to him. Dad eats his and then says "Well, it's almost as good as your Mother's." I laugh. "Well, she had more practice." Jimmie and Ashley clear the table while Ryan and I lay the boys in their cribs. "So, August eighteenth?" Ryan whispers across the nursery. I nod. "Arthur and I are setting up a fitting for the tuxes, probably in a couple weeks." Ryan says his voice asking really. "Okay, just let me know. Jimmie's friend Mike lives in Connecticut so he'll probably need some notice to make arrangements." I explain. Ryan nods. We join Heather and the boys in the living room. Ashley soon joins us. I peek in the kitchen to see Jimmie and my father washing the dishes. I almost burst out laughing. I don't think I've ever seen my father wash a dish in my life! I point at them and motion for Heather and Ryan to look into the kitchen. Their expressions show that they think it's as funny as I do and we all laugh quietly as we sit back on the couch. We continue to visit and the guys join us when they finish. "Well, thanks for dinner." My father says rising. Ryan rises too. I hug my father "Thanks for coming Dad.". Ryan and I hug goodbye "See you in a couple of weeks; I'll call you or Jimmie to let you know the date. OK?" he says. I nod. Heather gets up and shoves the boys to get upstairs to bed. "Come on Ash, you too." I say to Ashley. She sighs deeply and rises stretching, then goes to her room. Jimmie and I are alone in the living room.

"So, how about that bath?" he asks smiling his little crooked smile. I nod. I follow him down the hallway. He shuts and locks our bedroom door behind me. I go into the nursery to check on the boys. They are both still sleeping. I hear the water running in the tub. I enter the bathroom and Jimmie has lit candles in the sconces on the walls. He exits the room and I undress and enter the tub. I love this tub. The water is so hot, but that's how I like it. Jimmie comes in with a drink for me. He hands it to me and sits in his boxers on the side of the tub. I sip on my drink and he turns on the jets, I soak, just relaxing and enjoying my bath.

"Did you have a nice birthday?" he asks. I nod.

"Thanks for cleaning up. How did you get my father to wash dishes?" I ask. Jimmie shrugs.

"He just came in and started doing it. I don't know, it was a little weird, wasn't it?" he smiles and starts rubbing my shoulders. I finish my drink. "Do you want another one?" he asks taking the glass and setting it on the counter. I shake my head.

"This is nice." I smile and close my eyes. I open them again. He has taken his seat back. "Why don't you join me?" I ask. He undresses quickly and comes in the tub setting behind me. I lay against him, my back to his chest. He starts massaging my shoulders and back again. "That feels so good." I say turning my head to face him. "Just relax." He whispers and continues. He massages my arms, then my legs. I thought he would have mauled me by now. He's been waiting for two months. Even longer considering that we weren't really able to do anything for about a month before I had the boys, mostly because I was uncomfortable. His hands feel phenomenal on my skin. I don't know what he is waiting for, I start massaging his legs that are wrapped around me. Then I roll over, the water sloshing. I stare into his eyes and straddle him. I kiss him hard and then back off, kissing his neck and running my hands all over him. He continues massaging my back. I know he's ready and so am I. We start slowly. It hurts at first. Then we get our rhythm and as soon as we do it's over.

"I'm sorry" he says "I couldn't help it, you're so beautiful." He kisses me. Why is he sorry? He didn't do anything wrong. "Why are you sorry?" I ask getting off of him and out of the tub. I dry off with a towel. I look to him to answer me. "I just wanted you to, you know, enjoy it more." He smiles. "I did enjoy it." I say. He shakes his head and gets out of the tub he removes my towel. "That's not what I mean.". He takes my hand and leads me into the bedroom. He sets me on the bed and he starts kissing me all over. I feel the churning in my stomach again. He continues. I stop myself from screaming as he starts pleasuring my body. I feel the blissful spasms again. I grab a pillow and allow myself to release quiet moans, the pillow stifling the sound. He takes it from me and climbs on top of me. I can't help myself. My body wants him; I keep pulling him closer to me. My fingers dig into his back. He continues, our bodies moving together as one. This time, it's much longer and when we finish, neither one of us feels the other isn't satisfied. We lay tangled up in one another trying to catch our breath. "I've missed THAT!" he whispers. "Me too!" I say into his chest. "I love you so much." I say kissing his chest again. He squeezes me gently and kisses the top of my head. "You have no idea." "I have no idea about what?" I ask. As I say it, I hear the boys through the monitor. I throw on his shirt and go to change them. He brings in two bottles and he takes Ryan and I take Shawn. He still hasn't answered me. As I burp the baby I ask him in a hushed voice, "I have no idea about what?". He looks up from feeding Ryan, his eyes look funny, like he's looking through me "You have no idea, how much you mean to me, you don't realize how beautiful you are, and not just on the outside, but the inside too, where it's most important.". I notice his eyes are glossy like he's about to cry. "I am the luckiest guy in the whole world, and I can only hope that you never figure that out." I lay Shawn down and take Ryan from him; I burp him and look Jimmie in the eyes. "You are so good to me, I'm not all that wonderful, and you know you're not so bad yourself." I say I know it isn't the heartfelt speech he gave me, but I'm not very good at that stuff and he knows that. He smiles and takes Ryan laying him in his crib. We go back to bed. I want to ask Jimmie what he thinks about me staying home longer with the boys. I roll to face him "hey babe?" I whisper. He sits up on his elbow and rubs my arm "Again? You're a monster!" He kisses me on the cheek. I smile "No, I just wanted to ask you, what do you think about me staying home for a while longer? I mean, if you think I should go back to work I will, but I would like to stay home with them just until they are a little bigger. What do you think?" I ask biting my lip almost afraid he's going to say that I should get back to work; I know the wedding will deplete my savings a lot. He nods his head and rubs my arm again "You don't have to go back until you're ready. I think it's great that you want to stay home. I want you here." He smiles and kisses me again. I smile rolling back over to get some sleep.

5

Meeting Mike

Ryan and Arthur have scheduled the appointment with a tuxedo rental place to pick the styles and colors for the tuxes for the wedding this Saturday. May is upon us and the kids are excited to be winding down at school. The boys are getting bigger and bigger every day. They are awake a lot more now. Mike is driving up Friday night and will be staying with us. I am a bit nervous about this. He's Jimmie's best friend. I'm never even spoken to him. Jimmie is excited that he is coming. I am trying to make sure the house is perfect, linens cleaned and food prepared. Today is Wednesday. Grocery day and I have to run some errands, paying bills and things. Heather reminds me that we need to go dress shopping eventually. UGH! I hate clothes shopping, and I am sure the wedding dress shopping will be an all-day event. We will go on Saturday while the guys are out doing their tux thing. I run my errands, taking the boys infant carriers into places is getting a little less tricky for me and I am really working out my arms! Grocery shopping is a bit difficult though, I have learned to attach the carriers in the front of two carts and I push one while pulling the other, I'm getting the hang of it.

Once home, I unload the boys, and then the endless groceries. I have to stop putting things away in order to feed the boys. We are going to have a full house this weekend and I've got a lot of preparations to make. Ashley and Trysten come home from school; I send them out in the kitchen to finish putting away groceries. Ashley hands me an envelope addressed to the parent or guardian of Ashley McCann. I open it she has been selected to receive several awards at the end of the year ceremony. I fill out the card that we will attend with 10 guests. I place the card in the return envelope and make sure it's in her backpack. Its funny last year and every year prior to that anytime she had something at school it was just me. Mary tried, she attended a few, but usually it was just me. It is so wonderful to have Ashley surrounded by people who love and adore her. I write the award ceremony date on my calendar, and it will also remind me to tell everyone else. It's a whole new world for her, her days spent at school, and then home talking on the phone with her friends. She gets to go to parties and Mariah's house. I never allowed her to go anywhere in San Diego. I was too nervous about something happening to her.

Heather returns from work and I make dinner. Jimmie is late tonight, must be tied up at work. The kids, Heather, and I eat and she helps me take care of dinner. Jimmie is still not home. I am starting to get worried. I try his cell, but he doesn't answer. The seven of us settle in the living room watching the television and hanging out. I hear Jimmie's truck and get up to fix his plate. He enters the door, clearly he's been drinking. He comes into the kitchen, his eyes trying to read my expression to see if I'm upset with him. I smile and put his dinner in the microwave to warm it. He sits at the counter, and I set his dinner in front of him. "Hey, how was your day?" I ask being extra sure my voice doesn't sound upset. "Good, I guess." He says and starts eating. I return to the living room and turn off the television. "Time for bed guys." I tell the kids. Heather and the boys go upstairs and Ashley goes to her room. "Brush your teeth, Ash." I instruct my daughter which gets a growling mumbling response from down the hall. I change the boys' diapers and then set them in their cribs while I get their bottles ready. I go back into the kitchen. Jimmie is finished eating, but he's still sitting at the counter. I take his plate and rinse it, while I warm the bottles for the boys. "Sorry I'm late." He says, his voice sounding guilty. I shrug, "its fine, I was a little worried, but you're home now." I say. He stands and gives me a hug; I smile and then leave to feed the boys. I hear him getting into bed while I am finishing up feeding Shawn. "Do you need help?" I hear him ask. "No, I've got it, thanks." I say loud enough for him to hear. I lay my sleeping infant in his crib, and then take the bottles to the kitchen to rinse them. I wash the dishes up before I go into bed; I can't stand waking up to a sink full of dirty dishes. With Jimmie sound asleep in bed, I slide in and face the opposite way.

The next morning, the boys wake up just before Jimmie's alarm goes off. I hurry to warm the bottles and make the coffee. I sit feeding both of them; Jimmie comes into the nursery. "Good morning beautiful. How's my girl?" he says and then kisses my head. He kisses both the boys and goes to get ready for work. I bring the boys out into the living room, setting them in their bouncy chairs. They love to kick and make the music play and the lights flash. They smile and make excited noises! It's adorable. Jimmie sits watching them from the kitchen. I go to get the kids up; he stops me before I leave the kitchen. "Hey, I need to tell you something.". I nod urging him to go on. Ashley comes out of her room entering the living room. He sighs deeply and doesn't say anything at all. I figure it's something he doesn't want to say in front of her. "Never mind. It's not important." He says and gets his lunch from the counter. I hug him extra tight before he leaves. He holds on for a little longer than usual too. "I love you." He says into my hair. "I love you too, now get out of here, you're going to be late.". I say and go on about my routine. That was odd. I wonder what he wanted to tell me. Obviously it's something he doesn't want Ashley to hear. My day goes on as usual, Jimmie comes home on time and we all eat dinner together. He, Ashley, and the boys play kick ball in the backyard. Then everyone comes in for showers and bedtime. Once we are alone in our room, Jimmie says "Sara, I've got to tell you about Mike. He's my best friend, but he's a bit of a dog." I shrug "Okay?" He continues "I had a girlfriend in high school Emily, we were together for a long time. When I went away to college, Mike slept with her. I found out about it, and we broke up. I was so mad at him for a long time, but finally realized he did me a favor. If it wasn't him, it would have been someone else. We got together and patched up our friendship, but I haven't seen him in three years. We talk sometimes on the phone and stuff, but we always promised each other we'd never get married and if we did, we had to be in each others weddings. I know it's stupid. I don't even know why I felt like I had to tell you about that. I guess him coming here, with you it makes me nervous." He explains. "Why does it make you nervous? You think he won't like me? I have to say I am a bit nervous about that myself." I whisper in the dark. He rubs my arm and pushes my hair off my face with his finger. He tucks my hair behind my ear, and says "I'm sure he'll like you, maybe a little too much.". I take his hand "I'm with you; I don't want to be with anyone but you." I say kissing his hand. "You're mine." He says and it sounds a little creepy. I nod "I'm yours." He pulls me into him and we make love.

Friday midday Jimmie comes home from work early. He has picked up several cases of beer and lots of liquor for Heather, Arthur, and me. Ryan and Arthur arrive shortly after the school bus drops of the kids. Ashley runs to show Ryan the letter for her award ceremony. He promises to come. Heather comes home from work, she and Arthur start mixing drinks and drinking them on the back deck. I wait. Someone has to be sober around here. As I start setting dinner on the table, I notice a blue pickup truck pulling in the driveway. It must be him. Jessie starts barking. Jimmie goes out to greet our guest. Heather and I are still setting the table, "Holy MOSES! Look at that!" she says. I turn and see Jimmie's friend. He and Jimmie are getting his bags out of the truck and coming onto the porch. I look at her to see what I am supposed to be looking at. "He's hot.", She whispers. He's alright, he's got black hair, short cut, he's built like someone who works out at a gym every day, and he's about the same height as Jimmie. He looks a bit intimidating to me, definitely arrogant, I can tell by the way he's walking. I shrug and shake my head at her. "Whatever! Arthur agrees with me don't you?" she says. Arthur moves his hand to motion a so-so to her. I walk back into the kitchen through the living room while Jimmie and Mike are coming into the house. "Hey Sara, this is Mike. Mike this is my fiancé, the mother of my children, Sara.". Jimmie says. Mike sticks out his hand for me to shake it; I do and smile politely "Nice to meet you." I say shaking his hand. His eyes are as black as his hair. He smiles and doesn't let go of my hand. Jimmie must notice, "We can put your stuff right up here, hope you're hungry Sara's a Hell of a cook and dinner's just about ready. Isn't it babe?", he says leading Mike up the stairs. "It's coming out of the oven right now, go ahead and get settled. Make yourself at home." I say heading into the kitchen. Heather and I fix the kids plates and then call everyone in for dinner. I put the boys in their high chairs and set them one on each side of my chair so I can feed them some mashed potatoes and gravy. I love having them in with us while we eat dinner. Everyone seated the adults start fixing their plates. I see Mike giving Arthur and Ryan weird looks; I don't like it at all. Heather is trying very hard to get him to look at her; I find this just as annoying. Jimmie kicks my leg under the table, I look at him, he winks and smiles at me. I continue feeding the boys. Jimmie introduces everyone to Mike and they all make pleasant conversation. Heather continues to ask him questions. I find out he's a personal trainer, he works at a night club as a bouncer, he has never been married, he has no kids, and lots of other stuff. The guy is full of himself. I find it hard to believe he and Jimmie are friends. Jimmie is proud, but not arrogant. Heather seems very interested in him. Then of course they have to turn the conversation to me, no one is ever happy to just let me be a spectator. "Sara, this meatloaf is awesome. Did you make the gravy too? I know this is Mom's homemade bread recipe. It tastes just like hers." Ryan rants. Arthur "MM's' in agreement with him. "Thanks." I say picking at my own plate. "He loves those potatoes, he wants more, look at him. Feed me Mama" Jimmie jokes as little Shawn watches my fork. I give him another taste of them. He opens his mouth wide, like a little bird. I can't help but smile, Mike is smiling at us too. "What's for desert Mom?" Ashley asks. "She made coke a cola cake" Tyler says adding "I licked the mixer.". I give him a, "You weren't supposed to tell" look. "She still made me eat breakfast though." Tyler says trying to save me from his mother. "What's that? I've never had it before." Mike asks. "Sara's always trying different recipes. She cooks and bakes every day. It's a wonder we all don't weigh an extra hundred pounds." Jimmie laughs. I shake my head "It's just a chocolate cake, it's no big deal.". I get up going to the kitchen I cut the cake into pieces and bring it and a stack of clean plates into the dining room. I set it on the table so everyone can serve themselves and take the boys in for their bath. I finish cleaning the boys up and put them in their playpen. The adults are still visiting in the dining room. I go in and Ashley comes from the living room to help me clear the table. "Thanks for dinner, it was delicious. The cake was too! I can't remember the last home cooked meal I've had.", Mike says to me. "You're welcome.",I nod to him. Jimmie, Ryan, Mike, and Arthur retreat to the back deck. Heather comes into the kitchen "Do you mind if I sneak out there with the guys?" She asks. I shake my head and wash the dishes. After checking on the boys, who are just rolling around in their play pen, I make myself a drink and join the other adults.

Heather continues flirting with Mike; he doesn't seem to be responding though. Arthur says "So, big day for you tomorrow, are you excited?" looking at me to answer. Excited about dress shopping? No, but as the bride to be, I can't really say that can I? I nod my head, "Yeah, it'll be nice; Liz is going to watch the boys while we look at some shops." I say in response. Jimmie takes my hand, "It will be good for you to get away for a few hours. Maybe we can all meet at Mel's around four?" He asks glancing around the table for everyone to respond. "Sure sounds good to me." Mike says drinking his beer. I sip on my drink for a while and listen to everyone gabbing. Then I go check on the boys again. "No wonder you're so tiny, you never sit still." Mike says jokingly to me. Heather says "Yeah, she started doing sit ups before the boys were even a week old. She never stops. It's exhausting just watching her." Using her voice in her cheerleader tone. The boys are fine, laying in their pen. Ashley sets talking on the phone on the couch, "I'll get you Mom, if they cry. Go visit." She quickly picks the phone back up and starts talking again to Mariah, I assume. Back on the deck, the guys and Heather are laughing at something hysterically. I take my seat between Arthur and Jimmie. "We were just talking about you." Ryan says. Why am I not surprised? "So, you're not much of a shopper huh?" Mike asks. Heather shakes her head and says "You have no idea. This girl is impossible. She would probably rather get married in jeans and a t shirt.". Her hands waving dramatically as she says it. Jimmie takes my hand under the table. I smile at him. "She doesn't need to worry about it, that's all, she's beautiful in anything." He says in my defense. I squeeze his hand. "I would give anything to see it, hopefully. I'll be able to join you ladies at the fitting.". Arthur says. I love him, he's so fun, I would rather he could join us and help me pick a dress, he knows exactly what I like. "We could stop by, after we're done. If you want to?",Mike says to Arthur. Heather again being overly dramatic says "No way! Its bad luck, Jimmie can't see her in her dress!" I sigh; Heather is getting on my nerves. I squeeze Jimmie's hand and lean over to him and whisper "Is it too late to elope to Vegas?" He chuckles and kisses my hand "You're fine. I promise I won't even come in the store. Heather, that way Arthur can see what dress she picks." Everyone seems to be in agreement with this and I nod along with the others. Every time I look up at Mike, his eyes meet mine, it's weird.

I go inside to put the boys to bed and to get Ashley off the phone. I do all the necessary things to prepare everyone for bed. I leave Jimmie and his friend to visit on the deck and I take a very long bath. Heather comes into my room after I have been in bed for a while. "You OK?" she asks me. I sit up and nod. She sits on the bed beside me, "I like Mike a lot." She says. "Yeah, he seems nice." I say. "OK, sleep well. Tomorrow's a busy day." She chirps like a little bird. "Goodnight" I whisper and she exits. Jimmie comes in much later. He slides into bed next to me; he wraps his arms around me and squeezes me pulling me into him. He buries his face in my neck, then he starts kissing my neck. He whispers "I love you so much." Into my ear. I lift my hand and place it on top of his. "I love you" I whisper. Then he rolls me over and we make love. The entire time, he stares into my face and keeps telling me over and over that I'm beautiful, that he loves me, and that he's so lucky to have me. He usually does this, but this time, it sounds almost desperate. Like he's not worthy of me or something. Once he's done, we lay snuggled up together. "I love you" I tell him. "You're mine right?" he asks. "Yeah, of course I am." I say. "Good." He states and kisses my cheek.

The boys wake up just before three a.m.. I find Jimmie's t shirt on the floor and pull it on to cover myself. I go into the kitchen to get their bottles, and am startled to see Mike sitting at the counter. He is just sitting in the dark, alone. I let out a startled sound, and he turns facing me.

"Geez, you scared me." I say catching my breath. I continue to prepare the bottles. I place the bottles with water in the microwave and set the timer. He stands and walks toward me. "Sorry, I didn't mean to scare you.". I turn to see him, and he's almost right in front of me. I am uneasy about how close he is to me. Then he touches my arm, "Jimmie's got it made. You and your sister living in this house. He has it all." He whispers his hand running up my arm toward my shoulder. "We are very happy. We all get along great." I say moving to the side to put some distance between the two of us. He steps closer to me, and thankfully the timer goes off on the microwave. I grab the formula and start mixing the bottles. "You are so tiny. How did you ever have twins?" he asks. I shrug "I had a c section.". He is coming closer to me again. Standing right behind me, my heart races, and my brain goes into panic. He pushes himself against me. I turn and try to push him away. "Come on Sara. I just want to see what you've got under there.", He says pulling up the shirt. I slap him as hard as I can as he is trying to put his hand on the inside of my thigh. I lift my knee him and hit him the stomach, and he backs off. "What's going on in here?". Arthur's voice deep and angry asks from the living room. I shake my head, looking at Mike, who is obviously ashamed of his behavior. "Nothing, Just a misunderstanding" I say and I take the bottles and retreat to the nursery. My heart is racing. Every muscle in my body is tense. I feel like I might be sick. I breathe deeply and exhale slowly. I change and feed the boys. I don't know if I should wake Jimmie up and tell him about Mike. No, he's drunk. He's just drunk and being an idiot. I calm myself down, and finish putting the boys down. I climb back into bed with Jimmie, snuggling up to him, feeling safe with him holding me. My panic starts to slowly subside. I feel my eyes starting to tear up. I exhale slowly, letting the tears fall silently. "Hey, you OK?" Jimmie whispers. I nod. "Are you crying? What's wrong?" he asks. I don't have the heart to tell him. I don't want him to be upset. He will flip out, blame me even. "Nothing, I'm fine. I'm just tired I guess." He settles back to his pillow, and holds me until I fall asleep.

6

The Dress

In the morning I wake early and make breakfast for everyone. I leave everything out for them to serve themselves and go to shower. I wear a simple button down pink plaid shirt and jeans. My hair in its usual pony tail, I pack the boys' diaper bag and put them in their carriers. Arthur and Ryan are up, eating the pancakes I have made for them. Arthur rises from his chair "Hey, let me help you with that." He says taking Shawn's carrier and the diaper bag. "Thanks" I say handing it to him. Mike comes down the stairs and hurriedly opens the front door for me. He looks at me almost apologetically, and then to Arthur as if in anticipation for him to say something. "Thanks" Arthur says as we go out the door. We put the boys in the car, and Arthur takes my hand. "Sara, I came down for a glass of water last night. I saw what happened, did you say anything to Jimmie?" he asks in a whisper. I shake my head. "Mike was drunk. I'm fine. You didn't say anything to Ryan did you?" I ask worriedly. He shakes his head. "It isn't fine. The guy's an ass. I won't say anything as long as you don't want me too." He assures me. I hug him and get in the car to drive the boys' to Liz's.

Liz is excited to be watching the boys today. I tell her their schedule, and she nods listening to me. Then she says "I've raised a couple of boys of my own. I'm sure I can handle a few hours." I nod, "I'm sorry, I'm just a little nervous leaving them for the first time." I explain. She gives me a hug and I leave heading back to my mother's. The guys are all gone by the time I get back. Heather, Ashley, Donna, Britney, and Deb are waiting for me. They all load into the car and we head into the city to begin the endless day of trying on dresses.

The first two stores bring nothing that "we" are interested in. I liked the simple dresses, but Heather didn't so we moved on. Our third stop is a huge Bridal store, bridesmaids' dresses and rows and rows of gowns. Heather begins trying to find a style that suits her. She seeks help from one of the attendants. "We need sophisticated, but sexy, and they have to be chapel length." She tells the attendant. The woman brings several gowns, I like one, it has an empire waist, mermaid bottom, capped off the shoulder sleeves. Heather tries it on. Everyone agrees on it for the bridesmaid's dress. The woman directs Ashley, Donna, and Deb to measure for the gowns. Heather finds one that will compliment theirs. Still, sleek but it only has one shoulder and it's embroidered with tiny beaded flowers. It's very pretty. She insists her dress has to be different because she's the maid of honor. Then it begins, they bring me dress, after dress. I try on at least twenty. The woman must feel sorry for me, because she comes into the dressing room to speak to me alone. "What are you looking for in a gown? Perhaps something a bit simpler?" she asks. The last one had so much netting underneath and the train was so long I thought I was going to trip over it all. I nod and she disappears, appearing again moments later with four different dresses. I try on the first one, its sweetheart neck lined, tight waist and a ball gown bottom. It has tiny little embroidered roses with tiny pearls all over the bodice and again on the short train. I like it, I look in the mirror and she adjusts the off shoulder capped sleeves. I go out to show the girls, getting claps and cheers from Donna and Deb. Ashley gives me the its OK look and Heather gives me the same. I go back and try another, another sweetheart neckline, A framed, chapel length, lace bodice and silk. It's alright; I go out and find Arthur, Shawn, and Ryan sitting with the girls. Ryan and Arthur look like they are about to cry. "Hey guys!" I say. Heather gives me the thumbs down and I go back to try on the other dress. As the attendant helps me get the dress out of the bag, I am in love with it. It's perfect. I put it on. I love it. It has a sweetheart neckline; thin straps, tight waist, a long skirt with a bit of a bell, and trains only a little. Its bodice is silky with tiny embroidered roses holding tinier little gems. One side of the dress is the same, curling it around again across the bottom of the hem. I love it. The attendant sees this. She brings me a small veil; she pulls my hair out of the pony tail and places the veil on my head. It has the same tiny little gems on it. She smiles and nods as if to say, this is the one. I go out to show everyone. No one says anything. I stand on the little platform and the attendant pulls the bottom of the dress to show them the hem. Arthur nods at me, his eyes glassy. Ryan gives me thumbs up. Ashley nods and smiles excitedly, Donna and Shawn nod in agreement. Deb is crying and Heather smiles. This is it! I smile "What do you think? I like this one." I say. I look to them to answer, but hear Mike's voice from behind me, "Jimmie's right, you'd look beautiful in anything." I shudder at the sound of his voice and roll my eyes. I get down and go to get changed. The attendant takes my measurements; I pay for all the dresses and give her my phone number to call when they are here so we can do a fitting. I meet everyone, Jimmie included at the front of the store.

"So what's the damage?" he asks me. "You can buy me a drink." I smile at him kissing him. Everyone goes back to my mother's first to disperse. Heather, Jimmie, Mike, and I go in Jimmie's truck down to Mel's. I sit in the back with Heather. Jimmie and Mike tell us about their day tuxedo shopping with Arthur. "I have to hand it to him. He knows all about that stuff." Mike says. Jimmie nods "Yeah Art's great. He actually had to tell the guy how to measure for the pants." I laugh. Arthur does know his stuff. "How about you guys? How awful was she Heather?" Jimmie asks. Heather smiles "She was impossible, but you knew that. I have to say, I am surprised at the dress she did choose. It's very...." she trails off looking for the right word. I say "perfect." Jimmie looks at me through his mirror giving me a wink. We pull into Mel's and Jimmie opens the door for me. He extends his hand, which is no longer necessary, but I take it anyway. He puts his hand on my back and opens the door to the bar leading me in. I love that he still does that.

Ronnie is working the bar; she gets Jimmie and me our beers and looks to Heather and Mike. "What can I get for you?" she asks. Heather says "A white Russian please." Mike orders his beer and Ronnie gets it for him. Then she starts mixing Heather's up for her. Jimmie takes my hand and swivels my stool to face him, "You should have seen your Dad in a tux!" he laughs. I smile thinking of how awkward that must have been for him. Heather smiles too, "He wouldn't wear one at mine!" "Well, he's had a change of heart." I say in our father's defense. "He was so funny, fought with Ryan and me over who was going to pay for them. I let him do it. Whatever makes him happy.",Jimmie tells me. "I'll catch up with him." I say which earns me another odd look from Mike. "No, I'd let it go. He wanted to, you know how he is." Jimmie says his voice pleading. I nod he's right, my father would be offended if I tried to pay him back. "So what about the dresses? How much are we talking? Thousands?" Jimmie asks sounding worried. "She already paid for them." Heather says. Jimmie starts getting red. I squeeze his hand. "All you have to do is show up." I say teasing him. "What about the honeymoon?" Mike asks obviously feeling left out of the conversation. I hadn't even thought about that. We won't be able to go anywhere too far away. The boys will be just shy of six months old. My face must show the concern. "It's all set." Jimmie says. "Oh yeah?" I ask. "It's a surprise, a gift really, from Ryan and Art. They're sending us somewhere. You'd better get a passport." He explains. I sigh, "We can't.". He rubs my knee looking into my eyes, "We're going. Shawn and Donna will keep the boys and Ashley. It will be fine. Besides, I can't wait to get you all to myself." I giggle a bit. He still makes me have butterflies in my stomach. He smiles his crooked grin and we both swivel back facing the bar. There is no sense in arguing with him. He's right; Shawn and Donna will be fine with the kids. Heather can manage, its fine. It's our wedding, our honeymoon. Ronnie comes over and asks "What does the dress look like?" Heather explains it much better than I could have, she makes it sound elegant. "She looks like a princess in it." Mike says his voice almost sincere. "She looks like a princess right now." Jimmie smiles. "I'll never forget the day you walked in here, when you came back from California. That was the most romantic thing I've ever seen in my life. I cried for an hour. You two are so great together." Ronnie recalls. I nod and hit Jimmie with my knee. I remember that day too. It was one of my favorite days. "If you think that was romantic, you should have seen him at the hospital." Heather says. I don't remember anything romantic about the hospital, but I was probably unconscious. I will ask her about it later. Mike pipes up "All this lovey dovey stuff is sucking the man out of me! What about the bachelor party?". He is such a Neanderthal. I wait for Jimmie to respond. He doesn't. "Well, I thought I'd come up a few weeks before the wedding and we'd go out or something." Mike explains. Heather chirps "Or something? Meaning go out to see strippers or something? Well if you're getting them, we are too!",I shake my head and don't even get to protest because Jimmie does. "Oh no. Not happening." He says. "I don't want them anyway." I affirm. Heather pouts "Well if he gets them so do we, that's the deal.". She sips her drink waiting for either Mike or Jimmie to address her. "OK, we'll do a party; we'll just do it together." Jimmie says. Now Mike is the one who is frowning. "I don't want a party." I say. "If you're having one, you're having one where I can be right there. You know how I feel about you going out." Jimmie says flatly. Heather objects "It's supposed to be your last night being single, what fun is it if the two of you are together?" Mike nods in agreement. "Well that's the way it's going to be, or not at all." Jimmie says. They nod and he squeezes my hand. "Sounds to me like you've got a trust issue." Mike says to Jimmie, I know this is meant to offend him, but it doesn't. He straightens his posture and says "No, not at all. I trust Sara, she's not like that at all, believe me. I just don't trust everyone else. Bars are filled with guys like you." Mike looks guilty, he glances at me quickly, he must know I haven't said anything. He still has a jaw, and hands, if I had told

Jimmie about what happened he might still have a jaw, but it would be busted. Instead of defending himself he just laughs. We finish our drinks and head back to the house.

That night Jimmie and I are in bed, he snuggles up to me, wrapping his arms around me. "You shouldn't have to buy your own dress. I want to." He whispers and kisses my neck. Why? That's so silly. I nod, "If it will make you feel better, then OK. I just don't see what difference it makes." I whisper to him. "It just does. It matters to me. It bothers me, so just let me alright." He explains. I nod and squeeze his hand. He's so sweet, a bit unreasonable at times, he wants to pay for it so whatever, it won't matter in a few months anyway. "Another thing that bothers me, I know it's probably just me being a jealous idiot, I don't like the way Mike looks at you." Jimmie says quietly into my ear. I should just tell him what happened, I should but I don't know how. "I don't like it either." I say. He sits up on his elbow, rolling me over to face him. "You don't? So, it's not just me?" he asks. I shake my head. Before my brain can catch up to my mouth I say "He kind of got a little too friendly with me last night in the kitchen." Jimmie's face tightens and starts to get red "He was drunk, it was no big deal really. Arthur was there too. It's fine, don't say anything." I try to back pedal and repair any damage I had done. His face calms "What happened? What did he say?" he asks. I try to remember and make it a little less frightening than it had been. "Nothing happened. He just got a little touchy feely with me. I slapped him though.",I explain. He gets out of bed, and puts his pants on. "What are you doing?" I ask. I need to stop him from doing something he will regret, Mike's his friend. "Did he put his hands on you?" he asks his voice angry but still quiet. "Jimmie, he was drunk, let it go. Come on, don't."

I plead with him. He is out the door before I can talk any sense into him. I hear him go upstairs, and into one of the bedrooms. Then I hear him yelling at Mike. I hear Arthur and Ryan too. I hurry to get dressed. Heather comes down the stairs into the living room. The men all come downstairs and head out the door. They are yelling at each other in the yard, Heather asks "What the Hell is going on?" "Mike got a little hands on with me last night in the kitchen." I explain. She shakes her head "Well Jimmie just busted in on him and me going at it, it was all I could do to get out of the way!" She was in his room! The guy is a sleaze ball. "I can't believe the nerve of him! Going after you, and then coming up and putting the moves on me, I hope Jimmie kicks his ass!" she says disgusted. Ryan is standing between Mike and Jimmie, Arthur is talking and Mike is shaking his head. "Arthur saw the whole thing last night." I say sounding nervous. "Did you tell Jimmie?" Heather asks. I nod "I just told him, that's why he came bursting in on you. Sorry about that." I say. I'm not really sorry. I'm glad Heather found out what a jerk Mike is. Ryan is holding Jimmie back from trying to rip Mike apart. Mike stands in the lawn shaking his head as Arthur is talking. I see Ryan quickly looking to Arthur then Mike, for a moment I fear that Ryan might even hit Mike. Ryan shoves him in the chest and Arthur quickly jumps between them, trying to calm Ryan down. Arthur stands between Ryan and Jimmie and Mike. He motions for Mike to follow him. Arthur pulls on Mike urging him to follow, Mike walks into the front door, Arthur is behind him. He never looks at Heather or me, he goes straight upstairs. He comes down moments later with his bag. He walks out the door and gets into his truck and leaves. Jimmie is still ranting in the front lawn.

Ryan and Arthur are trying to calm him down. Heather goes out to see if she can help, I know I can't. I retreat back to my bedroom. I sit on the bed waiting for him to come back in. Heather comes in. She sits on the bed next to me. She looks upset. "Arthur makes it sound like he tried to rape you or something." She says more asking than telling. I exhale "He was just drunk, being an idiot, he did get a little too hands on. I slapped him and kneed him." I say to make it sound a lot lighter than it actually was. "Why didn't you say anything?" she asks "To me?" "I knew it was just him being an idiot. I don't think he's a rapist or something. People do stupid things when they're drunk." I explain. She shakes her head "No. It's not OK; you don't have to put up with that, from anyone. No one should touch you unless you want them to! Especially in your own house. You must have been scared to death!" Heather says putting her arm around me. Really, it's not that big of a deal. It's fine. Nothing happened. She gets off the bed "Jimmie's calm now. Ryan and Arthur are in the kitchen with him. I'm sure he'll be in soon." She opens the door and Jimmie's in the hallway. Heather exits and he enters closing the door behind him. He walks over to me, kneeling on the floor; he lays his head in my lap as I sit on the edge of the bed. "Why didn't you tell me? I knew you were upset last night. You were crying. I knew it! Why didn't you tell me?" his words rushed and upset, but not angry. I shake my head "He was just drunk and being an idiot. I knew you would get upset. He's your friend. With the history I wasn't sure if you wouldn't....." I stop myself from saying it. He stares at me "I don't care if he was drunk. I don't care if he was being an idiot. I know I am a psycho, I know I fly off the handle and get pissed off. You are my life Sara. He's not my friend. I don't even know him. I should have never brought him here, to this house with you." I shake my head. "It's fine, nothing happened. I'm fine." Jimmie sits up, he rises standing in front of me. "Something did happen Sara! That piece of garbage had his hands all over you. Arthur said he saw you squirming to get away from him, he said you slapped him and had to knee him in the gut to get him off of you! That's something, that's not just a bit too friendly, that's wrong!" he yells. I exhale slowly trying to calm down. His tirade is making me very uncomfortable. "I swear, if I ever see him again, I'm going to rip his head off!" Jimmie screams waking the boys. I get off the bed and start to go into the nursery to get them, I know tears are coming; I can't handle it when he yells. I pick Ryan up and rub Shawn's back. Then the crying subsides and both boys are asleep again. Jimmie comes in as I lay Ryan back down. "I'm sorry. I'm sorry that you don't feel like you can come to me and tell me when something's wrong. It's my fault; I fly off the handle all the time over stupid things.", Jimmie says apologetically. "Are you afraid of me?" he asks his voice full of hurt. I shake my head, "I'm not afraid of you, I'm afraid of what you might do. Honestly, I thought you would think...." I stop again. "What? What did you think I would think? That you lead him on, that you came onto him?" Jimmie asks shaking his head. "Sara, I know you better than that, I would hope that you have more faith in me than that!". I nod my head, that's exactly what I thought he would think if I had said anything. I am crying again. He walks over and pulls me in hugging me. I bury my head in his chest, just letting the tears fall. He leans down and kisses the top of my head. "I keep breaking my promise to you." "What promise?" I ask him. He pulls away from me so he can look me in the eye. "I promised you that no one was ever going to hurt you again. I've failed you on that, twice." I remember when he made that promise, the circumstances have been out of his control, and he can't put me in a bubble. "It's not your fault, none of it was, you can't...." I say but he stops me pulling me into him again kissing me. He picks me up and carries me into the bedroom. He sets me on the bed, and then lies next to me, just holding me. "You're mine." He whispers "I love you, and anyone who tries to take you away from me is going to lose." I nod and rub his hand with mine. "I love you too, psycho." I whisper.

7

Couples Counseling

The week passes and we put the incident with Mike behind us. He has called Jimmie several times to apologize, but Jimmie told him he wants no more to do with him under any circumstance. We all go back to our regular routine and our "normal" life. Jimmie has stayed out late a few nights but I figure its OK, because he is still stewing. I'd much rather he sat at Mel's and stewed than sat at the counter stewing in the kitchen. He and I have couples counseling tonight at the church. Maybe that will pull him out of his wallowing. He has barely touched me or talked to me at all since last weekend. Today though, he comes straight home from work, at least he remembered. He walks into the house as I am finishing up making dinner. Heather is home, so she and Ashley will be watching the boys. I smile at him when he enters the kitchen. I look at the clock it's 3:45 our appointment is at four. I remove my apron and set it on the counter and go into the living room. "Heather, we're heading out, we should be home in a little while. I've got my cell if you need me." I say and she nods, not even looking at me while she continues to read her book on the couch. I look to Jimmie, "You ready?" I ask. He nods and puts his hand out for me to take it. I do. He opens my door and I get in, he goes around to the driver's side and takes his seat. He drives to the church, never speaking to me. Once we park, I open my door and get out. I don't understand why he is not talking to me. He meets me at my door shutting it behind me. He takes my hand again and we go inside the church. The pastor is in his office waiting for us. "Come on in" he welcomes us. We sit in two chairs across from his desk. He begins talking about marriage, what makes a good marriage, trust, honesty, loyalty, devotion. We nod along and listen, and then he asks us about how we feel about our relationship. Why do we each want to marry the other person? He looks to me to answer first. I suck at this stuff, but I try. "I want to marry Jimmie, because he is honest, and trust worthy. He is a huge part of who I am. He makes me feel safe." This causes Jimmie to stare at the floor. "He is my heart, he's my best friend, being with him is right, it's not forced, it's natural. It's the way it's supposed to be." The pastor nods, I think he notices Jimmie staring at the floor. He says "And you James, why do you want to marry Sara?" Jimmie kicks the invisible rock with his foot. He remains silent for a moment, then he looks up at the pastor. "Sara is my life. She's a true person. There's nothing fake or superficial about her at all. She's a wonderful mother. Sara is everything that is beautiful in this world all wrapped up in one tiny little package. Being with her makes me a better person.". The pastor nods again. "Well, you two seem to have your minds made up, neither one of you doubts your relationship. So, I'd be happy to perform your service on August 18th." He rises and shakes Jimmie's hand. "Thank you" I say and Jimmie leads me out of the church.

At the truck he opens my door. I get inside and he remains there, "Sara, I'm sorry, I've been so distant this week. I am pissed at myself, and I've been taking it out on you. I meant every word I said. You are my life, you and the kids are everything I just...." he says I stop him by kissing him. "It's alright, I know that you were upset, it's fine. I'm not mad at you at all." I tell him. He smiles and shuts my door, once he is in he says smiling "Well, I'm mad at you!" "What did I do?" I ask. He leans over the seat taking my hand "You never told me how much your dress was, so I could pay you back for it." We're back to that now? I sigh "It was $1279 for all the dresses. I don't know how much mine was, but I'll find out and let you know OK?" I tell him. "Really? That's it?" he asks surprised. I nod, "Yeah, I think Heather's was the most expensive one, I liked the more simple dresses. The one I picked is perfect. It's not too much. It's just enough." He smiles laughing to himself "Heather's dress was more than yours?". I nod "Yeah, some of the ones she picked out for me were ridiculous! One was more than ten thousand dollars; it was the ugliest dress in the place.", I explain. He starts the truck "I'm glad you found one that you liked. It doesn't surprise me about Heather's dress choices though, she's got very expensive taste." He smiles again "I'm glad it doesn't run in the family." I laugh and we head back toward the house. "Do you want to stop at Mel's? Just for one quick, it's nice to have you all to myself." He asks. I nod and reach into my purse to check my phone, no one has called or texted me. We pull into the bar and I wait for him to open my door, he leads me into the bar and pulls a stool out for me to sit. He's so corny, but I'm used to it. I wonder where he picked up his gentlemanly ways. Someday I'll ask him. Ronnie brings us our beers and we drink and gab with her and Mel for a few minutes. "You should have your bachelor party here" Mel suggests to Jimmie. "We're having one together. Right?" Jimmie asks me. I nod. I really don't see why either one of us needs to have one at all. "You know, years ago. One of the guys got married, we did a hay wagon and pulled it around with a tractor. We went around to a bunch of the outlying bars. It was a good time. I betcha Oliver's got a tractor and a wagon. That'd be fun" Mel suggests. Jimmie smiles, I can tell he's thinking about it. Since I really don't care what we do, I'll let him figure it out. "What do you think? Does that sound like fun?" he asks me. I shrug "Well, it'd definitely be something we'd all remember." I think it does sound fun. I try to imagine Heather in her heels trying to get on and off a hay wagon. I laugh to myself. Jimmie and I leave assuring Mel we'll think about it. Once back in the truck Jimmie says "That was nice, I miss you. I mean, I miss being with you. You need to take more time for you. I don't want you to lose yourself in babies and laundry. If you want a break, you need to take one.". I nod. I know I am not a whole lot of fun to be around anymore. All I do from sunup until after sundown is cook, clean, dishes, laundry, and diapers. I hope Jimmie isn't getting bored of me, I don't think he is, but he has been going out a lot lately. I push the thought out of my mind, things are fine, and he's just stating the obvious.

That evening, after putting the boys and Ashley to bed, I run myself a very hot bath and make myself a drink. I lay soaking in the tub, I turn on the jets and let the water rise much higher than it really needed to be. I sip my drink, and try to relax. Jimmie comes in from the bedroom; I thought he was already asleep. He sits on the edge of the tub. He doesn't say anything. I look up at him wondering what he's doing, but I don't speak either. I sink into the tub covering my head with the hot water. "I could just sit here and watch you forever." He whispers grinning his crooked dimpled smile. I wipe my face off and sip my drink. "Well, that doesn't sound like much fun." I joke. He leaves the room, I continue to shave my legs and wash up. Jimmie returns with a CD player and a handful of CDs from my car. He sets the radio on the counter and puts a CD in the player. I had burned this one; it has a bunch of my favorite songs. "Skip to 3" I instruct him, and he does it. He turns and stares at me when he hears the song begin. "This is our song.", He smiles. I nod and continue with my bath. He sits on the edge of the tub again, both of us just listening to the song. He rubs my shoulders and I begin to relax. "You going to join me?" I ask. He shakes his head, "No, I'm perfectly fine right here. Besides, if I get in there, your water is going to be overflowing.". I smile at him, and then I finish my drink. I hit the plug with my toe and get out of the tub. I still can't get over the way he stares at me. He looks at me as if he were looking at something unreal, like I am some idyllic thing of art. I towel dry and wrap myself with a towel, then start combing out my unruly hair. He stands and comes behind me; he puts his arms around me pulling me closer to him. "You said some nice things about me to the pastor. It was nice to hear." He says quietly. I nod "I know I don't say them to you. I should, I'm sorry; I'm just not very good at saying the right thing." I explain "but I try to show you, in my own way. I think I do.". He kisses my neck and turns me to face him; he picks up my chin with his finger making me look him in the eyes. "Sara, you do. You show me every day. Words are just words. What you do for me and for our family, every day without complaint, without an ounce of gratitude even from me most of the time."He says. I lean into him kissing him; he picks me up and sets me on the counter. His hands all over me. We keep kissing. We attempt to make love in this position, but he is a bit too tall, and I am too short. He carries me into the bedroom and we resume. While we are still tangled up in each other, breathless and satisfied, I say "You make me feel so loved." He does. He makes me feel loved and adored. He makes me feel beautiful, with just a look. I know there is no one I will ever love more than him, and I also know that know one will ever love me as much as he does. He kisses my head and I fall asleep lying on his chest, his arms around me feeling safe and loved.

8

The Break

Saturday morning, I get up before dawn. I change the boys and bring them out to the living room and set them on a blanket on the floor. I make coffee and bring the boys into the kitchen setting them in their high chairs and feeding them breakfast. My mind wandering to Kayla, wondering if she had her baby yet, how she is doing. I wish she had reached out. Funny how during certain moments the oddest most random things pop into your brain. Ashley wakes up and comes out "Can I go to Mariah's tonight?" she asks. I nod "I'll call Deb in a little bit OK?" She nods and goes in to shower. My father's truck pulls in the driveway, sending Jessie with her tail flapping to the front door. He enters and I get him a cup of coffee. "Good morning Dad. How are you? We haven't seen you." I say and he takes his coffee nodding "I've been busy. Is Jimmie around?" I shake my head "No. He's sleeping still. I can get him up if you want.". He shakes his head "No. It's fine. How have you been?" he asks. We visit for a while. Heather gets up. She and the boys join us in the kitchen. It is long after 8am before Jimmie gets up. He and my father head out to the deck working on something with the pool I believe. Heather, the kids, and I go about our morning routine. I call Deb and talk to her about Ashley coming over, of course she says it's fine. I bring Ashley over there and am shocked when I return home to find two Sheriffs' cars in the driveway. I run to the door, frantically. What happened?

Upon entering the living room I find four policemen, Heather, Jimmie, and my father sitting in the living room. "What's going on?" I ask worriedly. "Ma'am, Tom Richards is missing. He has been awaiting trial, his attorney went to meet with him this morning and he was gone." We need to leave. We need to get out of here. I need to go get Ashley. We aren't safe here. He'll come. My mind panics. I know I am shaking. Jimmie's jaw is tight, his face red. I think he is reading my thoughts. The police go on, talking. "Where were you Thursday night, Mr. Goodwin?" Jimmie says "here." He wasn't here, he was out, he didn't come home until after 1am. I don't say anything. "Well, I was at Mel's then I was here." He explains. "And what time did you come home?" the policeman asks. "It was late. I'm not sure. Why?" Jimmie asks confused. The officer writes it down and then looks at Jimmie "Well, given the history, I just would like to know." Heather is crying, shaking, my father trying to calm her. "What should we do? Should we leave or something?" she manages to get out. I'm on the same wave length. I want to put as much distance between that man and my family as I can. "No, we are going to put an officer in a car right in the driveway until Mr. Richards is found." The officer explains. "Thank you" my father says. The officers leave and Heather goes upstairs to bed. My mind is racing, my body tense. All my muscles, even my damn teeth are tight. I'm terrified. Jimmie and my father go back out to the deck. I take the boys and retreat to the nursery.

We spent a long time just playing. I wish I could just lock us in here until the police say Tom is found. Jimmie comes into the room. He stands in the door way, watching me play with the boys. He smiles at us, and then sits next to me on the floor. He takes one of the brightly colored toys and pulls the string making it vibrate and light up. Shawn smiles a big toothless smile at him. "He's probably long gone by now. Fled the country or something." Jimmie says quietly his words soothing my fears. "We don't know that." I say flatly. His eyes meet mine; I can tell he's just as afraid as I am. I hear the door bell and Jessie begins to bark. Jimmie gets up and goes out. I carry the boys out to the living room. I see two more policemen, they are talking to Jimmie but I can't hear what they are saying. Then he nods and comes to me. "I have to go to the police station. They want to ask me some questions. Call Shawn, have him and Deb come get the boys. You can follow us down there. Everything is fine." He says the words but I still don't understand. "Why?" I ask the officer. "Ma'am, we just have to ask him some questions." He answers me. Jimmie follows them out the door; Heather stands beside me as we watch him get into the back of the police car. "Do you think he did something to Tom?" she whispers, her hand on my shoulder. I shake my head "No. I don't think so" My mind races. Jimmie would kill Tom if he had the opportunity, I am sure of that, but I don't believe he did. I call Shawn and explain what's going on, my words rushed and almost sounding irrational. He and Donna arrive in minutes to get the twins. "Where's Ashley?" Shawn asks as he puts the boys into Donna's van. "She's at Deb's" I explain getting into my car to go to the police station. "Do you want me to come with you?" Shawn asks. I am sure he's worried about his brother. I shake my head "I'll call you, as soon as I find out what's going on." I say.

He and Donna leave and I drive into Greenville to the police station.

I enter the building and tell the receptionist why I am there. She directs me to sit and wait. I wait an eternity. Hours pass. I fidget with my purse strap. I tap my foot impatiently. I look out the window, and I see Amy Pitcher coming into the building. She walks right past me without even looking at me. What the Hell is she doing here? She walks to the receptionist and tells her "I was called down here to speak to Sargent Collins" she says. The woman directs her to go through the door to the left. I am curious and angered by her presence here. I wish someone would just tell me what is going on. Moments later Amy comes back through the door. "Hello Sara" she says her voice smug and condescending. I wave her off like I would a mosquito that was flying around me. She leaves. An officer in street clothes comes out, "Sara McCann?" he asks as if there were anyone else waiting in this tiny little area. I nod. He motions for me to come with him. I follow him through the door and to a small desk. He sits on the other side, motioning me to sit in a chair. "Can you tell me what time your fiancé came home Thursday night?" he asks. "It was late, around 1am I think." I say. There is no need for me to lie. He nods. "All right thank you." He writes something down on a pad of paper. "What is going on?" I ask. He looks up at me "Well. Tom Richards is missing. Your boyfriend has threatened to kill him on several occasions. Don't worry though, his alibi was confirmed. We can concentrate on finding Mr. Richards." I nod. I can feel my face warming. His alibi huh? Amy Pitcher was his alibi. That's good. He's not a murderer; he's just a lying, cheating bastard! Jimmie comes out of another room, and sees me sitting with the officer. He walks to me, I rise and we walk out of the building. I cannot even look at him. I want to scream, he takes my hand and I pull it away from him. We go to the car. He gets in, and I start the car. I drive to Shawn's I don't say a word. I think he knows that I know, because he doesn't say anything either. At Shawn's I go in to get my boys. I put them into my car while Jimmie and Shawn talk. Donna can see that I am upset, she watches me unsure as to if she should say anything. "Thanks for keeping them" I tell her as I put them in the car. "Anytime, is everything alright?" I shake my head. I can't contain it anymore. Tears start to fall. "No, Jimmie was with...." I manage to get out. She hugs me, I let her, but then I pull away. "He was with another woman; she came in confirmed his alibi for the night Tom went missing." I say. Donna's jaw drops; I can tell she doesn't know what to say. I bite my lip, trying to stop myself from crying. Jimmie and Shawn look over to us. I think they heard me. Jimmie starts walking over to the car. I get in and start the engine. "Sara, wait, it's not what you think." He says I put the car in drive and go back to my mother's. I don't even want to look at him. I am in my autopilot mode. I get home and bring in the boys. Heather hugs me "Where's Jimmie?" she asks concerned. I tell her about what happened, at the police station, at Shawn's then I break down. She and I sit on the couch her arm around me. She just lets me cry. Shawn pulls into the driveway; Heather meets Jimmie at the door. "Give her some time. She's upset. I'll tell her. No! You need to leave. She doesn't want to talk to you right now. Don't make me have the cop tell you. Go on. You can call her later." She says. "Sara!" I hear Jimmie yell. "Please! Just listen to me." He yells. I get up and go out to the living room, Heather moves from the doorway. Jimmie comes in he tries to hug me, but I push him away. His eyes tear up, "Please, Sara! Don't be like this. I was at the bar. She was drunk. She couldn't drive. I took her home, that's all I swear. I never touched her. I swear to God." His voice pleading and his words rushed. I don't know if I believe him, "Why didn't you tell me? If you had nothing to hide, why didn't you tell me?" I ask my own voice breaking. He shakes his head, kicking the invisible item with his foot. The boys wake up and begin to cry; I walk away from him and go to take care of them. Shawn's truck pulls out of the driveway. Jimmie follows me, I begin to change Ryan's diaper and he takes Shawn from his carrier. "I got it!" I tell him my voice angry. He continues to change him and then gives him a little teething toy to play with. I put Ryan down and walk out of the living room, into our bedroom. I make the bed, and pick up the laundry. "Sara, I swear. Please don't be mad." Jimmie has followed me. "What would you think? If the tables were turned? You are out all the time. You say I'm disappearing? You say you miss me? You think I don't realize that I haven't been loads of fun? Well, that's called being an adult. That's being a responsible parent." I rant at him walking past him with my load of laundry. He continues to follow me to the laundry room. "OK. I get it. I'm an asshole. I drink too much. I know that. You can be pissed at me all you want. I didn't touch her. I love you, and I'm not leaving. Not with Tom out there somewhere, not knowing what he's going to do." He says flatly and walks out into the kitchen. I go about my laundry and cleaning. When I pass him sitting at the counter, I don't look at him. Even over dinner, I can't look at him. After dinner he goes to bed, and I lay on the couch. Heather is walking on eggshells. I know our argument is making her uncomfortable; she goes to bed with her boys. The night ticks away. I start to drift off, and I feel like I am falling. I sit up and realize, Jimmie is carrying me into the bedroom. He sets me on the bed, but I don't say a word. Anger and pride choke my words; he leans down and kisses my head. Then he leaves the room.

Sunday morning, I wake up alone in my bed. I go out into the living room to find Jimmie snoring on the couch. I feel a twinge of sadness, I wish I could believe him, but I don't. I make coffee and drink a cup. I decide to go for a walk. The boys are still sleeping so I put Jessie on her leash and go out the door. Maybe a walk will help me clear my mind. I wave to the police officer who is in the car and walk down the road to the creek. Jessie and I continue walking down the wooded road. My mind going over and over as to if Jimmie is telling me the truth about Amy. I hear a car and move to the side of the road. The driver isn't slowing down, it sounds like he is speeding up. I turn to see a car, heading right for me! I jump into the ditch, glimpsing the driver as he speeds past. I only see the blonde hair, the small shape of his profile. It resembled Tom! I hurriedly pull on Jessie's leash, quickly realizing she's hurt. She lies on the side of the road, she's breathing, but I see she can't stand. Oh no! I start to cry, I am terrified that Tom might turn around, I pull my phone from my pocket and call the house panicking.

"Hello? Sara? Where are you?" Jimmie's voice is rushed and concerned.

"Jimmie I'm up the road, I just saw Tom, and he hit Jessie with his car. Come quick. She's hurt." I cry and hang up. Moments later I hear his truck start and see him coming. "Get in" he directs carrying our poor dog. He and I head into town, to the vet's office. Thank God we live in a small town, where the vet's office is really the downstairs of his house. My heart is still racing and I am scared to my core. "Where are the boys?" I ask terrified. "They're fine. Heather is there, and I told the cop what happened." The vet meets us at the door and Jimmie carries Jessie in. He lays her on the table and the vet looks her over. "She's got a broken leg. I'll have to do some x-rays but I think she'll be all right. You can leave her here with me. I'll call you" the vet explains. Jimmie takes my hand and we walk out the door to the truck. He pulls me into him, I allow it, because he does make me feel better. He holds me there, for a long time. I cry, letting out my fear, my anger, everything. Jimmie opens my door and I get in the truck, we ride in silence for a while. His jaw tight. Eyes wild "Sara, what were you thinking? You can't just...." he stops himself. "I don't know what I would do if something happened to you" his voice calms he takes my hand. It was stupid of me to think I was safe. I didn't think. Once we are back at the house, Heather clings to me as I walk into the house. She's so scared. I hold her trying to calm her down, the officer comes in and asks me to tell him all the details. What kind of a car? I can't be sure, I think it was black, definitely a dark color. The officer goes back out to his car and we all try to settle down. Heather has to work this afternoon. Jimmie drives her. My father comes over. It is surreal; Tom is out there, somewhere. We can't do anything about it; we are all just sitting and waiting. Deb brings Ashley home and I feel a bit better that we are all together. Ashley cries when Jimmie tells her about Jessie, but reassures her the vet called and she'll be able to come home in a few days. After dinner, my father leaves to get Heather and brings her home. The children all in bed, I go into the bathroom to take a bath. I sit, but can't relax. I get out and go to bed. Hoping sleep will come to me, Jimmie is out on the couch still. My anxiety is so high I know I won't be able to sleep. I swallow my pride and go into the living room. I stare at him. His legs too long for the couch. He can't possibly be comfortable. I know I'm not going to sleep without him in the bed beside me. For my own selfish need to feel safe, I walk to the edge of the couch. I stroke his forehead. His eyes open, he looks up at me, his eyes read longing, sorrow, they look so sad. He sits up and I sit next to him, I take his hand and wrap his arm around me. He sighs "Can you come to bed? Please?" I ask him. He smiles at me and takes my hand leading me into our bedroom. He holds me while we lay in bed, his arms around me, my head on his chest. Lying here with him I feel safe, I want to believe him that nothing happened with Amy. "What happened? You want me to listen. I'm listening." I ask him. "Nothing, she was drunk, she went to leave the bar. I hadn't even talked to her. Ronnie told her she couldn't drive. She took her keys. Oliver drove my truck, I drove her car with her in it and I left her at her house. That's all." He explains. "That's all?" I ask not believing it. There has to be more to it than that. "She didn't say anything? Nothing happened?" I ask urging him to continue. He sits up and rests his head on his elbow. "Oh, she tried. I just told her there was no way. She definitely wanted it to, but I didn't. I love you. No woman in the world could make me cheat on you. NO way, under no circumstance would I ever do that." Jimmie says searching my face for a response. I nod "I believe you." He hugs me and kisses my neck. "Good" he says quietly. "You know, I think you didn't tell me, for the same reason I didn't tell you about Mike." I say pausing he nods "If we are going to have a good relationship, no more secrets. Just tell me and I'll tell you, even if it hurts, even if we know that we're going to be mad. Deal?" I say looking him in the eyes. Searching for any sign of dishonesty or shame, I don't see any. He says "Deal" and then kisses me. We don't stop kissing, I kiss him everywhere, I climb on top of him. I put his hands over his head and keep kissing him. He tries to hold me, but I put his hands up again. His face reading that he is surprised, I feel empowered, I take him, he allows me to keep his hands over his head. Our bodies moving together, mostly me though. He seems to be enjoying this. I lean down and kiss him "You're mine" I whisper and release his hands. "Always" he says and then he really gets into it, pulling me hard onto him. My muscles begin to spasm, but I don't stop, he rolls me over and we continue. We haven't been this wild in a long time. I grab the headboard as he is pushing me harder and harder. The next thing I hear is a crack, and then a crash. He doesn't stop, I realize I have pulled the headboard from the bed frame, and it is broken. A big crack through the center of it, I laugh out loud as he falls onto me. We lay there for a moment, both trying to come back to reality. "We broke the bed, "I laugh quietly in the dark. He sighs "I'll fix it" he holds me next to him and I start to catch my breath. "Where did that come from? Holy Mother of God! I love you!" he says his breath labored "and you think I would ever even think of being with anyone else? Not a chance! You are everything." He sighs "just when I think, you've given me the best sex I've ever had, you go and do this? I'm not complaining believe me! You just keep surprising me." I climb out of our broken bed and turn on the lamp to assess the damage. "Like by breaking the bed?" I ask sarcastically. He gets out of bed and looks at it. "I'll fix in the morning, I don't care if you break a hundred beds." He smiles.

9

Jessie comes home

The week drags on with no news from the police about Tom. Jimmie calls home every few hours to check on us and make sure we're alright. It would be really hard for something to happen to us. There is a police officer in the driveway all day and all night. I offer the officers on duty lunch, some of them take it some don't. I am really just trying to keep myself busy. The house has never been cleaner. Heather thought she saw Tom on Monday, but when she called security and they apprehended the man, it wasn't him. She's seeing ghosts. Jimmie keeps assuring us that he is gone, that he must have skipped town, but I don't think he believes it himself. If he did, he wouldn't insist I stay home, and call me a hundred times a day. Today is Wednesday; the kids are off to school. It won't be long before school is out. We have to attend the awards assembly for Ashley next week. My Dad and Ryan promised her they would come. Dad has been stopping by this week, just being here with us. He usually stays for dinner and then leaves. Jimmie and he spend most of their time walking around outside. I call it securing the perimeter. If anyone came in here, I could press a button on the security panel and have the police, fire department, and ambulance here immediately. I feel a bit like a prisoner. I'm not supposed to go anywhere or go outside alone, I hate it. I'll be glad when they find him and lock him up in a maximum security prison where he belongs. I know Heather is scared, but even she is getting sick of the round the clock surveillance. Dad, Jimmie, or Shawn brings her to and from work depending on her schedule and theirs. I offered to do it but my father shot that idea down before Jimmie could.

Ashley and Trysten come home from school I fix them their snack. Ashley misses Jessie badly; I happily tell her "Jimmie's bringing Jessie home today." She smiles "That's great! I can't wait to have her back! I miss her.". The kids do their homework and I check it for them while I start dinner. Jimmie comes home and brings a hurt but alive Jessie into the house. She's wearing a big cone on her head. She looks ridiculous. She's got a brace holding her back legs; her left is bandaged up so she doesn't put weight on it. The three legged coned wonder comes in tail wagging she goes right to Ashley licking her face while Ashley hugs and fusses over her. I pat her on the head and she nudges me with her nose. "Hey there girl" I say smiling. I go back to making dinner while everyone gets comfortable. Tyler's bus pulls up and he comes running in the house and goes straight to his bedroom. I think he was crying. I go to the bottom of the stairs listening intently trying to hear if it was just my imagination. I hear him. I go up and find him crying into his pillow. "Hey buddy, what's going on?" I ask gently as I sit on the bed next to him. He rolls over to face me "Peter in my class said my Dad was trying to kill everyone again." What do I say to that? I rub his back and don't say anything. "You're safe, don't worry. Everything is going to be alright." I tell him. He sits up and I hug him, he rests in my arms. "I know. You would never let anything happen to us. You saved us before, it's just scary." Tyler whispers. Jimmie has come up stairs to check on us he is standing outside the door. "You don't have to be scared buddy. You're right. I'll never let anything happen to you, or your brother, or your Mom. We're family, and families protect each other." I say trying to comfort him. "But, my Dad's my family too." Tyler cries again. I hug him again, I look to Jimmie hoping he can read my mind, I don't know what to say to him to make him feel better. Jimmie comes in the room and sets on the bed, "Hey little man! What's up? Rough day?" he asks Tyler. Tyler sits up again, wiping his face. He releases himself from me and starts talking to Jimmie retelling him the same thing he just said to me. I leave the room, if anyone can understand what he's going through its Jimmie. His own father had been abusive to his mother. I hope he can bring him some comfort. I go down stairs and finish making dinner. Moments later Jimmie and Tyler come down the stairs and head out back to play catch. I smile at him as he walks through the kitchen, he gives me a wink. Dad comes just in time for dinner, we eat and then Jimmie leaves to bring Heather home from work. The kids are winding down for the night, Jimmie asks "Do you mind if I head out? Just for a little bit?" I am sure this afternoon with Tyler brought up some feelings he just doesn't want to deal with. I nod "Sure, go ahead. Thanks by the way, for earlier with Tyler." I kiss his cheek before he leaves.

Jessie sits by the door tail thumping like she does when Jimmie comes home from work. I look out and his truck still isn't here. Maybe she needs to go out. I put her on her leash and take her out to the back yard. She is tugging toward the woods, but I don't allow her. She continues panting, tail wagging she's not doing her business. "Come on Jess, do your business" I tell her, she sniffs the ground again tugging on the leash trying to head into the woods. "Alright girl lets go to bed" I tug the leash forcing her to come back to the house. I go into the bathroom and draw myself a nice hot bath, before I get in, I check and double check the locks on the doors and make sure the security system is armed. Then I soak and try to melt the day away. Jimmie comes home after midnight; I am in bed, but not sleeping. He gets into bed with me "I'm sorry, I don't know why I feel the need to leave. I sat down there tonight. I wasn't having fun. I was just drinking, sitting by myself. I don't know why I even do it.",He says. "It's just something you do. It's alright." I say trying to make him feel better. "Well, I'm not saying I'm going to quit, but I'm going to stop staying out so late. It isn't fair. It isn't alright. You deserve better than that. I'm sorry." He says his voice high. I sigh. He gets like this sometimes. "OK if that's what you want. I'll support you in it any way I can." I say kissing his hand. "You're too passive, why don't you scream at me or something? Tell me I'm not allowed to go to the bar. Tell me that I can sleep on the couch if I stay out past nine! Why do you let me do whatever? You never bitch or complain or nag that I don't take the garbage out. What's wrong with you? You're not human, you're a dream, I've been in a coma and this is all just a wonderful dream." Jimmie starts off sounding angry and then he's joking. I laugh "You never take out the garbage." He sits on his elbow "Seriously though? Why don't you?" he asks. I shrug "You do what you want, if what you want is to be at Mel's and you'd rather be there than here with me then why would I want you here? If you want to be somewhere else? You're an adult, you can decide where you want to be, how much or how little you want to drink, and as far as the garbage and things around the house.... I don't want you to do it because it's my job. You go to work every day and that's your job. Taking care of this house and everyone in it is my job for now." He squeezes me and kisses my head "No it's mine; it's my job to take care of you. There is nowhere else I would rather be than with you" Jimmie whispers and holds me until I fall asleep.

10

A View from Someone Else's Eyes

I am waiting. Waiting among the trees for him to come, I know he will. It's dark. From where I sit I can see the officer on watch in the driveway, the idiot is playing some game on his stupid phone, he's a kid really. I climbed into this tall maple around dusk. I have been waiting for hours. I can see the girls and the kids in the house. Sara's such a good mother, she just keeps going about her business. I watch her through the window. Heather seems to be following Sara from room to room. Sara must be checking the kids' backpacks for homework. I need to remember that awards assembly next week, she'll be upset if I forget. Getting close to bedtime, Sara is making the boys their bottles. God she's beautiful, not just in the way that most men find women beautiful, hers is different. She's more than just a pretty face. Heather shuts off the light in the living room. It's not as easy to see into the house now. I can still see shadows crossing in front of the windows. Ashley's light is still on, and the nursery light, I can't see into either of those rooms, nor do I want to, I am just following the lights and figuring what is going on in the house. It won't be long now.

Uh-oh Sara and Jessie are in the backyard. Jessie knows I am here, her tail wagging she tugs on the leash. That dog must weigh as much as Sara, she's so little. There is no way she can see me. I'm too far into the tree line. The dog just won't give up, "Go on girl." That dog is smarter than most people I know, she's been a good dog. Jessie gives me peace of mind. She's here to protect the house. You don't have to worry about it tonight girl, I'm on guard. Sara tugs on her again, and they head back into the house. Time ticks away, the on duty officer keeps nodding off in his car. That's alright. I don't need him to mess up my plan. Tom is not going to get a second chance to hurt my family. I am however going to get a second chance to protect them. He'll come, I can feel it in my bones. I've been waiting night after night since he took off. I sit and I wait.

I hear a branch crack behind me. I stand and wait, hoping it's him, but also fearing what will happen if it is. I see the weasel sneaking around, through the trees. He isn't smart enough to avoid stepping on branches, leaves are unavoidable, but it isn't hard to step over a branch. Well, no one ever said he was smart. The damn shoes he's got on, loafers, in the woods really? Sliding down the tree and standing with my back against the trunk. He's coming I can hear him, if the damn cop in the car had a lick of sense he could hear him too! Tom might as well be ringing a damn bell! I see that he's got a gun, but I'm not worried about that. Right as he steps next to the maple I reach out my arm, grabbing his throat choking him, the way I know he has choked Heather many times, the way he choked Sara the night of the fire. I squeeze harder at the thought of him hurting either one of them. I can feel his windpipe breaking beneath my hand; I feel his throat fighting for air. Eyes wild meeting mine, he knows that I'm out for vengeance. His hands fumble to get his gun, then try helplessly to fight me off. I take his gun from him with my free hand and hit him in the head with it. His whole body relaxes, I know he isn't dead. I throw him over my shoulder and carry him through the woods to the truck parked out on the road.

I know the perfect place to dump garbage. I put him in my truck. I even buckle him in. I drive with his gun in my lap waiting for him to wake up. A quick jab to the nose and he'd be out again. He's a big man pushing around women and little kids, but he wouldn't stand a minute against a man in a fight. He didn't stand a chance with me, sneaky little weasel. He'll never get a second chance. His chances are up. I drive through the night and turn down the road to the Old Wells family farm. I pull into the tractor path into the woods. I carry Tom over my shoulder and grab my chainsaw from the back of my truck. He so light, it doesn't even phase me to carry him and my saw, through the woods to a swampy area.

I look around, taking in my surroundings its close. I've spent a lot of time walking these woods, hunting years ago. I keep walking. I see the perfect one ahead, a soft maple tip up, from a storm. A nice big tree, roots ripped from the ground. I found it last week, when I came here looking for a good spot to bury the trash. Perfect too, because someone has been cutting their firewood for the winter. I lay Tom inside the hole where the roots once sat. I aim the gun, it's been years since I've shot a gun. I almost pull the trigger, but he isn't worth a bullet. I throw the gun on top of his lifeless body. Pull starting my saw, I am thankful this is the kind of area where no one would think twice about hearing a chainsaw in the middle of the night, if they even heard it. I cut the trunk and flip the stump and roots on top of Tom's body sealing his fate. It begins to sprinkle. I see the lightening in the distance. There's a storm coming. Good, tomorrow no one will even be able to see my footprints.

I don't feel remorse, or even guilt. Killing him meant no more to me than killing a fly. Now, we are free. We are safe, my family is safe, we can move on and be happy. Tom would have killed the girls and the kids if I hadn't had stopped him. I did the right thing. He wouldn't have stopped, even if the police took him in. He's been arrested three times now and look how well they keep an eye on him. He was free to come to the house tonight with a gun. Trying to hurt my family, he wanted his second chance. He didn't get it. I got mine. No one will know, but I will know. I will know that I did what I had to do to protect my family. I drive back home through the night.

11

Ashley's Big Night

The morning of the awards assembly, Ryan and Arthur come just after the bus leaves taking the kids to school. Heather, Ryan, Arthur, and I visit and talk about the wedding. Jimmie's friend Jeff from work is going to take Mike's place as an usher. We all met him once when we were filling up the pool, Arthur makes arrangements with the store to have him fitted for his tux. The girls and I are all going in for a fitting tomorrow. Arthur and Ryan want to see the golf course that Jimmie and Heather have selected for the reception so we take a drive out to it. The manager has no problem letting us into the hall to look around. Heather and Arthur begin discussing how they will decorate it. Ryan and I walk out to the pier. "It's really pretty here" I say looking out over the lake. Ryan nods "It is. Are you getting excited?" I shrug. "I guess, honestly I haven't really had much time to think about it. We are all worried about Tom, where he is, what he's doing, if he's going to try something. Heather's a nervous wreck." I explain. He shakes his head "Don't worry about Tom, he's gone. He'd be an idiot to stick around. The whole state is looking for him." I nod and exhale slowly. Ryan's probably right. We join Heather and Arthur back in the large reception room. Heather begins explaining the layout to me. I nod in agreement. She knows more about this stuff than I do. We all leave and head back to the house. I am making everyone's favorite for dinner. I put my own spin on Jimmie's mother's Parmesan chicken recipe, salad, bread, and Ashley's favorite chocolate cherry cheesecake for desert. The kids come home from school; Ashley takes a shower and gets ready. Jimmie comes home from work, my father with him. We all eat dinner, Ashley and I leave because she needs to arrive early. "It's nice Mom, you know, having everyone come to something of mine." She smiles as I drive. I nod. "Not that it wasn't nice before, you always came. It just seems weird you know? Having a bunch of people in the audience for me, I bet you think I'm being stupid." She says staring out her window. I shake my head and reach over taking her hand "I don't think you're being stupid. I'm happy that you finally have the family you deserve." I say. She smiles at me, allowing me to hold her hand. We arrive at the school just in time. I take my seat in the auditorium making sure to tell the other parents that I am saving the rest of the row for my family. Jimmie arrives a bouquet of flowers in one hand an infant carrier in the other. My father steps behind him carrying the other and a camera! Arthur, Ryan, Heather, Trysten, and Tyler follow they also hold flowers, Heather has a star balloon saying "You're a star!" I smile and wave to all of them showing them where I am seated. Jimmie sits next to me, he takes my hand as the rest of our family takes their seats. Dad fidgets with his camera, "So what's she getting an award for?" he asks looking over to me. I hand him a program that I had picked up on my way in. I've read through it a dozen times while I waited. It doesn't say who wins what award, just in which order they will be handed out. The room is getting full and it's after seven o'clock. I see the line of kids waiting to take their seats on stage. Ashley is with them. The principal, an older but a prominent looking woman takes the podium. The kids file in to sit. The awards ceremony begins with a speech from the principal. They start with the fifth grade, then the sixth, going through the top ten students, then the highest average in Math, English, Science, Social Studies, and so on. Finally they start with the seventh grade top ten from 10th to 1st. I listen intently waiting for Ashley's name, the principal keeps reading the names, each student going up to receive their award and then standing in the line. After the ninth name I hear "Highest average for the seventh grade Ashley McCann" I clap and Jimmie whistles. Dad snaps buttons on his camera, Heather shouts, everyone claps. I can feel the tears welling up in my eyes. My heart over flowing with pride and love for my daughter, I try to blink them back Jimmie takes my hand and I see his own eyes are glassy. I smile and squeeze his hand. The kids all sit back down. Ashley receives four more awards "Presidential Excellence Award" for having a ninety and above average for all four semesters, highest average in English, Math, and Social Studies. My father snaps more pictures, we all shout, whistle, and clap. When the awards are finished, Ashley comes down. She hugs me, I squeeze her tight "I'm so proud of you!" I say. Heather gives her the balloon and Ryan her flowers. She hugs them and then Arthur. Dad picks her up like a little toddler, swinging her above his head. She laughs and hugs him as he sets her down. "Good job kid!" My father says to her. Jimmie hands her the flowers he got for her, and she takes them from him. Then she wraps her arms around him, hugging him, knowing Ashley it isn't easy for her to show people affection, like me, she tries not to. He hugs her, and kisses the top of her head "You did great! I'm really proud of you" Jimmie says. Ashley's eyes are teary, "Thanks guys! Thanks so much for coming!". "Come on guys, let's go get some ice-cream!" Jimmie says and the boys cheer.

We all head out of the school and into our separate cars, this time I bring the boys with me. Jimmie helps me load them into the car. "I'll follow you?" I say getting in to drive. He nods and goes to his truck. We all drive to the ice cream shop and have ice cream. Ashley is positively glowing! She loves this so much. I feel a bit of regret; I regret not coming back sooner. I regret staying in California for so long, where our lives had been so empty. This is the life that my daughter deserves. I smile at my family, crazy as they are; we all love each other so much. I know my mother is smiling down on us from wherever she is. I think my father is thinking about my mother too, his eyes lost somewhere, the unmistakable smile on his face. Jimmie takes my hand under the picnic table, as I give a taste of my ice cream to the boys. Their mouths opening like little birds, trying to reconnect with the spoon. "Sorry guys Mommy's a tease" Jimmie says taking my spoon and giving them each more ice cream. I kick him with my foot. Ashley is going on and on about how happy she is, that she had no idea until tonight that she was the top average. I smile at her, how could she not know? She's very bright, she studies, she tries as hard as she can at everything she does. My father pats my back "She must get it from her mother" I smile at this, Ashley has gone to talk to one of her friends "her father wasn't too smart, you know?" he says to Jimmie. Jimmie nods "Well that's stating the obvious! If I ever meet him, I intend on thanking him.". I look at him confused "For what? For donating his DNA to make a wonderful beautiful intelligent daughter?" I ask.

He shakes his head "For taking off. It was the best thing he could have done." He says taking my hand.

A young boy about Ashley's age is talking at the side of the building to her and her friend. I see the way Ashley's expression changed when he walked up. "You see that?" I say to Heather. She nods "You're in trouble now Mom." Jimmie looks over and sees the boy talking to her, he starts to stand, but I pull him back to his seat. "Don't! She'll be so embarrassed." I say. He smiles his little crooked smile "I can be cool" he says sarcastically. The boy is writing something on a piece of paper. He gives it to Ashley and walks away. She and her friend do a silent screaming celebration and quickly stop before he turns. I smile, oh boy. Ashley's got her first crush. She joins us back at the table, "Who was that?" Jimmie asks sounding very paternal. "That was Damien. He's in my Science class." Ashley explains. Ryan smiles "And was that the reading assignment he wrote down for you?" his voice sounding much like it does when he's being the over protective big brother to me. My father furrows his brow "You're too young to be thinking about boys." She rolls her eyes and sighs looking to Heather or me to defend her. I am trying very hard not to laugh. I can see that she is getting self-conscious "They're kidding, Ashley. It's fine. No dating until you're sixteen. That's my rule you know that." She rolls her eyes again. Jimmie squeezes my hand "Sixteen?" I nod affirming that he heard me right. "Not thirty-five? I think thirty-five works better, don't you think? Bill? Ryan?" We all laugh even Ashley. Our ice cream finished we all head back to the house. Ashley thanks my Dad for coming as he is getting ready to leave. Jimmie walks him out to the door, "You know, you should be thankful." Dad says to him. Jimmie nods "I am thankful, every day." He states. "Well, you should be. You only have one daughter!." Dad says almost laughing. Jimmie smiles shaking his head and closes the door behind him. Ashley doesn't seem upset by my father's comment, nor does Jimmie. He really loves her just like she was his. I knew this before now of course, but it seems funny that someone else could see it. "OK, smarty pants get to bed. It's getting late." I say smacking her playfully with the dish towel. She nods and retreats to her room. I return to my dishes. Jimmie comes in and starts putting the dishes away. "I love you" I say quietly to him. He smiles 'I love you too." The dishes are done, I turn to him taking his hand "Thank you," I wish my words could express how thankful I truly am for having found him, for the way he is with my daughter, Heather's boys, me. I don't know what else to say. I hope he can see it. "You don't need to thank me. I'm....honored is the only word I can think of. She's a great girl; you've done an amazing job raising her. She's a part of you that means she's a part of me." He says his voice quiet, and his words heartfelt. I squeeze his hand hoping he knows that his words have touched my heart. I am so lucky; he's such a good man. I pull on his hand leading him into our bedroom. We check on our sleeping babies and then head into our room.

12

Girls Day

I get up early to go get Liz, today I have invited her to join us so she can pick her mother of the groom dress. Jeff and Jimmie have left before I return to the house. Heather, Liz, Ashley, Donna, Deb and I get into my car Ryan and Arthur are watching the boys. We drive into the city to the dress shop. Heather finds Liz several dresses that she likes, while the girls try on their bridesmaids' dresses. Liz picks her favorite and it's her size. I pay for it while Heather tries on her dress. "What a lovely color." Liz says complimenting the dresses. "It's like the color of sunset. It's beautiful." She continues. I have never thought of it that way. It is like the color of a sunset. The attendant brings my gown and I try it on. It's super tight through the waist, nothing a few more sit ups can't fix by August. The bust is tight too, but it doesn't seem to be noticeable. I love this dress. I couldn't even imagine another one that I would rather have. The attendant brings the headpiece and fastens it in my hair. I think I'll have my hair down at the wedding. I go out to show everyone how it looks. Liz cries "Oh, how beautiful. I love the embroidery." She touches the dresses tiny flowers delicately, and then pulls me in to embrace her. "It's a lovely dress, but you make it gorgeous" she says. "Thanks" I say. I go back to undress and zip my dress and the headpiece into the bag. I carry it out to the girls. I get my receipt from the clerk just in case we need any further alterations. We head out all of us carrying our bags of dresses.

"Who's going to watch the boys during the wedding?" Liz asks. "Loretta, she's our aunt. She'll be in from P.A. for the wedding. She'll keep them during the service." Heather answers for me. "How about lunch ladies? Anyone in a hurry to get back?" I ask. They all nod and I pull into the next restaurant I see. Over lunch the talk is all about the wedding. Heather goes over all the details with Deb, Liz, and Donna. "I never thought you'd get married." Ashley says to me smiling. "Neither did I." I laugh. "I was married twice." Liz says looking over her menu at me. I nod. Donna smiles at me. We order our lunches and continue visiting. "Did you have a big wedding too?" I ask Donna. She nods "Yeah, half the town and hundreds of relatives that I hardly know." "My first wedding wasn't big. I got married in the court house. But my Patrick he made sure I had a beautiful wedding, he wanted the whole thing. He insisted. He was a romantic. I miss him dearly." Liz says her voice trailing at the end of her sentence. Our lunch finished, we head out back to the house. I carefully carry my dress into the bedroom and put it in the closet. Its large black bag concealing everything from Jimmie and Jeff as they watch from the deck. Jimmie has come into the room, "So this is it huh?" he asks. I push on him playfully "Don't even think about it!". He smiles taking my wrist from my attacking hand and quickly grabbing my other one. He's got my hands tied with two of his fingers, and he still has a free hand. He playfully tries to grab at the bag "Oh, yeah? What are you going to do about it?" he jokes. "Don't!" I whine. I know he won't I'm just playing along. He kisses me, "I could get used to this" he says referring to me being helpless. I bite his lip a little "I thought you were the one who liked to be restrained." He smiles pulling me in to kiss him again. I pull my face away, teasing him, I lose, he's much bigger and stronger than I am. Knowing that Liz, Deb, Donna, and Jeff are out waiting for us, I pull away again "Come on, we've got company" I say. "I can't wait, I hope Arthur and Ryan send us to a deserted island in the middle of nowhere, so we can just lay around naked all day." He kisses my neck. I know he's looking forward to the honeymoon, but I'm not. I'm still nervous. I don't want to leave Ashley and the boys. I don't know where Tom is or what he's going to do. Jimmie reads my mind again "They will be fine, I promise." I nod. We go back out to our guests. Heather is showing Liz, Deb, and Donna the floral arrangements she and Arthur picked out. I love the coral colored lilies. Shawn comes with Owen, Britney, and Michael. Shawn and Jimmie open the pool for the season. The kids can't wait to jump into the water. I smile to myself watching Ashley outside with the other kids. It's so funny, a little over a year ago, we were on our own. No one came to visit us, she had no one to play with, now our house is constantly full with people, kids, and noise. Not the annoying noise of city traffic, construction, and sirens but a nice chaotic noise. The kids laughing and playing, the adults visiting and chatting. I love it here. I am making a pasta salad for dinner and Donna comes into the kitchen "So, about this party." She begins. I roll my eyes at her. I really don't want a party. "Well, I was thinking, what if Liz stays here, with all the kids? That way Shawn and I can come together. The older ones will help her with the boys." Donna's voice is almost pleading. I think she might actually be looking forward to getting out. Why wouldn't she? She's a stay at home mom; I've never heard her talk about going anywhere except the grocery store. I nod "That would be fine with me. As long as she's OK with it." I say, instantly regretting it. My brain alerts, what about Tom? What if we're all gone and Liz is here alone with the kids. I don't want to alarm Donna, but Tom is dangerous, he tried to burn the damn house down. She must sense my distress "Your brother says he'll hang out here too, if you aren't comfortable with Liz being alone." Jimmie comes in and stands at the counter. "Everything will be fine, we won't be out too late, besides all Mom has to do is yell out the front door, there's a cop in the driveway. Come on, stop being a worry wart!" he says smiling at me across the counter. I nod "All right, but..." I start to say but before I can finish the two of them go back into the living room to tell everyone that the party is on. I finish making the salad and go in to listen to the plan. I notice Jeff and Heather are getting friendly, Heather sits next to him, her legs crossed toward him, he is doing the same toward her. Their body language speaks for itself. I smile; Jeff seems much nicer than Mike. At least he isn't hanging all over her, or staring me down like a cat does a mouse. The plan is Oliver Miller has a tractor and hay wagon. We are all going to load up here, with some coolers of course, and head to Mel's, then the Waterfront, a few more outlying bars, and then back to Mel's. Oliver has agreed to not drink and pull the wagon. The party isn't for a few more weeks, mid July. Liz is nodding and smiling "Sounds like fun" she says looking to me to become more involved in the conversation. I nod "Sure, sounds good. Although there is just one problem I can foresee already," I smile already having decided to pick on my sister, everyone looks at me for further explanation "How is Heather going to get up and down on a hay wagon with those damn shoes?",I laugh. Ryan explodes laughing hysterically. Everyone looks at Heather's spiked heels. Her face gets red and she slaps my arm "I have sneakers." She says defensively. "Well, I've never seen them. You'll have to dust them off, and wear pants. You won't want hay poking your legs, you'll get a rash" I laugh. Heather never wears jeans or sneakers. She always looks like she's going out on a date, or going to work. She wears dresses and skirts most of the time, and always heels. Every pair of shoes I've ever seen her in has at least a three-inch heel. Jeff smiles. Heather sits back in her chair arms crossed. Jimmie takes my hand squeezing it. Everyone begins talking again, Jimmie is sitting on the arm of my chair, and he leans over whispering "I've missed you" into my ear. I'm right here. I shake my head confused. I look up at him, and then realize I really haven't been joking around much lately. That's probably what he means. I pull his hand and he leans down "I'm right here" I whisper into his ear. He squeezes my hand. Ryan shouts "All right you two, knock it off." jokingly at us. Jimmie gets up and goes out to the kitchen, Shawn follows him. They grab the platter of hamburgers and hot dogs from the fridge and go out on the back deck to start the grill. My father comes joining our little get together and we all laugh, talk, eat, and enjoy our evening together. Ashley and Britney can't wait to show the guys their dresses, they try them on and come out to the deck wearing them "Two princesses" Shawn jokes messing up his daughter's hair. My father nods and smiles "Pretty color, never saw that shade of orange." Jimmie smiles at me and gives me a wink. "It's like the sunset" I say taking Liz's description of the color from earlier. "Go get it off, before something spills on it" I say tapping Ashley on her behind. "So where's yours I'd love to see it" my father asks me as he sips his beer. I look to Heather for defense, but instead she says "Go in your room and try it on, holler when you're ready. I'll babysit Mr. I can't wait." She nods to Jimmie. I get up and go to my room and put on my dress "OK! I'm ready" I yell. Ryan, Dad, Arthur, Shawn, and Donna come into my bedroom. My father looks me up and down, then turns his head looking away from me. Ryan and Arthur nod in approval. "Looks really. Nice" Shawn says and leaves. Donna pulls on the back, like the attendant did in the dress shop to show Ryan and my Dad the small train. "Here, put this on" she hands me the little veil. Ryan looks away. Why are they doing that? They wanted to see it! Arthur's eyes are glassy, "You are going to be the most beautiful bride this town has ever seen." He says almost in a whisper. I'm not all that and a bag of chips, but Geez these guys make me feel like I'm some angelic creature in white standing before them. "OK?" I ask just wanting them to leave the room, so I can get the dress off. I pat my stomach "It's a bit tight, through here. I'll have to be careful not to gain any weight before the wedding" I say. "You're skinny enough, they can take it out if they have to" Ryan says and puts his hand on my shoulder looking over me into the mirror on my dresser. "Are you happy?" he asks. I nod "Yeah. It's the perfect dress. I love it! It's not too much." I say fluffing the netting beneath the bell on the dress. Donna goes out to break up an argument between Owen and Britney. "That's not what I mean. Are you happy?" Ryan asks again. I nod "Yeah, Jimmie's wonderful to me. No complaints at all." He's always been the over protective brother. My father nods, "He'd better be." Dad walks over and hugs me, very awkwardly, he pats my shoulder. "I don't want to wrinkle you or get your dress dirty" he laughs and then leaves the room. Ryan and I stand in my room; he is looking at the floor. "You know. I'm very happy for you. I am so thankful that you and I got to be close again. I love this; we've lost so much time. I love you, you know?" He says to me. I hug him and start to tear up, I blink back my tears. "OK, knock it off. Get that thing off before you get it dirty or something" He laughs and I am left to undress. I am barely zipping up the bag before Jimmie knocks on the door. I hurry and zip the bag, putting it back in the closet. "Are you decent?" he asks through the door. What difference does that make? I yell "No, not yet." He messes with the handle on the door but before he opens it asks "Did you put the dress away?" "Yeah, I'm just getting dressed hold on" I yell, as he opens the door. Thankfully he is alone, because I'm just in my underwear. He shuts the door and locks it. He walks across the room as I pull down my t shirt. "Come here" he says pulling me to him. He kisses me very hard. I'm almost surprised by this. His hands move all over me, then he pulls my shirt over my head. "We've got company" I giggle to him. "I don't care" he says continuing to kiss me. I feel weird about knowing everyone is out there and he and I are acting like this. "Later, I promise." I say pushing him away. He sighs and backs off "You're killing me" he whines. I push him onto the bed, and climb on top of him. I unbutton his pants and pull them down. He is definitely ready; I straddle him as he sits on the edge of the bed. Our bodies move together. I push him to lay him down. He tries to sit up, but I push him down again. "Oh Sara!" he whispers. He definitely likes it when I am more aggressive with him. I am slowly beginning to allow myself to let my inhibitions go. I continue and he pulls my hips onto him as I move. Moments later he is finished. "Well, that didn't take long" I joke. He smiles "Well, what do you expect? You attacking me like that, I'll make up for it later." He pulls his pants back on. I go into the bathroom to clean myself up a bit. Moments later I go out onto the deck. Jimmie hands me a drink he has made for me. I am sure my face is red, no one says anything to either of us, not knowing or not caring what just happened. My embarrassment slowly subsides. Our guests leave, I put our kids to bed, and Jimmie makes good on his promise spending a very long time making love to me afterward he whispers "I'm still mad at you" I pinch him "For what! What'd I do to you?" I ask. "You never told me how much the dress was" he says I laugh, really? We're still on that? I really don't see what difference it makes who pays for what. He obviously isn't going to let the argument go so I just tell him "It was about $350 for the dress, the alterations, which by the way I have to be on a strict diet until the wedding because if I breathe I'm going to pop the stitches were another $75, and for the headpiece was $180." He nods "Well you really can't buy your own wedding dress. It's just wrong on so many levels of wrongness." He holds me and I fall asleep.

13

The Phone Call

The end of the school year is fast approaching, bringing with it lots of final exams, end of the year parties, and field trips. The thing I love the most about being home is that I can actually participate in these activities with Trysten, Tyler, and Ashley. Of course I bring the twins along. They are growing so fast. The older kids and I spend our afternoons swimming in the pool. The babies float around in their little floats, but not for too long because their fair skin will burn easily. Jimmie has been keeping his resolve to stop hanging out late. He usually comes home before dinner, and hasn't stayed out past nine in over a month. Jeff and Heather are becoming more friendly. They haven't been out on an official date yet, but he stops over once in a while. He never says he's here to see her though, he always finds some excuse to talk to Jimmie about something. Last Sunday it was to ask him about a repair on his truck. Jimmie confessed later to me that it had to be an excuse because Jeff is one of the best mechanics on the farm. I would like to see Jeff and Heather get together. She is a nervous wreck when he's around. It's cute really, Heather is usually so confident, but this "hick" as she would call anyone who works on the farm, makes her seem quiet and self conscious. Jimmie says Jeff asks a lot of questions about Heather. I don't see why he doesn't just ask her out.

Jimmie tells me that he thinks she's too good for him, way out of his league, obviously he hasn't given up on the idea entirely though. Everyone is getting excited about the wedding. Invitations went out last week. Heather took care of all of that for me, thankfully because I wouldn't have invited half the people she did. I haven't seen some of them for years. I don't know why everyone thinks it's customary to invite every single relative to a wedding.

Today I have an appointment with the caterer for the reception at Lakeshore Golf Course. I need to choose the menu. Jimmie offered to come with me, but I assured him that if anyone knows how to feed people it's me. The only request he gave me was that we have an open bar. I also need to go to the D.M.V., to fill out paper work for my passport. Ryan and Arthur are giving us a honeymoon for our shower present. I am still really nervous about going anywhere with Tom still missing, but the police, Jimmie, Ryan, my father, and Shawn have all assured me that the kids will be fine. I know I am not going to get my way. I informed them all that I am going under duress and that I will annoy every single one of them by calling a hundred times a day! I tried very hard to convince Jimmie to go to the cabin. I almost won, I brought it up while we were making love, when he protested against the idea, I stopped. He almost gave in, but opted for a cold shower instead. Oh well, that was my last attempt. Of course I gave in to him, the next night. He promised me he would make triple sure the kids were all right. I am not going to be able to get out of this trip! I know I won't have fun. I will be worried sick the whole time. Jimmie knows it too, but for some reason he's Hell bent on us going. I just wish I knew where it was we were going, but I guess I'll find out when we do our party in a couple weeks. I know

Heather has gotten me some really fancy lingerie, I found two bags from the boutique where she works in her room while I was picking up laundry. I didn't look at them too much, I just know they aren't for her because of the size on the tag that was hanging out of the bag. I don't wear that stuff anyway.

Later at the Lakeshore Golf Course, I meet with the caterer and choose the menu. We're going to do a buffet that way everyone can pick what they want. I chose to make my own menu from their selections. I chose prime rib, ham, and turkey for the main course. I also select several salads, two pasta dishes, and several appetizers. The bill for everything including the open bar for our three hundred invited guests is well more than fifty-five hundred dollars. The DJ of course is separate that is another five hundred. Over all the whole wedding is about twelve grand. I guess that's not too much considering some of the other weddings I've looked up online. It's a lot to me, but for once in my life I can afford it.

I arrive home just before Ashley and Trysten get home from school. I go through their school papers and prepare dinner for the family. Tyler comes home waving a sign up for baseball. I stick it on the fridge for Heather to review. Heather comes home from work, followed by Jimmie. Jimmie is excited for Tyler to join baseball, Heather fills out the form and the boys go outside to play catch. Just as I am about to call them all in for dinner, Jeff pulls in so I set one more plate on the table. "Dinner's ready guys" I holler as I see Jimmie toss the ball to Jeff who tosses it to a grinning Tyler. I feel guilty for calling them in. They were just getting started. Jeff follows Jimmie up to the deck talking about a tractor. "Why don't you join us for dinner?" I ask him. He shrugs and looks to Jimmie "Come on in, it's fine." Jimmie says ushering him into the house. Heather comes down, obviously not knowing Jeff was here, because she's in her pajamas. When she saw him in the kitchen she rushes back upstairs coming back moments later wearing the outfit she wore to work. She glares at me across the table as I feed the boys. "Mom, I'm getting better at catching. Jeff even threw me a fast ball! I caught it!" Tyler says excitedly. "I'm good too. I just don't want to play." Trysten says looking for attention. "Maybe we can all play after dinner?" Jeff suggests. "Unless you guys have other plans?". I think this is a great idea. I love a good game of ball. "Sure! Let's all play. I love baseball." I say nodding. Jimmie says "You do?" surprised. "Yeah, she played softball all through school, from like fifth or sixth grade right up until she...um. Until she was a junior. Right?" Heather explains. I know that she was going to say until I got pregnant. I don't know why she didn't say it. Ashley knows I was only seventeen and a senior in high school when I got pregnant for her. "Yeah, I didn't play my senior year obviously. They kind of frown on pregnant girls on the team." I nod. Jimmie smiles at me, reassuring me that Ashley wasn't a mistake. "I did not know that." He says very surprised. "She even won trophies, for softball, and cross country too." Ashley nods. "Well, I never played on a team, but I'm sure I can whoop your butt!" Jimmie says jokingly to me. I smile at him and then narrow my eyes "You wanna bet?". Jeff laughs "Are they always this competitive?" to Heather. She smiles "No. They're flirting." She waves her hand at us to tell us to knock it off. I kick his leg under the table and we both feed one of the boys each. I love how he helps me at dinner. We finish dinner and I bring in the strawberry shortcake I made this morning. "I helped pick the berries."

Trysten says proudly. I nod "You did buddy, thanks for helping. Do you want the first piece?" I ask. He nods. I serve him up a big helping and then pour the whip cream on top. "Geez, I haven't had strawberry shortcake in years." Jeff says. I serve him up a piece and then everyone else. The boys love the whip cream. Jimmie gives them each a little bit with a taste of the strawberries. They do their little wide mouth bird action that we all find irresistibly adorable. When we are finished, I wash the boys up and Ashley and Heather clear the table. Heather washes the dishes and I put the boys in their swings on the deck. The guys and Trysten and Tyler are starting to throw the ball around the yard again. "Come on, go change. Let's play ball." I say to Heather as we finish the dishes. She shakes her head at me "I'll look like an idiot. I can't play baseball.". I sigh at her "Come on. It's just for fun. Who cares? It would mean a lot to the boys. I'm sure. Chicken?" she pushes my arm and goes upstairs. Well, I don't know what she's doing, but I'm going to play. I bring two beers out for the guys and join them playing catch. Ashley comes out with her sneakers on moments later. I throw the ball a few times to Trysten and Tyler, and then once really hard at Jimmie. He is shocked when he has to dive to catch it. "You've got quite an arm!" He laughs. "She was the pitcher." Heather's voice says from the deck. She has on a pair of jean shorts and one of my plaid button up t shirts. She's even wearing sneakers! I almost laugh but I don't want to do anything to send her running back into the house. We form teams. Jimmie, Trysten, Ashley, and Heather against Jeff, Tyler, and me. My father's truck pulls into the driveway. He walks out back to us. "You're just in time." I holler as he walks across the lawn. "In time for what? Dinner?" He asks. "No, we're playing ball.

Come on you're on my team." I tell him. He joins us in the out field. "OK but I'm pitchin." He says taking the ball from me. I nod and take position at third base. I can see Jimmie is loving this back yard baseball game. They strike out the first round, and we take bat. I hit one so hard Jimmie has to run into the woods and scavenge for it. "Holy crap!" he laughs retrieving the ball. I skip around the bases, just to be a bit funny. Heather laughs and Jimmie kicks the invisible item with his foot. Tyler gets out and then Jeff hits, Jimmie catches the ball throwing it to Heather who doesn't catch it, but does get it in time to get Jeff out on second base. I think he might have let her. Dad hits, but Trysten gets him out at first base. We switch again. Jimmie hits and I catch it before it hits the ground. "OUT!" I yell and my Dad gives me a high five. Heather hits her second ball, but Tyler gets her out at first base. Ashley hits and makes it to second safely. Jimmie hits again sending the ball flying, Ashley makes it home, and I slide taking him out on third base! Dad and Jeff are laughing hysterically. We switch again. Jeff hits. He makes it to first. Tyler hits Jeff makes it to second, but Ashley takes Tyler out at first. Dad hits Jeff makes it to third, again my Dad gets taken out at first this time by Ashley. I hit and the ball is gone into the woods again. Officer Reynolds is on duty and has come to watch our game, he stands against his car clapping when one of us hits. Jimmie and Jessie look for the ball. Meanwhile, Jeff makes it home and I walk the bases twice, just to be a smart ass. Jimmie and Jessie come back with the ball. He smiles at me "OK, what's the damage?" He asks. "What do you mean?" I ask not understanding. "I bet you I could beat you. I obviously didn't. So what do I owe you?" he asks. "Ice cream!" Tyler yells. I nod. "Good idea buddy" I say as I mess up his hair. "OK let's go get ice cream." Jimmie says and heads to the deck to help with the babies. "Okay thanks for dinner Sara. I'll see you tomorrow Bill, Jimmie." Jeff says waving goodbye. "Hey, wait a minute. Why don't you join us? You were on my team. Jimmie owes you ice cream too." I say jokingly. Heather scowls at me. He looks at me unsure at first, but then Heather says "Fair is fair, come on you can ride with us. You too Dad." The men and Heather's boys load into her van and our family rides in Jimmie's truck. I take his hand across the console. "Sorry if I wounded your pride" I joke at him. "You didn't. I just had no idea you were that good. You keep surprising me." He says and kisses my hand. We all enjoy our ice cream. Heather seems to be lightening up a bit toward Jeff. "I can't believe I got you." She laughs. "I haven't run in years!" she continues. I still believe he let her. Dad huffs a bit, he must think the same thing I do. We all finish and head back to the house. I prepare the children for bed and then join the adults on the deck with a drink. I am happy to see Heather and Jeff laughing and joking together. Dad leaves after he finishes his beer. "Heading out, see you tomorrow. I don't like drinking here with that cop sitting there." He says and hugs me. "Night Dad" I say and he leaves. Jeff switches over to soda, must be my father's comment made him think about it too. He stays until a bit after nine, then he bids us a goodnight and leaves. Heather retreats to her room and Jimmie and I head into bed as well.

"I'm going to go in to take a bath." I say to Jimmie and kiss him on the cheek. I head into our bathroom and begin running the water when I hear the phone ring. It's very late for someone to call, unless it's an emergency. I look at the clock it's nearly ten. I shut the water off and go out into the living room to over hear Jimmie on the phone. "This is James." He says. He looks at me across the room. He nods at me. "Well, thanks Paul. We appreciate it." I hear him say. Paul? No, it can't be. "That would work out fine for me. I'll have the lawyer send you the paperwork." Jimmie says into the phone. Lawyer? Paperwork? I am so confused. "I would like to say just one thing" he pauses "I understand that." He says pausing again. "Listen, no one wants anything from you. Sara, Ashley, and I are perfectly fine. They were perfectly fine before without me and certainly without you. I understand. You were very young. So was Sara. Ashley is a beautiful, intelligent, young woman with nothing but the brightest future in front of her. I hear you man. I don't really care." Jimmie says into the phone his voice sounding not angry but adamant. What the Hell is going on? I wish he would just give me the phone. It's obviously Ashley's father Paul. "Let me just say Thank you. Yes you heard me. Thank you. Thank you for walking out on them. Thank you for being a horrible father. I am sure you're not a horrible father to your other kids. Whatever! I'm just saying Thank you. You'll get the paperwork by Monday." He hangs up the phone. He almost throws it onto the receiver. I stand anxiously awaiting him to explain what just happened. "That was Paul." he nods. I nod obviously, "He wants to sign over his paternal rights to Ashley." Jimmie explains. "He's never had any custody or anything? We've never even been to court. He's never paid me a dime! What the Hell is he trying to pull?" I am angry. Jimmie takes my hand. "It's just a form from the attorney. It says he'll never fight you if let's just say I wanted to adopt her give her my name. He wants to sign saying that he relinquishes his rights. He doesn't want to see her. He doesn't want you to sue him for child support. That kind of thing.",He explains. I exhale deeply. Paul is such a piece of crap. I already got the best of him thirteen years ago. Jimmie loves Ashley, but we've never discussed him adopting her. That's something I would discuss with her, if he even ever brought it up. Jimmie pulls my hand wrapping it around his waist. He kisses the top of my head. "I told him Thank you." He whispers. "I know. I heard you." I say. "If he hadn't had been such an ass, you might have been more open to getting involved with someone else after he left. You might have met some rich handsome movie star out in California." He sort of laughs. I laugh too and shake my head "I'd still chose you." I say. He looks at me confused. "What did you say?" he asks. I lean up and look him in the eye "I said, I'd chose you. If I had a chance to do it all over again. I would still chose you. You are my match. We are exactly right and always will be." I say and kiss him. He sighs pulling away from me "Go take your bath, Momma. I'll be in. I'm going to lock up.".

Jimmie watches as I lay soaking in the tub. He is so weird, why does he stare at me? I get out and let my towel fall, walking naked into the bedroom. I lay under the covers and he crawls in next to me. He holds me, massaging my arms, my back, kissing my neck. He whispers "I love you" into my ear. His breath on my neck sending a churning in my stomach. I roll over and push him making him lay on his back. I lift his arms above his head. I lean down to kiss him, but I don't I kiss his neck, his chest, his belly. I kiss him everywhere. I climb onto him and take him, then retract. I tease him some more. His arms fighting my hand trying to hold them in their position. He may be the masculine stereotype in our everyday life, but in this room I rule, and he likes that. I bite his neck playfully. He can't take much more teasing. I kiss the inside of his groin, I know I am driving him insane. I take him again, moving very slowly. Then I release his arms. He pulls me harder and harder. I move away from him. I won't allow him to kiss me. He hates it when I do that! I kiss his neck and push him into the bed. He pulls me off of him and rolls me onto my belly. He takes me from behind his hands pulling my hips into his. Moments later he is about to finish, but I'm not nearly done. I pull away from him, and he knows what I need him to do. He continues pleasuring me, and when my muscles spasm I let out a sigh of bliss and relief. Then I climb onto him again holding his arms down, moments later he is finished and we lay tangled beneath our sheets. "I can't wait until we are alone" he whispers in the dark. "Why that wasn't good enough?" I ask quietly and jokingly. "No, it was perfect. I would just love it if you could let go, I know we can't. We always have to be quiet." He whispers. "Where do you think we're going?" I ask. "Heaven" he says. I giggle into his chest and fall asleep.

14

Ashley's Dad

After Paul's phone call, my mind was reeling for days. Why all of a sudden the interest in signing over his rights? Why did he feel he had any rights at all to begin with? What would Ashley have to say about all of this? I hadn't brought up the discussion with her. I have been avoiding it. Jimmie and I have talked about it very briefly, he took care of the paperwork and even mailed the large envelope to Paul's attorney. He hasn't mentioned adopting Ashley again. I think even he is avoiding this conversation, not because he doesn't love her or anything, it's just neither of us have talked to her about her father's wishes. I really wish Jimmie was just her father, I wish he had said that he wanted to adopt her. I almost asked him about it, I wanted to, but I don't want him to feel pressured into doing anything. Honestly what difference does it make? Jimmie loves Ashley. Ashley loves him. I love both of them, who cares what her last name is? It really isn't all that pressing of an issue to me. Father's Day is this Sunday, I am preparing for a get together with Ryan, Arthur, and my father. It will be fun. We are going to have a cookout, swim in the pool, maybe get another backyard baseball game going.

Jeff keeps stopping in, still using Jimmie or the wedding as an excuse. Heather and I have talked about him. She is interested, but is waiting for him to make his move. I told her she should just ask him out, but she insisted that would seem desperate so she won't do it. She also swore me to secrecy so I haven't said anything to Jimmie. Ashley is winding down at school. After today, she only has three more half days all filled with finals and then she is off for the summer. It will be nice to have some company during the day, I get a bit lonely during the boys long naps. Usually walking outside with a tray of cookies for the on duty officer. Officer Reynolds likes chocolate chip the best. Also I feel paranoid because I am so afraid to leave the house, so scared Tom will run me off the road or plow into my car as I am pulling out of the parking lot. I get my groceries as quickly as possible, I've even begun leaving the boys with Liz or Donna while I shop. I know Tom is out there. He is, and I am not going to make it easy for him to hurt my babies. Jimmie keeps assuring me that Tom took off for Mexico or Canada, but his eyes read that he is just as afraid for our family as I am. Once I have all my provisions I hurry to Liz's to pick up the boys. Ashley and Trysten will be home from school soon.

The bus arrives bringing the older kids home, Ashley seems down a bit. "What's up girl?" I ask her as she sits slumped on the couch, a bag of chips in her lap. She smiles and shrugs "Not much. You?" she asks. I sit next to her and put my arm around her. "Rough day?" I ask. She shakes her head. "No, it's fine. I'm good." She tells me. I wish I believed it, I rub her arm lovingly and get up from the couch. Jessie takes my place, and begins thumping her tail. I look out to see Ryan's S.U.V. Pulling into the driveway. "Uncle Ryan's here, Arthur too." I say to Ashley. She smiles and her eyes brighten a bit. "Cool, are they staying the whole weekend?' she asks. I nod. "Good, it will take her mind off of the stupid dance!",Trysten says sarcastically. "What dance?" I ask. "Nothing, it's stupid! I'm not going." Ashley slumps into the couch again. Well, if she's not going to tell me about it, I'll just call Deb. I'm sure Mariah knows all about this dance and why it's got Ashley's panties in a bunch. I open the door for Ryan and Arthur greeting them with hugs then they take their bags upstairs, and I retreat to the kitchen with the cordless phone.

"Hey Deb" I say as she answers.

"Oh Hi! Sara, how are you?" she asks.

"I'm good, hey, do you know anything about a dance?" I ask.

"Oh yes! The Father Daughter Dance. It's a seventh grade tradition. Kinda like the girls moving on to being young women, it is their last year as little girls. You know? Next year they are really considered Jr. High." She explains. Father Daughter Dance, that explains a lot. "OK, when is this dance?" I ask. "Tonight" Deb explains. Oh well, that puts a damper on things. I don't even have time to get her a dress or anything. "What time? What's Mariah wearing and John? I need details here Deb." I explain. "Oh, It's at seven tonight in the gym, and we've got a cute little dress, it's not too dressy, just enough for Mariah. John's just wearing a nice shirt and slacks. He got her flowers and everything. He's such a good father." She tells me. "Yeah, he is. Thanks Deb." 'You're welcome, "she says and I hang up. I go back to the living room. "So, Father Daughter Dance. Huh?" I ask Ashley. She looks at me and forces a smile. "It's fine, Mom. Really, I get it." She says to assure me. "Do you want to go? Why didn't you say something sooner? I'm sure Jimmie would go with you." I ask her. She shrugs and shakes her head. "I don't know, I guess.". "Well, it's not too late." I say trying to get her to tell me what to do to make her feel better. "Not too late for what?" Ryan asks as he comes into the living room. "It's nothing, a stupid Father Daughter Dance. Everyone is going." Ashley explains. I defend Jimmie. "This is the first I've even heard about it. You can't get mad if you didn't even ask anyone to go with you. I am sure Jimmie still will, do you want me to call him?". Ashley shrugs. "Or Grandpa? I'm sure he would go." I try to find another solution. "What am I chopped liver?" Ryan asks jokingly. "I'd be honored to go. Would that be all right with you Ash?". She nods and smiles. Arthur comes in, "Can Arthur come too?",she asks. Ryan nods. "And I'll call Jimmie and explain Mom, so he doesn't have hurt feelings." Ashley says. She takes the phone into her room and Arthur looks at Ryan and I confused. "Where am I going and why would it hurt Jimmie's feelings?" he asks. Ryan puts his hands up in the air "I guess, we're going to a Father Daughter Dance with Ashley tonight." Arthur looks at him concerned. "Do you really think that's a good idea?" he asks. Ryan nods again. "She's going to need to pick a dress." I say heading into Ashley's room.

She's sitting on the bed with the phone in her hand. She looks up at me and then dials the phone. She seems nervous. "Hey, it's Ash. Nothing, everything is fine. Um. There's this dance at school." She says into the phone. "Yeah, tonight. No, you don't have to Uncle Ryan and Arthur are going to go with me. Yeah I'm sure. It's cool. I just didn't want you to get mad or anything. OK? All right, see you later. Bye." She ends the call. She lets out a relieved sigh. "So. What do you want to wear?" I ask her. She goes to her closet and picks out a really cute green dress, it's a bit sparkly and not exactly age appropriate for her, but I know she's wanted to wear it since Heather got it for her at Christmas. "Cool. Do you want me to fix your hair? Aunt Heather will be home soon, if you'd rather she did it." I say. I know she would rather Heather did it. I would rather Heather do my own too. "Yeah, Aunt Heather can do it." She says setting her dress on her bed.

"I think I hurt Jimmie's feelings." She says sadly.

"Oh yeah? He's a big boy. He'll be fine." I say. She didn't mean to hurt his feelings. I know that. "I guess. I just. I don't know. Jimmie's cool, he's really nice. I just know I'm not his kid. He shouldn't have to do this stupid stuff with me. He's got his own kids." Ashley says. I sit next to her. "Ash, Jimmie loves you. We're a family." I say trying to assure her. I know my words fall short, but she nods. I leave her alone to change. I go out and begin making dinner. Tyler comes in followed by Heather. I call everyone to the table for dinner. We visit, talking mostly about the wedding. After dinner, Heather and Ashley go into the bathroom and Ryan and Arthur go upstairs to get ready. Jimmie comes home just as they are all ready to leave. Ashley comes into the living room looking more like a woman and less like my child. I almost burst into tears. Heather has woven her hair into a fancy braided twist. It looks so pretty. She even applied very light makeup to her face. I let it go, realizing it is a special night. Ryan and Arthur pose for pictures with her, and then I do too. Jimmie seems out of place, not sure what to do so I encourage him to get in one or two as well. We all say goodbye and my princess is off to the ball with her two escorts.

Heather brings me a drink and Jimmie a beer as we sit in the living room. "You know that she really wanted you to go with her." She says to Jimmie. He looks at her confused "She asked Ryan and Arthur. It's fine." The door bell rings and Jessie runs to the door to greet our visitor. Jimmie opens the door to Jeff. He directs him into the living room and I grab him a beer. "What are you guys up to tonight?" he asks. "Oh, Ashley just left to go to a dance with her uncles. We're just hanging out." Jimmie says. "Heather's right." I say to him when he sits next to me. Jimmie raises his eyebrows "She is?" He asks. I nod "Girls are weird, they never want to just ask for what they want. They wait for the guys to figure it out. Don't ask me why, but I know that she really did want you to go, she was just afraid to ask. Happens a lot to us women doesn't it Heather?" I explain getting a very glaring look from Heather. She nods and says "Why can't you guys just be telepathic? It would make life much easier." Jimmie rises. "Why can't you girls just say what you want? Men are not complicated. We're easy. Just tell us what you want us to do and most of the time we'll do it." He says. He smiles down at me. I laugh and say "Do the dishes, take out the garbage, and change the boys before you put them to bed." He shakes his head at me. "I can't. I've got a date with a beautiful girl." He says and heads into the bedroom. Heather smiles at me, "Tell him to stop and get her some flowers.". She says. Jeff drinks his beer and shakes his head, "Sure starts early with girls doesn't it?" he asks.

Jimmie comes out moments later looking very handsome in a pair of black slacks and a button down shirt, although he is fumbling at tying his tie. I rise and fix it for him. "Thank you, for doing this for her." I say and kiss his cheek. "All I can say is, won't we be the talk of the town by morning? Ashley and her three Dads." Heather laughs. Jimmie laughs "Must run in the family, you McCann women are so....." I raise my eyebrow at him waiting for him to say the wrong thing. He smiles his crooked little smile that shows his dimple "hard to say no to." He says and I smile. He leaves and I go back to visiting with Heather and Jeff. "So, Jeff. Are you bringing anyone to the party?" I ask, I know Heather was curious about this as well. She had wanted me to find out if he was bringing someone. He shakes his head. "No, just me.". I nod. "You are welcome to stay here that night, you know, so you don't have to drive." I tell him. This sends a flush of red over Heather's face. She must be having naughty thoughts. I wish she would just tell him she likes him, it's getting annoying. "So Heather, why didn't Ashley just ask Jimmie in the first place? Did she say something to you?" I ask. Jeff feels awkward, perhaps I should have asked her this later. "You know how it is, you can't just ask." She says. I look at her and then at Jeff "Well, like Jimmie just said. If you just ask, you'll probably get what you want." I get up and leave the two of them alone, hoping that they will at least strike up a conversation. The tension between the two of them is crazy. They both like one another, but each of them are too shy or too stupid to say anything.

I get the boys ready for bed, put away the dishes and then rejoin them in the living room. I feel like a third wheel. Neither one of them is talking, so I take the boys into the nursery and put them in their swings. Ryan and Arthur return. I can hear everyone laughing in the living room. "You should have seen her face, when he asked to cut in while we were dancing. It was priceless." Ryan says beaming. "She was really surprised he showed up.". Good I am so glad she was happy. "They should be back soon. They were talking to a couple of Ashley's friends parents when we left.". Arthur explains. Ryan and Arthur take their seats on the couch, talking with Heather and Jeff. I mix up drinks for Arthur, Heather, and me and bring them in. "So. Tell me. What happened? Was she having fun?" I say hoping they will elaborate. "Yeah, she was. She was beaming. We all took turns dancing and playing games with her. It was great. Makes me want to adopt." Ryan laughs. Arthur rolls his eyes. "I'm just thankful we have a niece and nephews to enjoy. I don't think I could handle it on an everyday basis.". I laugh. Kids are great, I love being with the kids. "You know Paul called?" I say to Ryan. He looks at me surprised. "Oh yeah? What did he want?" he asks. "Jimmie talked to him. He wanted to sign over his paternal rights. Jimmie mailed him the paperwork." I explain. Ryan shakes his head and gets up from the couch walking to the kitchen. Jeff looks to Heather "Who's Paul?" He asks. "Ashley's father." She explains. Ryan returns bringing Jeff and himself a beer. Ryan never drinks beer. I don't say anything though. "Thanks" Jeff says taking it from him. Ryan opens it and drinks one long pull then says "Well, Ashley's already got a Dad. So his loss I guess. Actually she's got several. I dare anyone to challenge that." He states sounding very protective and paternal. Arthur pushes him with his shoulder, bringing a smile to his face. His mood lightens considerably when Jimmie and Ashley pull in the driveway. They come in and join us. "So did you have fun?" I ask. She nods and smiles. "Thanks again for taking me Uncle Ryan and Uncle Arthur. I was so surprised when Jimmie walked in! I was the luckiest girl there. I had three dates." She beams, her smile reaching through her eyes. It is so great for her to have these three wonderful men to love her and watch over her. She doesn't need Paul. She never has. She doesn't need Jimmie to adopt her either. He loves her, just as much as he does our boys. She has several Dads and a grandfather. We don't need any piece of paper to prove it either. I go into the kitchen and get Jimmie a beer. I bring it to him and the six adults sit and visit. I've never seen Ryan drink. It's weird. Ryan is a lightweight. After his second beer he is already stammering and getting loud. At least he's a happy drunk. He tells Jeff, Jimmie, and Arthur stories from our childhood together. Heather and I laugh as he tells about the time Heather's boyfriend rode his bike to the house in the middle of the night. Ryan caught her trying to sneak out the back door and chased the poor kid down the road. He was our father figure. Dad was gone by then, and Mom had her hands full with the three of us. Heather always had lots of boys interested in her. "What about Sara?" Jimmie asks laughing. "How many times did you have to chase the boys away for her?". Ryan sits back into the couch thinking. "Never" he says. "Did you even have any boyfriends before Paul?" he asks. I shake my head. "No. He moved here in January of our senior year with his Dad. We never even went out on a date." I explain. Heather giggles "I remember that. I felt so bad. It was my fault really. I kept telling her she couldn't be a virgin forever, she certainly couldn't go off to college without trying it once." Her voice becoming somber. "I'm so sorry. I was so stupid." She says. I shrug. "So was I." I admit. Jimmie squeezes my hand. "You know we've never been on a date?" he says almost jokingly. "Are you asking me out?" I say sarcastically bringing laughs from everyone. He nods his head. "Yeah, I am. Will you go out on a date with me?" He asks. "Oh, I don't know...." I say. Then I nod "sure, when?". He thinks for a minute "Tomorrow night. Just us." he says. I look to Heather. "Can you watch the kids? Oh wait. You have to work. We can't. She needs someone to pick her up, and..." I say and get cut off by Jeff "I can bring you to work and back home, it's no problem" he says his eyes almost begging her to say yes. She nods. Ryan interrupts as well "We can watch the kids. I think Arthur and I can handle that. Right?" I nod. "OK, so it's a date." Jimmie smiles. "Where are we going?" I ask. "I'll come up with something. And No you won't have to dig up or catch dinner." He smiles. I laugh. The night goes on and we are all well into the alcohol I offer Jeff the couch. "You should stay here tonight. It's no big deal really." I say. His eyes look to Heather and then to Jimmie. Jimmie nods "It's fine. We've got a guest room upstairs or you can crash on the couch. You're honestly probably better off upstairs. Sara gets up really early." He says. Jeff still looks like he doesn't know what to do, Heather gets up, "Come on up. I'll show you where the guest room is." He obediently follows her upstairs. Ryan and Arthur go up after them and Jimmie and I pick up the glasses and beer bottles from the coffee table. "This was fun." I say. He nods. "It was really nice of you to go to the dance tonight." I say. He smiles. He's being awfully quiet. "I think Ryan was upset about Paul. I told him about him calling and that you sent the paperwork to him." Jimmie takes my hand, "Ryan loves you guys. He just gets mad when people don't treat you like they should." He says. "Especially me." He almost whispers. "You treat me just fine" I say assuring him. "No, Sara, I don't. You have no idea, you deserve to have everything. You always worry about everyone else. You never think about yourself. I don't know how you keep everything straight. I'm trying. I just thank God you put up with me." He rants. I roll my eyes and finish picking up. Why does he feel that way? He does everything for me, for the kids, I can't stand it when he's so down on himself over nothing even. "So, where are we going tomorrow night?" I ask trying to change the subject. He smiles "Well, do you remember the night I picked you up and we went fishing?" Of course I do. I nod. "I was going to take you over to Jefferson, to that Italian place. You'd like it. I think we'll do that." he explains. I nod. I smile remembering that first night. He still sends butterflies through my stomach. I meet his eyes, and move to him to kiss him. He runs his fingers gently over my skin on my arms, barely touching me. "So, you think you'll get lucky tomorrow night?" I jokingly ask him. He pulls me into him and hugs me "I'm lucky every night." I take his hand and we walk into the bedroom where I intend to show him just how much he means to me.

15

My Date

Heather and I sit out on the deck early Saturday morning drinking our coffee. Jessie pacing nervously back and forth on the deck. I think she knows that Jeff is here and he usually isn't or something. Heather beams over her coffee cup at me. "So Jeff and I chatted for a bit last night before I went in to bed." she says. I smile back at her. "Really?" I ask inquisitively. She nods "He's really nice. He makes me nervous though. I feel like every time I talk to him. I sound like a moron." I giggle a little at this and sip my coffee. "No, you don't. You just think that because you're trying too hard. He likes you, trust me. He's shy. You need to just ask him." I tell her. She shakes her head "He's made no comments about me being pretty or jokes that he might like me. Usually men will hit on me, I don't want to throw myself at him. I don't want to come across as desperate or something.",she says nervously. "Men are easy. I am sure Jimmie or Dad have talked to him about being respectful to you. If not, geez Heather, you've been through a lot. Maybe he's seeing if you're even ready for that. Just because a guy doesn't treat you like a piece of meat, doesn't mean they don't like you." I tell her my voice and my words sounding very much like Mom. Heather smiles at me "I know, I guess I've just never had a guy be NICE to me before, it's weird. Speaking of guys, I better shower and get dressed before he gets up." She rushes. I shake my head. "Just be you, for once. If he still comes around after he sees you without makeup you'll know he's interested." I laugh. She doesn't get a chance to have it her way, because Jeff and Jimmie sit in the living room when we go inside. She and I make breakfast for them. Pancakes, bacon, eggs, toast, and juice we set everything in the dining room so everyone can eat as they wake up. I bring the guys in their coffee and Heather brings sugar and creamer. I am so glad she took my advice and is just being herself. It's better to let him see her for who she is, instead of always putting on the show. "Thanks for letting me stay, and for breakfast. I don't know how much of an appetite I'm going to have." Jeff says but fills his plate with bacon and eggs. Jimmie smiles at me as I bring in the boys and begin to spoon feed them their rice cereal. I mixed in a little applesauce with it just to make it taste better to them. They are getting so big. Shawn is chunkier than Ryan now, which is great because we can tell them apart. He has quite the appetite, always cleaning his bowl. Ryan is a bit more fussy. Jimmie helps me after he finishes his breakfast. I nibble at my toast in between feeding spoonfuls to the boys. "Eat Momma" he says picking the boys up one on each hip to go clean them up. "No, I'm good. I got it." I say taking Ryan from him. "She doesn't want to gain any weight before the wedding. You should see her sweating working out every morning after the kids leave. She's obsessing over it." Heather jokes. Jimmie frowns at me. "You're kidding right?" he asks Heather. She shakes her head. "I got these guys sit down and eat." he says his voice sounding a bit irritated. I do, I eat some eggs and drink my coffee. I shoot Heather a glare across the table. "You do not need to worry about it, get real Sara, you just had twins. Give yourself a break." She says to her defense. Ryan has come down "Worry about what? Fitting into the dress? I told you we'll just have them take it out a little if they need to." He says piling on his pancakes. Jimmie looks in from the living room "You know about all this nonsense too?" he asks Ryan. What is the big deal? "What nonsense?" Ryan asks. "I know she said the dress was a bit tight. You know how she is." He says almost dismissing the fact that I am still in the room. I don't want a big blow up argument. I just laugh "Oh well, if it doesn't fit, we'll just get it fixed." Everyone else moves on talking about other things, I finish and bring my plate to the kitchen. I go into our bedroom to get dressed. Jimmie follows me in. "You are not fat." He says flatly. I nod "I know, I just wanted to tone up a bit, you know before the wedding." I smile. He walks to me. "All right. I just hate hearing about this stuff from everyone else. Why don't you tell me?" I look at him confused "About me exercising? I didn't think it was a big deal. I did tell you the dress was tight." I tell him. He sighs pulling me into hug him. "It isn't a big deal. I overreacted. Sorry. I am looking forward to tonight. How about you?" he says. I nod. "It'll be nice." I say. He leaves and I get dressed. We all go about our routines. Jeff leaves thanking us over and over for letting him stay. Ryan and Arthur hang out with the kids, Heather and I work on laundry, Jimmie leaves for a bit to go to his brother's. Once we are alone Heather says "So, I told you we talked.". I nod and she continues as we fold clothes "He's never been married, no kids, his parents live over in Jefferson. He's an only child. He worked at a trucking company as a diesel mechanic before he came to work at Appleton. He's been there for nearly ten years now. His last girlfriend was about three years ago. She cheated on him. They were together a long time." She tells me. "So, did you tell him anything about yourself?" I ask. She shakes her head. "He didn't ask me anything. Probably because Dad or Jimmie have already filled him in on all my details." I nod and we continue to fold "Going out on your first date tonight. Are you nervous?" she jokes. "We did have a date. He took me fishing. We've just never been to a restaurant or a movie or normal date stuff." I say. "You should let me do your hair for you and your make up." She says. I nod, "OK."

Our laundry folded, I put clothes away and put on one of my swim suits so I can jump in the pool with the kids. My stomach is getting flatter, it's not perfect, but it's getting better. I put on my coral bikini, finally feeling I look good enough to wear it again. I lay floating around with the boys while the bigger kids swim. Arthur sits on the deck visiting with Heather. Jimmie comes back and I see his face flush red as he looks at me. I hope he isn't still mad about earlier. I motion for Heather to take little Ryan from me, she does and I carry Shawn out on my hip. I take him from her wrapping the three of us in a towel and we go inside. Jimmie takes Shawn as we enter the kitchen. "You're killing me Momma" he says to take the baby into the living room. We lay the boys down and put their clothes back on them. I leave them in their play pen and go to get my clothes together for our date. Jimmie comes in locking the door behind him. I am standing looking into the closet searching for something to wear. He stands behind me resting his chin on my shoulder, his arms around my waist. "I'm all wet. You're going to get soaked." I laugh pushing him away. He kisses my neck "I don't care.". I turn and kiss him hard pushing him down onto the bed. He removes my top and kisses my breasts then my belly. I unbutton him and kiss him everywhere. He flips me over so he is above me. He starts kissing the insides of my thigh, then he stops. He buttons his pants and smiles. "You better get dressed." he says almost laughing. He calls me a tease. I don't think so. I sit up, I remove my bikini bottoms and walk to him. I sit him down on the edge of the bed. I unbutton his pants again and pull them down. I pull off his shirt. I sit on my knees and look at him. I start to rub and kiss him. I pleasure him orally, his hand on my shoulder, almost afraid to move. I don't usually do this, I'm not sure if I am doing it right, but he seems to be enjoying it. After a few moments I climb onto him we make love, it's weird in the middle of the day like this, but I have to admit it's fun. "Sara.....I love you. So much." He whispers between breaths. I kiss his neck and continue. I whisper "I love you. You're mine." and then he finishes. I kiss him deep before climbing off and retreating to the bathroom for my shower. He's still sitting on the bed when I get out. He walks over to me taking my towel. "Later" I tell him. He sighs and kisses my neck. "When?" He asks continuing to kiss my naked body. I really want to throw him back on the bed, but I know we've got things to do. I push into him, "Later" I say. He sighs. I pull the coral shirt and black skirt from the closet that I wore on the night we went fishing for the first time. He smiles. "I was hoping you were going to wear that." He says. I smile and find some under clothes. He exits as I finish dressing, moments later Heater comes in with her tool box. That's what I call her makeup bag. She does my make up and hair for me. I haven't looked this good since before the boys were born. She finishes just as Jeff pulls in to pick her up for work. "Have fun" she says as she follows him out the door. "You too!" I say to her and she gives me an annoyed look.

I go over and over the instructions for the boys with Ryan and Arthur. "They'll be fine." Ryan says and practically pushes me out the door. Jimmie opens the passenger's side door for me. I get into the truck, and he gets in to drive. "You look really nice." He says and he hands me a bouquet of flowers that he had in the back seat. Roses, they are very pretty and smell nice too. "Thank you" I say smiling. I remember when he brought me the hand-picked daisies and lilies. "They're beautiful.". He smiles and starts the truck. We head into the city. I really do not miss living in the city. Just riding in the truck seeing all the traffic makes me nervous. We arrive at Antonio's restaurant, he walks to my door and opens it. "Where did you learn to be such a gentleman?" I ask him as he opens the door to the restaurant. "From my Dad, not my real Dad, my Mom's husband Patrick. He insisted that Shawn and I learn how to treat a lady." He says and we go inside.

This is so nice, just sitting here, talking without kids running up or babies crying. It is so easy to get lost in the everyday chaos of life. I really enjoy this time with Jimmie alone. We sit holding hands across the table, sipping on our beers as we look over the menu. "We should do this more" I say to him, his eyes meet mine. "I was just thinking that! We should. Once a month or something." He says. I smile and nod. "You shouldn't get buried in housework. You are far too beautiful to hide away from the world." He smiles. I roll my eyes and look back to my menu. I am thinking about having the Scallop Fettuccine Alfredo. The waitress comes and Jimmie orders an appetizer platter, and he gets lasagne. I order mine and we sit talking again. We talk about his job. I tell him about Heather and Jeff. He laughs a bit at this. I tell him about Deputy Reynolds whom I bring lunch to every day when he's on duty. I also tell him about some of the little things that the kids do, that I just never bring up because our evenings are rushed and busy. We catch up on a lot of things that we used to share, but somehow got put on the sideline. The waitress brings our appetizers and we snack and talk about the wedding. I tell him about the menu and the decorations. He smiles. "You're making me the proudest, happiest man in the world." He intertwines his hand with mine playing with my ring. "We need to get you a new ring" he says "You can pick it out this time. I'll have to get one too, I hope you don't mind if I don't wear it though." I raise my eyebrow at him "Oh you're wearing it." I tell him flatly. He smiles "I knew you were going to say that. I've already come up with a solution. My family, we have a curse. Wedding rings are dangerous especially in my line of work. My great-grandfather got his wedding ring caught on a planer and cut his finger off. My Grandfather cut off two of his fingers on a saw mill, the culprit a wedding ring. The men in my family don't do well with wearing rings and keeping all ten digits, so here's my solution. I'll get a tattoo of a band around my finger." He looks at me for approval. I thought my mother was superstitious. I nod in agreement. "It can say property of Sara Goodwin." I say sweetly realizing I just said my soon to be name. Jimmie smiles as I say it. "Whatever you want." He says. The waitress brings our food and we eat. I haven't had scallops since I left California, they're quite good. "We'll use the ring for the ceremony. You can get your tattoo later." I tell him. "Do you want to stop by the jewelery store and take a look on the way home?" He asks. I shrug "Sure." We enjoy our meal, and leave the restaurant.

Jimmie drives through the city to the jewelry store where he purchased my engagement ring. We go inside and start looking. The clerk shows us lots of options. Jimmie chooses a plain gold band. I really like one that kind of wraps around my engagement ring with two small diamonds on each side. It makes me think of our three kids. I eyeball it as Jimmie is fitted for his ring. I bet it's expense so, I move my eyes looking for something plain. "Do you see something you like?" the woman says to me. "How much is that one?" I ask about the wrapping one. She pulls it out and puts it on my finger to show how it would look with my engagement ring. I really like it. "We're having a sale on the wraps right now, and since you bought the ring here, you'll get the discount." She says. "It'll be $1749.00" UGH. Yikes. I am almost afraid to touch it. I hand it back to her. "I'll keep looking" I say. Jimmie takes my hand. "If it's what you want, I don't care. Get what you want." I shake my head "That's ridiculous, I can't justify spending that much money on a ring." I keep looking I select a small gold band, plain and perfect. It's only $100.00. The woman kind of gives me a look of disapproval when she fits me for it, but I don't care. I know Jimmie would have bought the other one, if I said I wanted it, but that's just stupid. I dig in the garden, wash dishes, play with the kids. What good is a ring you're afraid to wear? We leave the store and Jimmie opens my door for me. He is standing outside of the truck, "Are you sure you got what you wanted?" he asks. I nod "Oh yeah! I'd be too afraid to even wear that other one. You want me to wear it don't you?" I ask. He nods "Either that or you can get a tattoo across your forehead that says Property of James Goodwin." I laugh and he smiles. He rubs my knee "I love you. I'm so glad, you're you." he says and then shuts my door. We drive back toward home. We talk more about the wedding. I have to sit down with the DJ and get the play list together. Jimmie makes a few requests. I need to get something old, something new, something borrowed, and something blue per Liz's instructions, to which he laughs.

He pulls into Mel's and we walk inside. We sit and Ronnie brings us our beers. We continue going over the little details of the wedding. Once we finish our beers, we leave and head for the house. We really could have picked Heather up from the mall because it's just before nine, but I am sure Jeff has enjoyed doing his small favor for her.

Upon entering the house, I see that Uncle Ryan and Uncle Arthur are really out of their element. Dishes, food, toys, diapers, wipes, bottles, and clothes are spread from the kitchen, through the living room and into the dining room. The men are standing holding screaming infants trying to soothe them as Trysten and Tyler fight or play running around the living room. I stand looking at all of them disapprovingly. They all freeze seeing us enter. Trysten picks up his sword and hits his brother "Come on, pick up." He says. Tyler does carrying so many toys he's dropping them on his way up the stairs. I take the screaming Shawn from Ryan and he instantly stops crying. I put him in his chair and take Ryan from Arthur. I take the bottle that he was trying to feed him and Ryan starts sucking silencing the screams. "Magic" Arthur says, letting out a relieved sigh. Ashley comes out the phone attached to her ear. "Help get this mess picked up." I say to her. She looks at me surprised, as if she didn't know I was home, and then says goodbye to her friend. She and Arthur begin picking up the dishes. Ryan looks as if he's been defeated "How do you do this? Everyday? All by yourself?" he asks as if it's impossible. "It's all about the routine." I say. Tyler and Trysten come back down picking up the rest of their toys. They look almost afraid that Jimmie or I might yell at them. I know Jimmie never has, I have at times, but they know what they need to do, so I don't need to tell them. Ashley and Arthur wash the dishes and then she runs the sweeper cleaning up the floor. The boys come back down in their pajamas and go in to brush their teeth. "I did tell them to do that at eight thirty." Ryan defends himself. I nod "They just know they can't get away with it with me. Look at them, they know they're in trouble." I say. "The hand that rocks the cradle rules the world, "Arthur says in awe as he assesses the living room that a moment before was torn apart and full of noise, now it's clean organized and quite. "Ain't that the truth." Jimmie says smiling. I change the boys and put them to bed for the night. Jeff drops Heather off home and everyone prepares for bed.

16

Father's Day

Sunday morning I get up and begin making preparations for our Father's Day picnic. I have gotten Jimmie a few presents from the boys. The coolest one in my opinion is the rock garden I am making. I have made all the kids hand prints in cement and pie dishes cooling them into rocks and added paint and decorations. They look really nice. I even did Trysten, Tyler, and Ashley's. It will look really nice in the flower bed. I guess in a way that is more for me, but Jimmie will like it. I also got him some fishing gear and a new boat seat. His was getting a bit beat up. I got my Dad a new camera, he definitely needs one, his is ancient. Ryan and Arthur will like the cookbook Ashley and I put together for them. Heather and I drink our coffee and get breakfast for everyone. Jimmie is still sleeping. I let him sleep, its Father's Day after all. I do all his normal chores for him, I vacuum the pool, and begin mowing the lawn. Then I go into the house and do my usual chores.

Heather has been keeping an eye on the boys for me. They need their baths. Jimmie gets up well after nine a.m.. "Wow, I slept in." He says surprised. "I'll bring you breakfast, its Father's Day." I tell him nodding for him to return to the bedroom. I bring him in a big plate of eggs, sausage, and blueberry waffles. He smiles at me as

I set it down on the bedside table. "Every day is Father's Day around here. I feel bad. I didn't do anything for you for Mother's Day." He says sounding ashamed. I shrug. It really doesn't matter to me. "It's fine. Come on eat." I say. He does and I continue making food for the picnic. Dad arrives just before noon, the kids greeting him and trying to hand him their gifts. We all sit at the picnic table and the kids give their gifts to Arthur, Ryan, Dad, and Jimmie. Heather loves the rocks that the kids and I made. Dad likes his camera, although Ryan has to show him a bunch of times how to even turn it on. Jimmie likes his gifts from the kids and I. He seems sad though, I am not sure why. Perhaps he is feeling bad that he didn't do anything for me for mothers' day. I take his hand under the table giving him a gentle squeeze. He doesn't need to buy me stuff. He does enough for me. He forces a smile at me. Jeff pulls in sending Jessie's tail thumping. Jimmie gets up to go greet him. Heather smooths her skirt and sits up straight. I almost laugh at her nervousness. Arthur must notice it too. He rolls his eyes at me. "I don't know, why you don't just ask him out." Arthur says to her. She huffs and crosses her arms. Jimmie and Jeff come to the deck and I go in to grab them a couple beers. I bring one out for my Dad too. I ask Ryan "Do you want one?" to which he shakes his head, and causes my father to look at me strangely. "I hear you're getting very good at ball, Tyler." Ryan says. Tyler nods "Yeah. We've been practicing.". "Do you want to play with us Uncle Ryan?" Trysten asks. Ryan nods and Trysten and Tyler runs into the house to get their bat and ball. "You up for another game?" Jeff asks me. I shake my head. "Not today." I say. "Oh come on, chicken?" Heather says to me. So she and

I run out to the lawn to play with the kids. Soon we have another backyard ball game going.

I can't really play, because I have to keep stopping to attend to the boys who are a bit fussy today. Arthur takes my place and I bring the boys into the house. The game continues long into the afternoon. Even our on duty officer joins in the fun. I finish cooking lunch and bring everything out to the deck. I was too busy to notice the officer was our usual Officer Reynolds. I invite him to join us. "Do you have kids?" I ask. He nods "Just one, but she's got her own now." He says almost sadly. We all sit and eat and laugh. After lunch, I pick up. The boys are down for a nap, which is nice, because they have been cranky all day. Jimmie comes in as I wash up the dishes. "Thanks for everything today. It was nice." he says. "You're welcome. Thanks for the date last night. You're very good to me Daddy.",I say smiling. He shakes his head and kicks the invisible rock with his foot. "Even your boyfriend got to join us. Just kidding, but that cops sweet on you. You're Dad and I are going to work on some stuff. Do you need anything before we get going?" he asks. I shake my head and he heads out the back door, Jeff, he and my father get in Dad's truck and leave.

Heather goes upstairs returning moments later in her bikini. That's the Heather we all know and love. So glad she's coming back to us. She stretches out on a reclining chair. I change into my pink ruffled one and make two drinks for us. I hand her the plastic margarita glass and take a seat next to her. We turn on the radio and sit soaking in the rays. Arthur and Ryan are playing with the kids. "Thanks sis." She says drinking her drink. I smile at her and ask looking over my sunglasses "Where did the guys take off to?". She shrugs "I'm not sure, I didn't ask.

Jeff said something about working on a tractor today." She says. I nod, "So how are things with you two, you actually got a chance to be alone last night. How did it go? You ask him out yet?" I ask. She huffs at me "I'm not going to ask him. He's definitely sweet, he came right inside to get me last night, opened my door and everything. Must be Jimmie's rubbing off on him.". I smile Jimmie is sweet in that way. "That's good, did you kiss him?" I jokingly ask her. She sighs "No, but, I think he wanted to kiss me goodnight. He held my hand just for a second. It sent tingles up my spine. He pulled away though." I giggle a bit. It feels like we are young girls talking about our high school crushes again. Heather's got a good heart, she's just been through too much. Jeff is going to have to make the first move if anything is ever going to happen between the two of them.

We sit in the afternoon sun and the kids eventually jump in the pool. Ryan and Arthur join us on the deck. The boys wake up, and I put them in the pool for a little bit. Heather is turning red from the sun. "Can one of you start the grill? I've got everything ready in the fridge." I ask to Ryan, Arthur, or Heather. She gets up and lights the grill, returning from the house with a tray of meat and a spatula. She even makes more salad to replace the one we devoured at lunch. Then she mixes up a batch of chicken wing dip. Returning periodically to flip the burgers and turn the hot dogs. Ryan takes over the grilling, "You're going to get burnt" he tells her taking the spatula from her. The other guys return bringing a half empty case of beer with them to the back deck. Jimmie smiles and splashes the boys and me playfully from the edge of the pool. "Hey momma" he says smiling. I walk over pushing the boys floats and give him a peck on the cheek. I get out handing the babies to Arthur who sets them carefully on a towel on the deck. I wrap myself up and take the boys into the house. Jeff sits with my Dad at the table, I can see him eyeballing Heather as she stands cooking at the stove in her bikini. This makes me smile. When she notices they are back, her face flushes red. I walk in and put on a pair of shorts, she runs upstairs and comes back wearing a pair as well and a tank top. Dinner is ready quickly and Heather brings everything out to the table. I put the boys in their swings and give them each a toy to play with. "Dinner looks good Momma" Jimmie says. I shrug "I didn't cook it. Heather did.". He looks surprised "Wow, Thanks for dinner Heather." She nods and continues to eat "See, I told you I can cook." She jokes to Ashley. We enjoy our meal together and then the evening begins to wind down. The kids all bathed and ready for bed, Dad leaves, Ryan and Arthur leave. Jimmie, Heather, Jeff, and I sit enjoying the evening on the deck. "We should have a fire, it's a beautiful night." Heather says. Jeff gets up and starts to find some small wood in the edge of the woods. Jimmie stacks it up in a safe spot in the yard and he lights it. The small flames begin to grow, until it's a nice glowing blaze. The guys bring chairs down for us to sit in. We sit around the fire, "Tyler's got a game this week, Wednesday. You should come." Heather says to Jeff. It isn't a date, but it's a start. His eyes look surprised, and he can't even disguise the enthusiasm in his voice "Really? Yeah of course I'd love to. Ice cream after the game? It's on me this time." Jimmie nods approvingly, Heather smiles and pokes the fire with a stick. "We need marshmallows." She says sounding disappointed. "Next time." I tell her. I snuggle into Jimmie, the air getting cooler, and I love this. I love these moments. Our fire beginning to get low, Jimmie says "We better get to bed." I nod. We leave Heather and Jeff to sit and be alone. Once in the house, Jimmie and I head into our bedroom, I check on the boys and then crawl into bed next to him. He holds me to him very tightly. "You OK?" I whisper. He inhales deeply and then says "No, I'm perfect." and kisses my cheek. Everything is perfect, that's the problem. In my experience things don't stay settled for long. I feel like I am waiting for the ball to drop, for something bad to happen. For Tom to show up, do something to try to ruin us. For life to throw us a curve ball. I know I am pessimistic but I feel that I am realistic. "Where did you go?" he asks. "I was just thinking, everything is perfect. Except..." I say and he stops me by rolling me over and kissing me. "Except nothing. Everything is great. Just let it be great. Don't worry so much." He says. I kiss him back. What will be will be. Right now in this moment everything is just as it should be.

17

No More Protection

Monday afternoon, an officer knocks on the door. I don't find this to be particularly alarming, sometimes they need to use the bathroom. However, upon answering the door the man tells me that they are no longer going to continue to watch the house, there has been no attempt on Tom's part to come here, and they feel that we are safe. They will continue to patrol the area, routinely. Of course this sends me into a panic. I call and leave messages for Jimmie and my father. I lock myself into the house and pace the floor nervously. Jimmie calls and I tell him, he assures me that everything will be fine, he'll be home soon. I try to push the fear from my mind, unsuccessfully.

The kids arrive home from school, I know I am being bossy and short with them. I try to calm myself down. They continue unpacking their school bags and then hurriedly go into their rooms to pick them up. Tyler comes in, and finally Heather and my father arrive. "It'll be fine." Dad says assuring me. Heather nods nervously and goes to her room. I take my father's hand, just him being here calms my fears. I wish Jimmie were home. He will be shortly. Dad smiles and squeezes my hand. "He's long gone kiddo. Don't worry your little head about it no more." He says. I nod, I know my eyes are tearing up, but I bite my lip to stop the tears from falling. Jimmie pulls in sending

Jessie's tail thumping. He comes in walking straight to me. He picks me up pulling me into him. "It's fine. I promise. I'm not going to let anything happen to you." He whispers into my hair as I cling to him. He knows that I am terrified, maybe I am being a bit over dramatic, but Tom has tried to kill me twice. It is a bit frightening. "The kids only have a few more days of school, then they'll be home with you for the summer. You won't be here all alone, and if it'll make you feel better maybe Ryan can come stay, he's all done with school until August." Dad says. Jimmie nods "That would be great, if he doesn't mind.". Dad nods "He'll do anything for these girls.". Jimmie releases me and I regain my composure trying to busy myself with cleaning and then Heather comes down joining me in cooking dinner. I think we both need to be busy. Jimmie comes in and explains "I just talked to Ryan, he'll be here tonight." He says. Heather lets out a sigh of relief. I nod to him acknowledging that I heard him. We serve everyone's dinner in the dining room. After finishing dinner, Ashley and Heather pick up the dishes while I give the boys their bath and get them ready for bed. Jimmie, Dad, Trysten, and Tyler play catch in the backyard. Ryan pulls in just before nine. I hug him when he comes through the door. Heather does too, he pats my arm and squeezes it a little. He waves to Jimmie and Dad through the door. "Thanks so much for coming, it means a lot." Heather says. I nod in agreement and he just smiles. "I'm sure it'll all be for naught." He says. I hope we haven't inconvenienced him. Jimmie comes in "Sara's all worried, no more police watch." He says and rolls his eyes a bit. I'm a bit offended, but I don't say anything. "Well, she needs to feel safe. It's fine, I'm not doing anything except working on some research, I can do that just as easily here." Ryan says to defend me a bit. "Besides, think of the money I'll save on gas. I was supposed to be driving up here a bunch in the next couple weeks anyway to take care of wedding stuff." He continues. Dad comes in and shakes his hand "Good to see you son, Glad these girls can always count on you." Ryan nods to him, and I can tell that Dad's words have affected him, and he's trying very hard not to show his emotions. I help him take his stuff up to his room. Once we are alone, he says "God, you know, I'm still just a kid inside." I look at him understanding. We all have vied for our father's attention for years and when we get it, it's very hard not to show how much it means to us. "Aren't we all?" I say and hug him. "It's different for me. He's finally.... Never mind. It's just been a long time coming is all." I just nod. I know it's different for him than it is for Heather and me. Our mother's death brought out a side of our father that none of us had ever seen. He's really present in our lives, all of our lives. He is trying. Ryan knows that more than anyone. They finally have a relationship, I thought for a while, perhaps Ryan would hold a grudge against Jimmie for his relationship with our father, but he doesn't. Ryan said one day this past spring that Jimmie would never be good enough for me in Dad's eyes, his eyes, or even Jimmie's eyes for that matter, so that's one thing they can all agree on. I had tried to defend Jimmie, but Ryan just laughed at me. "I like Jimmie, don't get me wrong" he said. I don't understand men, they say us women are hard to get. I go back downstairs after telling Ryan thanks again and goodnight. I check in on Ashley and then the boys. Everyone is tucked in and ready for bed. I run myself a bath, hoping to release some of the tension in my body.

Jimmie comes in after a while, bringing me a large drink. I take it from him and sip while I soak. He sits on the edge of the tub for a moment, then sighs and goes into bed. Perhaps he senses that I really just need to be alone right now. I drink my drink and soak until the water starts to cool. Feeling much more relaxed, I get out and go into bed. Jimmie lifts the blankets for me to crawl in next to him. I snuggle up to him feeling safe in his arms. I can't help but feel sorry for Heather, she must be feeling so alone right now. Knowing my mind won't let me rest until I check on her, I get out of bed. "Where are you going?" Jimmie asks almost annoyed. "I'll be right back. I just need to check on Heather." I tell him. He rolls over and I head upstairs to check on her. I find her in her bed wide awake.

"Hey, you doing OK?" I ask quietly from the doorway. She nods and sits up "Yeah, I just feel so bad. I'm so sorry, for everything." She says sadly. This isn't her fault. She can't possibly blame herself. "This isn't your fault. None of this is your fault." I say flatly hoping that she takes some comfort from my words. She nods fighting back her own tears, I sit on the bed and hug her. Letting her cry, rubbing her back and trying to soothe her. How awful this all must be for her. I feel stupid and selfish for overlooking her feelings. She sits up and forces a smile at me. "I love you, you know." She says. I nod "I love you too," I tell her. I hold her hand and just sit in the dark silent room with her until she falls asleep. Then I return to the safety of my own bed and Jimmie's comforting arms. He calms all my fears. He unknowingly fights my nightmares away. In his arms nothing can harm me. I know that I am so blessed to have found him. He always says he's lucky to have me, but he has no idea how much he means to me. Why he picked me, against all the other girls he could have had, I will never know. He has unleashed a side of me I didn't know existed. He has opened my heart and my mind allowing me to feel things I would have never been open to before. I see the good in things and people. Looking at the world through his eyes, it's a beautiful place full of good things. I know that before I met him I never saw that. I only saw the danger, the fear, and the hatred within myself. Even the way I see myself has changed. I no longer feel the need to rise to some unrealistic expectation. I am just me, and he loves me. I am the lucky one. The morning comes and the routine that goes with it. Heather doesn't need to work today. Ryan sits in the living room while she and I keep ourselves busy until the kids return from their half day of school. Then we all go fishing in the creek together. Jeff drives by as we are fishing. He parks on the side of the road and walks down the bank. "Hey guys, catching anything?" he asks to all of us, but he is smiling at Heather. She nods "Yeah, we've caught a couple. Oh look. I've got one now!" She says excitedly. Jeff smiles as she reels in a mid size perch. I think he is impressed that she can take it off the hook and throw it back by herself. I smile to myself, trying really hard not to laugh as he stands jaw agape watching her. The three of us went fishing almost daily with Mom when we were kids, it's not something you really forget how to do. She sets her pole down and he assists her as they walk up to his truck. Ryan watches them attentively then he furrows his brow at me "I'm supposed to be on protective detail.". He laughs a bit. "She's fine. Jeff's nice. She invited him to Tyler's game tomorrow night. They're just taking it slow." I say quietly hoping the kids and Heather won't hear me. "Oh yeah? Tell that to him." Ryan says and nods for me to look up the bank. I do, just in time to see Jeff pulling Heather in to kiss him. I quickly look away smiling. Ryan reels in his pole and a nice size bullhead which he throws back. "That was a good one.",I smile at him. Ashley pouts a bit "Why didn't we keep it? We can catch enough to eat." She asks. Ryan shakes his head "Water's too warm. They'll taste muddy." He explains. She nods and continues to fish.

Heather returns and picks up her pole recasting. Ryan and I both look at her for explanation but she instead she says "What?" sounding irritated. We just look away from her and continue to fish. Later back at the house, the kids in the yard and Ryan working on his lap top in the living room I corner Heather in the kitchen. "So? Are you going to fill me in or what?" I ask playfully. She smiles coyly at me. "Not much to tell I'm afraid." She says. I huff at her annoyed "Come on, spill your guts." She smiles and pulls herself up so she is sitting on the counter. "Well, the other night when we had the fire, you and Jimmie went to bed. I told him I appreciated him picking me up from work and him playing catch with the boys." She explains. I nod urging her to continue. "He didn't say much, just that I didn't need to thank him. That he was more than happy to do it. He really likes the kids you know." She says. I just stand listening to her, waiting for her to continue. "Well then, I don't know we just got talking about stuff and I took his hand. It was nice, just being with him talking. I wasn't sure at first if he was all right with me holding his hand, but he didn't pull it away. I felt weird. I'm not used to a man just waiting for me to make a move. He told me that he liked me a lot, and he knows what I've been through so he's not in any hurry. He'd wait as long as it took, if there was any chance for him at all. I kissed him. I don't know. I like him. He's cute, he's sweet, so I kissed him.",She tells me. I smile at her "And then? Come on Heather, I know you better than that. You just kissed him and that was it?" She shakes her head. "Nope, that's it. I kissed him, but he pulled away. Then he said he had to go, that he would see me Wednesday night at the game. Then today he really kissed me. Maybe he was wishing he had the other night. Sometimes it takes men a while to let stuff sink in you know.". I think that's sweet.

It reminds me of how Jimmie used to be with me. He didn't want to do anything to pressure me. He made me make the move. "That's good. I think he's good for you. He's nice. He'll treat you right." I say and then begin to make dinner. Heather picks at the ingredients as I make the salad. "You know. I don't think I've ever just been myself with a guy. I've always liked whatever they liked, done whatever they wanted. Geez, you know I didn't even like the music I used to listen to when I was with Tom. He liked it so that's what I listened to." She says. I have seen this for a long time. Heather loses herself in whoever she is with. She just absorbs into an extension of them. "Just be yourself. If he's worth it, he'll love you for it." I say, instantly realizing I've heard our mother say this to Heather a million times. She smiles and jumps off the counter, getting the steaks from the fridge to start the grill. Ryan comes in from the living room "Oh NO you don't! You're not flash frying those." He takes the steaks from her. She pouts a bit and then opens the cupboards looking for something else to make. "Here mix up the fruit salad for desert." I tell her handing her the bowl and the rest of the berries.

Our family enjoys our dinner, Jimmie loves having Ryan here to cook the steak especially because he likes his a bit rare. The thought of eating half-cooked meat has never sat well with my stomach. I know I always overcook steak. I love Ryan being here too. He is really helping pull Heather out of her depression, and I feel safer knowing he is here. I think this might bug Jimmie a bit. He wants to be the one that makes me feel safe. He does, but he has to work. I hope someday, I won't feel the need to be protected, but that day is in a distant and unimaginable future.

18

Home Run

Wednesday comes and Jeff as promised shows up to Tyler's baseball game. He sits beside our family in the bleachers as we await the start of the game. Jimmie isn't with us. He is down in the dug out helping prep the team. I can't hear him, but I see him instructing Tyler how to hit the ball. I can visualize him coaching our boys' teams in the future. He's so cute. I smile watching him encourage Tyler's teammates. The coach shakes his hand and then he joins us in the bleachers. The other team bats first, leaving Tyler's team in the outfield. Dad arrives just as the first pitch is thrown, Ryan stands allowing him to see where our family is seated. He comes up the bleachers sitting next to Ryan, he nods to Jeff and gives Jimmie a short wave. He pulls out his old camera, not the new one we had gotten him for Father's Day and begins taking pictures. "Where's your new camera?" Heather asks him. He shrugs "I couldn't figure out how to work the darn thing. Too many buttons.". Jimmie laughs a bit and we all continue to watch the game.

I do sneak a peek at Heather who has lowered her hand to be right next to Jeff's. He hasn't taken it yet though. I smile as Jimmie watches the game intently. He, Ryan, Dad, and Jeff looking anxiously whenever the ball even comes close to Tyler. Finally one of the kids hits one right to Tyler, Jimmie jumps out of his seat shouting "GET IT!" and Ryan, Dad, and Jeff all rise to their feet. Heather jumps up shouting and clapping as Tyler catches the ball. "YEAH!" Jimmie shouts and sits down next to me again. The boys are startled by the shouting and begin to fuss a bit. Ashley takes Ryan handing him to me, then she sets Shawn on her lap. We go back to watching the game. Tyler's catch was the batting team's second out. Jeff has taken Heather's hand. I caught a glimpse of the two of them looking into each others eyes. It was only a moment, but I saw it. I take Jimmie's hand and sigh. It seems so long ago that the two of us had those awkward moments, now being with him is like breathing. He gives my hand a gentle squeeze, I think he might have noticed the two of them as well. Trysten comes up the bleachers rejoining us after his visit to the concession stand. Heather quickly moves her hand away from Jeff's. The batter strikes out and teams switch places. The game drags on, Tyler doesn't even get a chance to bat. His team strikes out. The teams are still tied with neither of them scoring. The next time Tyler's team bats, Tyler gets a turn. We all stand shouting encouragements and cheering for him. Heather is his biggest cheerleader, Tyler turns and gives Jimmie a nod. Jimmie nods in return. His first ball is a strike, Jimmie shouts "Just wait for it Ty. Keep your eye on the ball." to assure him. The next pitch, Tyler swings hard and the ball goes flying. We all are on our feet, cheering and clapping. Onlookers looking at us like we are a bunch of crazy people. Tyler makes it to third base. He makes it home before his team mate is taken out at first. The game continues. Ryan and Jimmie take the babies from Ashley and I. Time goes on the opposing team scores two runs before they reach their third out.

Tyler's team takes bat again. Two boys make it to first and third. The game is almost over only a few more minutes remaining. Tyler takes the bat smiling and nodding to Jeff and Jimmie. Dad readies his camera and snaps pictures as Tyler hits the ball, it goes over the fence. Our row of the bleachers explodes. All of us rising to clap, shout, and cheer on our little guy. Tyler throws the bat runs the bases. Bringing the final score 4:2, his team pats him on the back as he runs into home base. Jeff hugs Heather and gives Trysten a high five, his smile is genuine. His eyes read he is so happy to be here, in this moment, enjoying this special time with us. Dad shouts "Come on guys. Pizza and Ice Cream on me." He leads down the bleachers to go collect Tyler. He scoops him up and puts him on his shoulder. Tyler's face is so proud and happy. This is the life that he deserves as well. All of our kids so happy, healthy, protected, loved, special in their own ways surrounded by people that love them. We all follow Dad and Tyler out to the parking lot. Trysten jumps into Dad's truck with him and Tyler. Jeff and Heather ride in Jeff's truck, Ryan and Jimmie ride in Jimmie's truck and Ashley and the boys ride with me. We pull into the pizza shop, Ashley chatting all the way about kids that she knows. I have to admit I was a bit distracted. I was thinking about the way Jeff opened Heather's door, how he stood holding out his hand helping her into the truck. The look on her face said it all. She's falling hard for him. I glance out Ashley's window just in time to see Jeff and Heather lost in a conversation inside his truck. Our presence quickly brings them out of their moment and we all go inside to celebrate Tyler's win. The night is spent laughing, chatting, and eating pizza. Once home Heather and I get our kids ready for bed, Jeff, Jimmie, and Ryan sit out on the deck drinking beer and talking baseball. Once Heather and I are alone I take her hand, "So, are you going to tell me or what?" I ask. She shrugs her shoulders at me "He's nice. I'm just not sure, I don't know if I am ready." She explains. I nod "Well, take it slow then.". She nods and joins the guys on the deck.

I finish cleaning up and then join them myself. They are talking about the party. It's fast approaching, just like the wedding. We all make plans for the Fourth of July. We are going into town for the fair. The county fair is held yearly in Jackson the next town over. It will be fun. I remember when we were all kids. Mom used to take us to the fair every year. We would eat fried food, cotton candy, drink soda and ride the rides until we thought we would be sick. The boys and Ashley will love it! Ryan bids us goodnight and heads into the house. I take Jimmie's hand and give him a gentle tug "Come on in to bed." I say to him. He nods and finishes his beer. I think we should give Jeff and Heather some time to talk alone. Jimmie goes in to shower and I let Jessie out to do her business before bed. Jeff and Heather have gone out to the front of the house, I only see him lean in to kiss her and then Jessie and I retreat to the house. I join Jimmie in our bedroom knowing Tyler isn't the only one to hit a home run tonight.

19

Off to the Fair

The first day of the fa ir is a Friday. It always begins with a parade. Heather, Ryan, and I pack the kids into the car and make it to the fairgrounds just before the parade begins. The kids clap as each float goes by. Ashley sees several friends from school either riding in the different floats for the fire departments or other organizations or marching in the bands. Little Ryan and Shawn are fully enthralled watching the balloons tied to their stroller. I have to admit. I am out of my comfort zone. I do not like being around so many people. It makes me nervous. Ryan laughs "How did you ever live in a city? You are a nervous wreck!". I shrug and try to force a smile. I lived in the city before I had to look over my shoulder for a psychopath that was trying to kill me and my family. I wish someone would tell us something about Tom. If they had any leads as to his whereabouts, if he had used his credit card, anything. The police haven't told us anything. I wonder if they still suspect someone did something to him. The thought has crossed my mind. My anxiety is soon swept away because Jimmie, Dad, and Jeff join our little group. Jimmie smiles and takes my hand pulling me to him kissing me on the cheek before leaning down and messing the boys' hair. "Hey, I'm glad you made it." I say to him with a sigh. He nods and we continue watching the parade. Once it's over our family strolls down the boardwalk to the midway.

Trysten begs Heather for money to play the games. Jeff says "They're all fixed buddy, but here go try." and hands Trysten some money. Heather shakes her head and walks to buy tickets for rides. Ashley says "Hey Mom, I see some of my friends can I hang out with them for a while?". I don't like the thought of her wandering around without me, but I don't get a chance to say no. "Go ahead, meet us back here in an hour. Do you need some money?" Jimmie says to her. She shakes her head, and looks to me for approval. I nod and say "Take some money just in case. Do you have your phone?" She takes the money Jimmie was offering and nods as she walks away from us. Jimmie must have read my mind because he says "You need to relax. She's fine." and takes my hand as we continue to walk around. My mind settles a bit, I allow myself to get lost in the smells and noise of the fair. Ryan finds us bringing corn dogs and a bucket of fries. We find a table to sit at near the bandstand, where a band is playing some oldies songs. Heather and Jeff are over by one of the rides watching the boys ride. She waves seeing us, I wave back. Soon they join us. Heather gets the boys hot dogs and fries. Jeff gets a big turkey drumstick, he looks like a caveman eating it. Tyler watches enviously as Jeff takes a big bite. Heather and I dance while we sit, humming along to familiar songs. Jeff and Jimmie smile, I think they both think we are crazy. "Hey, we should ride the bumper cars." Heather says. I shake my head, remembering when we were kids, she rammed my bumper car so hard it knocked the little electronic pole in half. We got kicked out of the ride. Our mother was so embarrassed and mad at us. "Oh, come on. Go. Both of you." Jimmie says nodding us toward the ride. Ryan laughs "Just don't break anything." Heather and I head to the line for the bumper cars. I can overhear Ryan telling Jeff and Jimmie the story. I see Ashley across the fairgrounds. She is riding one of the spinning rides with a few of her friends. I recognize a couple of the girls, and one boy to be Damien. Heather and I ride the bumper cars, ramming into one another and several young college age kids. Once our turn is over, the group of boys follows us out of the ride. "Hey!" I hear one of them, Heather and I stop. "So, what are you two doing next?" one of the boys asks us. I almost bust out laughing, are they really trying to pick us up? Heather points over to the table where Tyler, Trysten, Ryan, Jimmie, and Jeff are sitting watching us. "Well, I probably should let my kids ride some rides." She explains sarcastically to the boys. They appear to be shocked then one says "Sorry ladies. Hope you guys have a nice night." Heather and I giggle and walk back to our table. "Still breaking hearts California?" Jimmie smiles taking my hand. I roll my eyes and pull him up so we can walk around a little more.

Jeff and Heather go off to let the boys ride some more rides. Ryan heads to check out some of the exhibits. Jimmie and I push the stroller through the crowd of people, looking at all the little tents set up to sell different things.

"Sara?" I hear a voice say. I turn to see Kayla, the young girl I had met at the doctor's office this spring. She is with Officer Reynolds. "Hey there! How are you?" I ask noticing she is carrying her baby in a carry pack. She smiles "I'm fine. You?". Officer Reynolds' face looks confused "Hello Sara. You two know each other?" he asks. I nod "Yeah, Kayla and I have the same doctor. Good to see you. Glad you're doing well." I say. Kayla shows me her baby's face, beautiful pink and new. "Yup. We're staying with my Dad. He got me a job at the station filing papers and stuff." I nod and smile. "Well, nice to see you." I say returning to Jimmie. "Your cop boyfriend has a new baby?" he says almost rudely. "That's his daughter and he's not my boyfriend I just fed him. I felt bad for him sitting out there all day." I say defensively. "Well...I can't remember the last time I got chocolate chip cookies." Jimmie says teasing me. I roll my eyes at him and we walk over to the ticket booth where we are supposed to meet Ashley. She's about ten minutes late, but no harm done. We find Heather, the boys, and Ryan and walk out to the parking lot. "No fireworks?" Ashley asks whining. I shake my head "I've got to put the boys to bed, we'll come out tomorrow night and watch them over the lake OK?" I say. Jimmie helps me load the boys into the car and we head home.

Once at home, I notice Jeff has not come to the house. Heather and the boys go upstairs to bed. Once Jimmie and I are alone he asks "Did you have fun?", I nod. His face flashes an old familiar look, I know to be his jealous look. "What? What did I do?" I ask. He shakes his head "Nothing. You didn't do anything. I guess I just forgot why I don't take you anywhere." He says with an air of indifference. "What's that supposed to mean?" I ask, it's been a while since I've had to deal with jealous Jimmie. "It's just, I guess, I still get mad. Especially the cop. I'm glad he's gone." He explains. I roll my eyes at him and get into bed. I don't understand why he gets so jealous over nothing. It's a bit ridiculous, I mean I rarely even leave this house. I think he likes it that way. Even I can see it isn't healthy for me, I was so anxious at the fair I thought I would pop out of my own skin. I really need to start getting out more. It isn't good for me to put myself in my own little bubble. I should start seeing Deb, maybe going to lunch with Donna or something.

20

Getting Out and About

I have started going to the town library for Story Hour with the boys. I know they don't have any idea what is going on, but I do it for myself. It's nice to meet other Moms. Heather and I have joined a Zumba class as well. We go on Wednesday nights. I confessed to her about my anxiety and even in her own depressed state she could see that it wasn't healthy. Jeff and Heather have reached a stalemate, he still comes by, but she hasn't made any further attempts to invite him out or anything. I really think the two of them need to grow up. Jimmie objected to the Zumba exercise class at first, but I assured him it was more for Heather than myself so he agreed. It's nice to get out of the house for a little while. I have met some really nice women at Zumba. I like having Ryan there too, he keeps me company during the day.

This Saturday is our pre-wedding party. Everyone keeps calling it a shower, I don't really feel like it's a shower. Nor is it a bachelor party or a bachelorette party. It's just a reason for everyone to get out and be a bit crazy. Heather refused for me to make the party preparations, she insisted that it was my party and it just wasn't proper for me to make the food myself. We have both invited some of the girls from Zumba class to come or meet us out on our bar tour. Ryan made sure I got my passport last week, I know now that he and Arthur have booked us a trip out of the country. Jimmie is thrilled about it, but I am still very anxious. I feel like Tom is peering around every corner, watching and waiting for us to let our guard down and launch his attack. Ryan suggested almost as a joke that I talk to my doctor about anti anxiety medication. I was very offended, although perhaps in a way I know he is probably right. I thought my anxiety was fueled by my isolation, but I think it is just an overwhelming fear of the psychopath on the loose that is trying to kill my family. I wish I just knew what was going on, but acknowledge that I might never know. Jimmie says I can't control everything, and I just need to trust and have faith. He says the words, but his eyes flash with fear and anger every time I try to talk about Tom. He's worried too, but he's just trying to be strong for me. Dad is very dismissive when I try to ask him about it. Ryan just gets angry, so I stopped trying to talk to him about it. I keep my thoughts to myself. In a house this full of people, it is difficult to have any privacy even within your own mind. Today I am meeting Deb for lunch at the mall, she is going to help me chose a few different outfits for my trip. Not knowing our destination is making shopping a bit difficult, so I asked Ryan some yes or no questions to help with wardrobe choices. "Is it south of here?" I asked to which he replied "Yes." "Should I pack a bathing suit?" to which he answered "Yes.". "Do I need to have something nice to wear?" to which he answered "Probably not. But you might want to pack something just in case." Our yes or no questioning went on for a while before I became too irritated by his ambiguous responses that I quit talking to him. Jimmie just asked me to get a carry on bag, he joked saying "I'm hoping we won't be needing any clothes." He's such a dork! He's not even the slightest bit curious as to where we are heading, perhaps he already knows.

I meet Deb in the mall food court. She is waiting for me, sipping on her coffee. I wave greeting her. I sit across from her "Hey girl! Glad you came, I half-expected you to cancel on me." She says. I shake my head "Why would I do that?" I ask. She shrugs "Oh, I know how busy you are." She says her voice seeming sad. "Well, I'm not too busy to get together with you." I say my voice sounding much like Heather's cheerleader tone. Deb smiles "I know it's hard for you to get away. Especially with the boys. I remember those days." She says. I smile, "So, what are you going to get for lunch? I'm thinking pizza for me." I say. She nods and we walk over and order two slices from the pizza shop. We sit again and talk about Mom stuff. The kids, housework, the wedding, and our men. We walk around the mall, I get a few things for Ashley and the boys. I find one outfit that I like for the trip, a very long flowing floral dress, Jimmie will like it. Deb finds a few things for her kids, I remember to get a luggage set.

Deb looks at me strangely as she is filing through some clearance items. "What?" I ask her almost sounding annoyed. She shrugs her shoulders at me. "Nothing. I just think it's funny." She says passively. "What's funny?" I ask. She picks up a shirt holds it up to me as if sizing me and says "Just that, you know, you and me shopping together, almost like normal people. We haven't really had much time for that stuff in the past year. It's just nice is all." She says. Deb usually isn't one to keep her mouth shut. I know this isn't really what she was thinking when she looked at me so strangely. "It is nice." I say as she hands me the shirt, it's only a couple dollars so I carry it along with some other things I liked. "So, is this going to be like a new norm for you? Are you allowed to leave the house now?" she asks. "What do you mean?" I ask her. "Well, it's just Jimmie doesn't seem to like you going anywhere. Honestly I was a bit worried about you. You have always been so independent. Since you've been with him, I don't know I guess maybe you've just been busy." She says. Jimmie doesn't control me. Does he? Have I really been avoiding going anywhere to avoid arguments with him? No, I don't think so. "Honestly, I don't go anywhere, because I don't want to. I am busy. You know how it is, kids, laundry, cooking, cleaning. Besides I have a psychopath that tried to kill me on the loose. Sorry if I haven't been social!" I rant at her. Her face is shocked and her eyes look wounded. I've hurt her feelings. "Sorry" I say immediately, "I've been really stressed out about Tom.". Deb's expression turns from angry to apologetic, "I'm the one who should be sorry. I didn't even consider that and I'm sure your hormones are still all out of whack from the twins. Have the police gotten any leads on him?" she asks. I shake my head "No. And Jimmie insists we go on our honeymoon. I don't feel comfortable leaving our kids, let alone Heather and the boys. Even with Ryan there, no one has any idea what Tom is capable of." I explain. She smiles sweetly "I'll check on her while you're gone. You and Jimmie deserve a honeymoon. Speaking of which. Do you know where you're headed? I know it was a big secret before." She asks very animatedly. I shake my head "Not a clue. I did have to get a passport so..." I shrug "Who knows? Jimmie's excited about it though." I explain.

We continue to shop and pick out a few things. We gab about the wedding, the party this weekend. She and John are excited about coming. Deb says "We're going to paint the town!" excitedly. I think everyone involved in this wedding is more excited about it than I am. The thought of this causes me to second guess everything. Am I doing it for them or for me? I love Jimmie there's no doubt in my mind about that. Why do we need such a big spectacle? I know I shouldn't feel this way, but it's how I feel. I am not enjoying the "experience" of being a bride like Heather and Arthur want me to be. I sense that Heather knows this, Jimmie too. I put on a big smile to everyone else. I know my lack of enthusiasm is really irritating to Jimmie so I try to show some excitement whenever the topic comes up. Deb and I finish our shopping and hug before we leave in our separate vehicles.

I stop at Mel's before heading home. I have one drink and visit with Oliver and Mel. I am leaving when Jimmie enters the bar. "What are you doing here?" he asks me as he raises his hands in question. "Having a drink, I was just leaving." I say. He shakes his head and heads out of the door. He's angry. I walk outside "What are you doing? Where are the kids? I thought you were shopping with Deb." He interrogates. "The kids are home with Ryan. I just stopped for ONE drink. I just left Deb and the mall. What is your PROBLEM?" I yell back at him. He shakes his head "Well, I've got to get back to work, I assume your going home? I'm not going to drive by here later and see your car?" He rants getting into his truck. I shake my head at him "You know, you're such a hypocrite! You go out all the time! You do whatever you want. I don't interrogate you! I'm done with this conversation. I'll see you later." I yell and get into my car. How dare he? I wasn't doing anything wrong. I drive home, as I do I question my own motives. Why did I go to the bar? Why did I do that? I don't really know. I felt like it. That's the only reason I can come up with.

Once home I bring in all my bags and the luggage and sit watching the babies sleep. Thinking about Jimmie's reaction to seeing me there bothers me. I've never given him reason to question my loyalty to him. What is the big deal if I stop and have one drink? I'm not drunk, driving around risking my life and anyone else on the roads'. I'm a good mother, I don't leave my kids very often if that's what he's upset about. I can't wrap my head around his actions. It really isn't very responsible of me to make extra stops on my way home, or to be drinking in the middle of the day. Ryan enters the nursery. "What's up?" he asks. I shrug "Not much, Jimmie's pissed off at me." I say. "What for?" he questions. "I stopped at Mel's before I came home. I had one drink. The way he acted you would have thought I'd been there for hours and I left the boys home alone." I say. "I don't know why he flips out over stuff." I continue. Ryan furrows his brow "He doesn't get physical with you? Does he?". I shake my head "NO! Never. He wouldn't.". "Well, I've seen him angry remember? I had to ask. Heather went years without saying anything because no one asked. I'll talk to him later. You have every right to go wherever, whenever you want. He doesn't own you." Ryan says his voice flat and paternal. "Don't!" I say. "I'll take care of it myself." Ryan nods and leaves the room. I go out and begin to prepare dinner. Heather comes in from the deck. She's really working on her tan. I should do the same.

Once dinner is prepped and cooking I change into my strapless suit and go lay on the deck. Heather and I sit tanning ourselves like reptiles soaking in the Vitamin D. I look up to see Jimmie sitting at the counter drinking a beer with Ryan. I can't hear them, I can only hope Ryan respected my wishes not to say anything to him.

Jimmie comes out, and he sits in the chair next to me. He sets his ice cold beer in the small of my bare back. I quickly sit up moving away from him. "Come on, don't be mad." He pleads. I huff and roll my eyes at him before wrapping myself in a towel and heading into the house where I resume making dinner. I am mad. I have a right to be mad. He can't just come home, make a joke and pretend everything is fine. I take my frustrations out on the poor boiled potatoes mashing them aggressively with the metal masher. Jimmie comes in and stands across the counter from me. "I'm a jerk, I'm sorry." He says, but his voice doesn't have any remorse in it at all. He sounds very passive, almost dismissive of his behavior. I look at him. I am sure he knows I'm upset. "You're absolutely right. You are a jerk." I say and put the mashed potatoes on the stove. I remove the casserole from the oven and then he explodes "What is with you lately?" he screams. "You running around all day, if you don't want to be home with the boys why don't you get a job!". I feel the heat in my face, I know the tears are coming but I push them away. "What's with me? What's with you? What do you care if I go anywhere? You're gone all the time!" I scream back. "I can go wherever I want. I don't need to ask your permission." I continue calming my voice. "I will go back to work. That sounds like a fabulous idea." I take a stack of plates into the dining room, and Jimmie follows me. "I don't want you to go back to work. I just don't understand the need for you to be in the bar in the middle of the day. Alone. I overreacted. I'm sorry. "he says calmer. "Well, I felt like it. You know I do like getting out. I have been cooped up for a long time. You could try to understand." I say as I continue setting the table. Ashley runs into the living room from her room "Are you guys fighting?" she asks. I nod my head and she goes into the kitchen and out the back door. "Look, I said I was sorry." Jimmie says still sounding very condescending. "We are going to be married in a month. My parents had this kind of relationship. My Dad was always trying to control Mom. It didn't work out so hot for them. Is that the kind of marriage you want?". I ask him. Seriously, he's acting possessive and I don't like it. I've never liked this side of him, this jealous irrational side. He looks to the floor. I am sure he's kicking his foot at the invisible item. He appears to be wounded. I take his hand, "You are better than this. WE are better than this. I love you, and if you love me you've got to let me be me." I say. He nods still looking at the floor. "OK?" I ask. He pulls me to walk around the table, I do and move in to hug him. "OK" he says hugging me.

21

Pieces

I sit alone in the kitchen. These are my only peaceful moments these days. It's just before dawn. Everyone is asleep. I quietly drink my coffee and try to collect my thoughts. Jimmie's outburst yesterday was short lived, he seems to have put the incident behind him. I wish I could put it behind me as well. Deb's comment about him being controlling, his outburst, and then his ability to so easily dismiss his behavior. I don't know why I didn't see it before, he is controlling. Is it because he is worried about me? Is he just as afraid of Tom as I am? Am I overreacting to all of this? Cold feet about the wedding maybe? Hormones? Maybe I am just crazy. Everyone around me is acting so strange, maybe it isn't them maybe it's me. Ryan drinks now, not just a beer here and there. I saw him making himself a drink and take it into his room, he won't drink the liquor around Heather and me though. There really isn't any reason for him to hide it. I don't understand why he feels the need to. Perhaps he doesn't want Arthur to know about it and is afraid Heather or I would say something. Dad isn't his usual self either, it almost feels as if he is avoiding being around us. He comes over and only stays briefly. Maybe I am pushing everyone away, maybe I am making them crazy. My brain picks through the bits and pieces of things that are bothering me.

Jimmie comes out of the bedroom. I prepare his cup of coffee and his lunch. I take my seat back at the counter looking out the glass door at my garden. Instead of his usual picking up his lunch and quick kiss on the cheek he sits on the stool next to me. He sits for a while sipping on his coffee, I wonder what he is doing, if he doesn't leave soon he is going to be late for work. He sighs deeply breaking the silence in the dimly lit kitchen. I turn to face him, his eyes full of concern. "Sara, I don't know what's wrong." He says. Really? My mind wants to scream, but I don't I just sit waiting for him to continue. "I'm trying my best, I know I slip. Thank you for sticking with me. I'm so sorry for...." he says and pauses "for everything." He takes my hand and kisses the top of it. I can feel the lump growing in my throat and my eyes beginning to tear up. I blink them back and exhale slowly shaking my head. "I am sorry too." I manage to get out. He stands and takes his lunch, "I better get going. I'll see you tonight. I love you." He leans down and kisses the top of my head. I guess he does understand that his behavior wasn't fair or right. I should be a bit more understanding of him as well. He's been through a lot too. I'm not the only one in this relationship that came with a whole bunch of baggage. My thoughts are interrupted by one of the boys waking up. I hear the mumbled cry and then the outraged scream of one of my infants in the other room. I go in and retrieve Ryan from his crib and leave Shawn to sleep. Then my whirlwind begins Trysten and Tyler waking up and coming down the stairs, breakfast, laundry, cleaning, Shawn wakes up, followed by Ashley. Ryan gets up coming down the stairs in an apparently hung over state, Heather I know is still sleeping. It must be nice to sleep the day away and allow someone else to take over your motherly duties.

I stomp into her room collecting the laundry from her floor. It is well past ten a.m.. She doesn't have to go into work until this afternoon, but I have about had it with her sleeping all day. She barely rouses as I deliberately stomp through her room and slam the door on my way out. I bark demands at Ashley and Trysten "Pick up the living room!" and "Go out and weed the garden" or "Could you help me with the boys please?!". My attitude leaves much to be desired this morning, I know, perhaps I just need to get some air. Let the house fall apart if it must. I take the babies out to the garden while I weed. The garden is growing nicely, the tomatoes should be turning red soon. I'll have plenty to make tomato sauce. I really enjoy the garden, it's the one piece of my day that gives me a sense of accomplishment. I could clean the house top to bottom and within ten minutes of finishing there would be another mess to clean. I have literally overtaken Heather's role as mother to her boys. Maybe I should just stop. I have three kids not five. She could take up some of the duties. She started to come back to us, but soon slipped back into her depression. I know she hasn't been contributing to the household bills either. I overheard Jimmie discussing it with Ryan, it's not his place to pay her share either. I know he didn't say anything to me because I am very defensive when it comes to Heather. I think I am going to confront her about things though, it can't go on forever. Tom is gone, where? Who knows? That leaves her as Trysten and Tyler's only parent. She needs to step up to the plate and do her job. They deserve better than what they are getting right now.

I continue to work in my garden pruning my tomato plants and weaving my cucumber wines through their cages. The cucumbers are just about ready to pick, by next week I'll have lots. I piece through the bits of my life that are bothering me. Piece by piece I sort and compartmentalize my problems. First order of business is to discuss Heather's behavior with her. I scoop up my boys and head into the house. I make lunch for the kids and wash up the dishes. Ashley is in the living room watching television with Tyler, "Can you keep an eye on them for me?" I ask her as I place the twins into their playpen. Ashley nods and I head upstairs into Heather's room. She is still asleep. I push on her shoulder trying to wake her up. She barely moves. "COME ON! GET UP! You're such a slug!" I yell at her. She snaps to attention and glares at me. "What?!" she whines. "You don't have to sleep all day, get your butt out of bed. Go downstairs. Your kids need you." I say and walk out of the room slamming the door. It isn't long before she comes down the stairs and straight into the bathroom where she proceeds to take an hour long shower. Once primped and ready for work she emerges from the bathroom looking at me as if I'm the one who's done something wrong. "What is your problem?" she asks. I shake my head and walk away from her before I say something I will regret. I know she's been through a lot, but haven't we all? Her boys especially. I have stepped up long enough, but now she needs to get her act together. I check on my boys who are playing on their mat in the living room. Trysten and Tyler are out in the clubhouse. Ashley is in her room, probably on the telephone. Feeling secure that the children will not overhear our conversation. I go into the kitchen and tap my fingers on the counter until Heather turns from the refrigerator to glare at me.

"You've got to start doing things around here. I have no problem helping you out with the boys, but you're taking advantage of the situation. Enough is enough. You're sad. I get it. Grow up. You're their mother." I say flatly, trying very hard not to yell. Heather shuts the refrigerator door and stands at the opposite side of the counter. "Is that all?" she asks. I nod and then her attack begins "I'm not LIKE you, I'm not strong. I can't do this by myself." She rants. "Everyone can't stay home and bake friggin cookies all day some of us have to work.". Work? Taking care of this house and five kids all day isn't work? "Heather, come on. Really?" Ryan has come into the kitchen. "Let's talk about what the real problem is here." His voice sounding very paternal and lecturing. "I'm not the one with the problem. Talk to Miss Sensitivity over here." Heather says defensively. "No, Heather you do have a problem. How about we check out what's in your purse, shall we?" Ryan asks grabbing Heather's purse, her face shows immediate concern, but she says "Go ahead." Ryan proceeds to open her purse, envelope after envelope of bills, piling them high onto the counter. "Last notice, past due, final notice. Shall I continue?" he says accusingly. Heather grabs at her bag as Ryan pulls out a prescription bottle. "Give me that!" she yells. "Who is Mary Lombardo? Why do you have her prescription? Oh maybe because you're drugging yourself every day and night. Doxepin, let's see...." Ryan says as Heather grabs the bottle from him. Why does she have so many overdue bills? Why is she taking someone else's prescription medication? "Just mind your own business. You wouldn't understand." She cries. Endless tears stream down her cheeks. As angry as I am at her, I feel so sorry for her right now. She looks so desperate, so broken. Ryan continues lecturing "It says right on the bottle that use of alcohol is strongly discouraged while using this product. You probably wash it down with a half a bottle every night! Enough is enough! You're broke. You wasted all the money Mom left you. Now you're just digging your hole even deeper, buying drugs. You and the boys had a fresh start, you had it made, and you're just going to throw it away.", Heather breaks at his harsh words, she falls into the stool at the counter laying her head down and sobs. I glare at Ryan willing him wordlessly to stop. He grows quiet and takes the pills from Heather's hand. He goes into the bathroom and flushes them down the toilet. I sit beside her silently just waiting for an explanation. I don't get one. Her sobbing finally subsides and she sits somberly, wipes her face and stares at me. "I am broke. Tom's account is frozen. I haven't been receiving any money from him. I know I shop too much. I like nice things. I've never had to NOT get what I wanted. I maxed out my credit cards months ago. I just don't know what to do." She says desperately. "We'll figure it out. I can go back to work. It'll be fine. Why didn't you tell me?" I ask. "I don't know. I thought I could fix it, I kept thinking things would get better. They started to for a while, but I don't know I guess I just don't know how I'm supposed to do this. I don't know how to work, be a Mom, manage money. I tried. My kids hate me. Jimmie can't stand to look at me. I'm driving Ryan to drinking. Even Dad won't return my calls anymore, and you, you just keep baking freakin cookies and playing house. Oblivious to everything that is going on around you." She explains. I should be offended, but I'm not. I know she's just lashing out because I'm an easy target. I'm not the only one who feels like the world is falling to pieces around them. Now it's time to pick up the pieces and get our life back on track.

22

The Roller Coaster

Life is funny, ups and downs, highs and lows. I like the middle the best. I take a lot of comfort in the mundane and everyday routine. Unfortunately, I was born into a family where everyone is hiding something and no one is what they seem to be. I do love my family, they are just insane. I am sure everyone feels their family is insane, but I think mine takes the cake. Also my life in general, before moving back to New York it was very simple, now every day brings something different. Sometimes it's bad, sometimes it's good, but it is a fact that boring and my life are two things I really can't use in the same sentence. Earlier today after Ryan confronted Heather about her debt and her drug use, I came to realize I am the most sane adult in this house. Which is a bit scary because even earlier this morning I was doubting my own sanity. Heather called in sick to work. She's having a long talk with Ryan upstairs in her room. Jimmie still hasn't come home from work. It's starting to get late. He's been doing this lately, going to the bar after work again, for a while he had made an effort to come home by dinner time. After the day I had with Heather I am not even going to address this issue with Jimmie. We have bigger problems to discuss, like how are we going to afford the utilities on the house, groceries, his truck payment, the loan for the house repairs, and all the other necessities in life. I regret spending so much on the wedding, had I known I wouldn't have. We could have kept things simple.

I busy myself with the routine, dishes, getting the kids bathed and their teeth brushed, feed the boys, make sure they have dry diapers before putting them to bed. Jessie starts pacing in front of the door just as I finish turning all the lights out. I see Jimmie's headlights pulling into the driveway. I sit on the couch waiting for him to come in. He opens the door, sending Jessie's tail thumping. I rise and go into the kitchen "You hungry?" I ask as I pass him. "Yeah, I guess." He says. I prepare a plate for him and set it in the microwave. "You mad?" he asks me. I shake my head, he's had too much to drink to have the conversation I was hoping to have with him tonight so I just set his plate on the counter and go into our bedroom to bed. It isn't long before he enters the bedroom, climbs in under the sheets and snuggles up behind me. I know he's naked, but I don't feel like making love right now. He kisses my neck and rubs my shoulders, I continue to pretend to be sleeping. He keeps persisting, so I finally give in. Once he is finished, I roll back over and return to the darkness.

For the first time in a long time my dreams are haunted, I wake with a jolt sitting straight up in bed. I am covered in sweat and my heart is racing. Jimmie sits up wrapping his arm around me, "Hey, shh, you're all right. Shh" he whispers as he comforts me. I cry, sob into his chest. I cannot even recall my dream, but I know this feeling. "You're OK. I'm here. You are safe." Jimmie whispers. I calm down after a few minutes and settle back into my pillows. "Are you all right? It's been a while since you've had one of those." Jimmie asks. I nod "I'm fine now. Thanks." I am sure that if I close my eyes sleep will not come, but the darkness will. My nights used to be haunted by an unseen danger, I would wake up terrified. Since my mother told me what happened to me years ago, my darkness has a face. It was easier to handle when I didn't know why I was so afraid, now my monster has a name. Jimmie continues to hold me until morning, his presence calming my fears, chasing the ghosts away.

I get up before the alarm goes off, I go into the kitchen to make coffee. There are shadows in every corner. I really need to get over this anxiety. I breathe deeply and exhale slowly trying to slow my heart beat. I gather Jimmie's lunch pail and start to pack his lunch. He comes to join me in the kitchen. "Good morning beautiful. How's my girl?" he asks as he kisses my cheek. I smile, "I'm tired. But hey at least it's Friday. Big party tomorrow right?" I say trying to make my voice sound enthusiastic. He smiles "Yeah. It's going to be fun. I'm looking forward to it.". I continue with my morning routine and he prepares for work. "Hey, before you go. Ryan and I had it out with Heather yesterday." I tell Jimmie. He doesn't appear to be surprised "Oh yeah?" he asks waiting for further explanation. I nod "Guess she's been having a really tough time. Financially." I say hoping he will tell me how long she hasn't been contributing. "I know." He says "Girl's got a lobster taste on a macaroni and cheese pocketbook.". "Well, I would like to put my savings into a joint account. I will go back to work after the wedding." I explain. He shakes his head at me disapprovingly "We can do a joint account, but I don't need your money. It's bad enough you've paid for the wedding. We're fine. Just keep doing the groceries and whatever you want with your money. You don't have to go back to work until you're ready. I don't give a damn about Heather and her tough time.

Maybe she should..... Never mind. I don't want to start the day off with a fight. I have to get going to work. I love you have a great day.",He says and leans down kissing my cheek. "OK, love you too. Bye" my voice hushed. I continue doing my regular routine. I do however wake Heather after her boys come down for breakfast.

Heather appears to be trying. She washes the dishes after breakfast. I rouse Ashley and the two of us take the boys outside to work on the flower beds. I love these moments with her and I. She's such a great kid. She's interested in learning about the plants, just like I always had been as a child. I am more than happy to share what my mother taught me about the garden. We finish our work in the flowers and move to the vegetables. Once back in the house I see that Heather has made herself busy with the laundry. As bad as I want to take over for her, because she isn't sorting it the way I do, I don't I walk past her in the hall and let her continue. I go into my room, collecting Jimmie's laundry from the floor and making our bed.

Heather knocks on my open door, I look up and meet her eyes. She walks slowly to my bed and sits on the edge. "I'm sorry. I just don't know how to fix it." She says apologetically. I sit next to her and she continues "You see, I've always had someone tell me what I was supposed to be doing. When we were kids, Mom always would tell me to act like a lady, smile, sit up straight. In high school, my friends told me what I was supposed to act like. Boyfriends before Tom, always told me what they expected from me. Do this, be this, like that. Tom was an ass, but he did keep me on a short lease. He had very clear standards of what he wanted in a wife. I was the one who was unfaithful, I was the one who had frivolous spending habits. I put us close to foreclosure and bankruptcy numerous times."

She pauses to catch her breath. Tears fill her eyes, and she exhales slowly. "That was no excuse for him to hurt you the way he did." I assure her. She shakes her head "No. I ruined him. I made him look like a fool to his friends. I slept with his boss, his coworkers, his cousin. I pushed him to it. The thing is now. I don't know how to be. I don't have anyone telling me what I am supposed to do." She admits. I guess in some demented way this makes sense. She blames herself for what he did to her. "I feel so bad. Not just for the things I did, but Tom almost killed us all. His own children, you, Ashley. It's my fault. Now we don't know where he is or what he's going to do. Every day I wake up thinking "Is today the day he comes?" and each night I lay awake worrying about it. The pills helped make me numb. I just don't want to live with this constant unknowing, I wish I could take it all back.". Heather cries. I take her hand and sit silently while she goes through her emotions of fear, guilt, sorrow, and anger. The roller coaster ride that is my new life continues to climb. I'm still waiting for the climax and the descent. She's right. Tom will come. He's filled with rage and hatred for Heather. He won't stop. Not until she's dead or we all are. Who knows what sadistic plan he has for us? He has nothing left to lose. One thing is for certain, he's coming and we're all in danger.

Jimmie doesn't want to listen to my concerns about Tom. He assures me that Tom is gone. We have a party, a wedding, and a honeymoon to plan. These are the only concerns he seems to have. His dismissal of my concerns is suspicious to me. Why isn't he worried? Ryan also seems very certain that there is nothing to worry about. My brother, the ever over protective and paternal older brother, not even batting an eye or furrowing his brow in concern over Tom. Also, my father, his absence has not gone unnoticed. This family has always been very good at secrets, and I have a feeling that the men in the family are keeping something from Heather and me. Maybe the police have shared some details with them? Perhaps I could call on my friend Officer Reynolds and see if he would fill me in on the investigation. I am sure he would if I brought him a plate of his favorite chocolate chip cookies. I'll find out, but for now I've got a party to plan.

23

Kiss and Make Up

It is Friday and I have a lot of work to do. I do my normal routine and then wake Ryan and Heather. I have made them each a list of simple tasks they should be able to handle in order to make sure everything is done before our guests arrive. I have asked Ryan to retrieve everything I need in town complete with cash and a specific list of items. He will carry out this task for me. I have asked Heather to help with the bed sheets in the guest rooms for our anticipated guests. She obediently goes upstairs and follows my instruction. Ashley is in charge of the kids today, I have asked her about this previously and she assured me it was something she could handle. I begin the seemingly endless mixing and preparing of the food for the party.

Heather had offered to have the party catered, but I refused. I like to cook, and honestly don't mind doing it myself. Ashley is up in the living room with the boys by the time Ryan returns from the grocery and liquor store. He also has some other bags, "I got some other stuff too," he laughs. "Thanks. What else do I have to cook?" I ask jokingly. He shakes his head "Art will be here this afternoon, I'm sure he'll want to decorate for tomorrow.". I nod, I did forget decorations, I am glad that Ryan thought of this or Loretta would have had a fit! Aunt Loretta and

Uncle Wayne will be here tomorrow morning. Heather has washed the bedding from the upstairs guest rooms, I should check to be sure she dusted the furniture. I'll do it after she goes to work. I continue making miniature cheesecake bites that Ryan requested in several different varieties: chocolate, strawberry, raspberry, and blueberry. I prep the vegetables for the salads and then take a quick break to lie on the deck with Ashley watching Tyler and Trysten swim in the pool. Ryan is in the kitchen with Heather, looks like the two of them are trying to put their argument behind them. I am really on edge today. My lack of sleep and nightmare have keyed up my anxiety. I go into the kitchen and make a drink while I prepare lunch for the kids.

Ryan peers over his laptop at me as I sip "Are we going to need an intervention for you too?" he asks jokingly. I shake my head "No. I'm just taking the edge off. I'll only have this one I promise." I say. He smiles "So, are you and Jimmie all right now?". I smile, "We're fine. He's excited about the party. I just had a rough night." I explain thinking he was wondering about my middle of the day need to have a drink. "You want to talk about it?" he asks concerned. I shake my head. "We've got enough problems to worry about. I'm fine." I say looking at Heather in the living room. Ryan shuts his lap top. "Heather, come here." He commands. She does, she walks into the kitchen and sits next to him at the counter. "Now I'm going to tell you both something. You two are my family. I love you both. I'm not going to let anything happen to either one of you. We are going to put all this nonsense of the pills, the spending, the drinking behind us. We are going to kiss and make up and be the loving "normal" family. Got it?" Ryan's voice paternal and at the same time joking.

Heather smiles at him and I can't help but laugh. "Since when are we a "normal" family?" I ask. Ryan reaches across the counter and messes up my hair. "Since never!" he laughs. Heather smiles and it seems we are all back to our "normal" selves. Arthur arrives bringing bags of gifts and some more alcohol. He also has dinner arrangements made for all of us this evening. "I have a special surprise for all of you." Was the only clue he would give us. After a day of cooking and prepping for the party, I welcome someone else to cook dinner. It is actually a relief that I don't have to worry about it. Just before four, my father pulls in the driveway followed by Jimmie. Dad gets out of the truck carrying several grocery bags. He doesn't come into the house but heads to the back deck and starts unloading his bags onto the table. I go out to greet him. "Hey Dad! Missed seeing you around. Been busy?" I ask as I exit the kitchen. "Hi there kid. Yeah, busy, you know. Work. Say I talked to Art earlier. He's here right?" Dad asks. I nod. My father doesn't normally reach out to Arthur, so I return to the house to let him know he's looking for him. Arthur has heard him and is heading out as I enter. "You go relax girlie. Let us handle dinner tonight." He jokes. I watch from the kitchen as Arthur and my father lay kabobs on the grill. Dad pulls out a few store-bought salads and a few bags of chips. Ryan laughs from behind me "That's something you don't see every day.". I nod. We both sit watching them cooking on the grill and drinking beer as they chat. Jimmie enters the kitchen from the bathroom. "Hey guys, what's up?" he asks and follows our gaze. "Bill's cooking huh? He told me at work that he and Arthur were making dinner tonight, Jeff's coming over too. Seems Arthur wants to make it a groomsmen weekend. Shawn's coming later, he's busy at work this week.". OK so it's a wedding thing, that's all right. It makes a bit more sense to me now. We all go out and sit on the deck watching Trysten and Tyler play. I bring out Shawn and Ryan to swing in their swings. Dad and Arthur must have been discussing Arthur's family. I listen as Arthur talks about growing up traveling the world with his archeologist and adventurous parents. He's had such an interesting life. We all laugh when my father pipes "I've never even left the county! Let alone the country!". He always liked to stick to where he knows.

Dinner is ready very shortly. Steak, onions, peppers kabobs, store made macaroni salad, chips, and fruit. It is good, but not the usual home cooked meal the kids are used to. "Thanks for dinner guys." I say in my mock Heather cheerleader tone. Arthur smiles "Well, it isn't much compared to your usual spread, but for a couple of bachelors I think we did just fine.". Dad laughs and drinks his beer, "I am a fan of those microwavable dinners, some of them ain't half bad.". I smile, I remember those first few days at Dad's apartment, he had nothing in his cupboards, just beer in the fridge, and a couple frozen meals in the freezer. Jimmie kicks my leg under the table "Yeah, other than Sunday's that's all I used to eat too! Now I would rather eat the box." He says causing laughs all around. Jeff pulls into the driveway causing Jessie to run to the front lawn to greet him. He comes to the back deck causing Heather to appear uncomfortable. I know he hasn't come over in a couple weeks. I wonder what happened with them? Oh well, I guess neither of them are ready for the relationship to move to the next level. Dad and Jeff shake hands and nods before he sits down and joins our little get together. "Would you like a beer?" I ask rising. "No thanks, brought my own this time." Jeff says rising to walk back out to his truck. "Good, you know this isn't a bar." Jimmie jokes.

Our evening continues, and the guys build a fire. Once chairs are brought down Heather, Ashley, the boys, and I join them. Jeff gets up and walks out to his truck. For a moment I think he's going to leave, but then he shuts and walks back to us holding a grocery bag. "Here, I brought these, just in case." He says tossing the bag to Heather. She catches it and opens it pulling out a bag of marshmallows. The kids run to the woods to find sticks. Then we begin roasting the marshmallows. I haven't roasted a marshmallow in years. It's fun. It's getting late so I go into the house and set the boys to bed in their cribs. "Come on in guys. It's almost ten." I holler out the door to Ashley, Trysten, and Tyler. They come in and do their usual bed time routine. Then I retrieve the baby monitor and go back outside with the adults. I don't know what I've missed but apparently I am the topic of discussion again. I overhear Dad and Jimmie as I am walking back through the night. "He showed me her picture that night and I was in love ever since." Jimmie laughs. Dad nods. Ryan asks "How can you fall in love from a story and a picture?" almost condescendingly. "I don't know, but something about her eyes. I knew, I just knew." Jimmie says staring out into the woods. I sit down next to him snuggling into him and he puts his arm around me. "I didn't know that Dad showed you my picture. I wondered how you recognized me the night we met." I say. He kisses the top of my head "I've dreamt about you from years. I could never forget those eyes." He explains. He's so sweet sometimes. "OK lovebirds, knock it off. Save it for the honeymoon." Ryan jokes. "So, whereabouts are you guys going anyway?" Jeff asks. Jimmie shakes his head "Doesn't matter. As long as we are far, far away.". I sigh, I still don't feel comfortable leaving, I wish we could just go to the cabin for a couple nights and call it good. "Well you guys will find out tomorrow!" Arthur says excitedly. Heather is the one to let out a long sigh this time. "I miss traveling." She admits. I know Tom used to take her on exotic cruises and lavish trips. I've really never had a vacation other than Aunt Loretta's house when we were kids. Jeff nudges Heather's knee with his "Where would you go? If you could go anywhere?" he asks. She sits up straightens her posture and sighs deeply. "I don't know. I like the ocean, I've always wanted to go to Alaska, but I've never had the chance." She explains. That surprises me. I would have thought she would say Hawaii or Australia, anywhere warm really. I am glad the two of them are talking again. Looks like we are all going to kiss and make up tonight. "I'd go to the jungle, if I had a chance." Dad says. I laugh "Well that's something I'd like to see, you in the jungle....." He smiles and finishes his beer. "Well kids, I better get going. You guys enjoy your fire, I've got to work in the morning. I'll see you all tomorrow night." He waves and pats Ryan on the back before heading to his truck. "I'm going to turn in too, late night tomorrow, don't want to be too tired to enjoy it." Ryan says and Arthur and he walk into the house. "Night guys" I say and then feel how tired my own body is.

I stare into the fire almost hypnotized by the flames. Heather seems to be doing the same. "You know, you two are pretty special." Jeff says breaking the silence. I look up at him for him to elaborate which two? Jimmie and I or Heather and I? "What do you mean?" Jimmie asks probably thinking the same thing I am. "Well, I mean, the fact that you two are together, getting married, living the dream. It's special." He explains. Heather obviously wounded says "Marriage isn't special if you don't make it special.". I smile at her hoping she takes comfort in my words "It's special when it's right.". I yawn again and snuggle back into Jimmie. "You getting tired Momma?" he whispers into my hair. I nod. I am falling in and out of sleep. "You really love her don't you?" I hear Heather say and then she continues "The day she had the boys and you were kneeling at the doctor's feet begging and pleading with him to help her, the way you cried and prayed when they told you she was hemorrhaging, then when they didn't come back and we waited an eternity for any news and you prayed to God to take you instead, bargained with him even. I heard you. I thought that's what I want. I want someone to love me that much. Then when they did come out and tell you she was OK, you cried again thanking God over and over again." She says. Jimmie responds "I've almost lost her, too many times.". His voice sad and somber. "Well, you haven't made good on your deal with God. You said you would never let a day go by that she didn't know how much you loved her that you would show her. That you would be the best father and husband she could ask for. You've got to keep that promise, not just because you made it with God, but because......." she pauses "It's what she deserves.". I open my eyes to see her rising and walk back to the house. After a long silence, sleep starts to take me again, I never heard about that before. I didn't know how hard the birth of the boys really had been on me. I don't know why Heather thinks Jimmie isn't keeping his promise. He's good to me with the exception of his jealous outbursts. "Well, I guess she told you." Jeff sort of laughs. "She's right." Jimmie says squeezing me gently. "Why do you say that? You're a good guy." Jeff asks. "I guess, but am I good enough?" Jimmie asks. I keep my eyes closed not to disturb their conversation. "Sure you are. You love her right? Loved her before you ever even met her. You provide for her. You take care of her. Protect her." Jeff says. "Yeah, well I suck at protecting her. As for taking care of her, she takes care of me. And providing for her? Well Sara would be happy in a shack with a dirt floor, she never asks for anything. She's not like Heather, that girl's high maintenance.". Jimmie says seriously at first then jokingly about Heather. "Yeah, I know. Kind of gave up on that. She'd never be satisfied by me. Bill told me about her endeavors with shopping. But hey she's gorgeous, she'll find someone." Jeff says sadly. Jimmie moves me a bit I rouse, "You know, Heather's not all bad. She just needs guidance, someone with a level head. She's been through a lot. She's used to guys treating her like a trophy instead of a lady. I don't think you've given up completely on the idea, and you shouldn't she's just not going to make the move. You are going to have to. She is used to men coming to her, she's not going to come to you. If you want her, you're going to have to be a bit more forceful.". Jimmie explains, guess he understands women more than he admits. Jeff sighs "You think I stand a chance?". "Not if you don't try." Jimmie says and sleep takes me.

24

Party Time

I wake up in my bed, the air is cool and the sun is not up yet. I look to the clock and a snoring Jimmie beside me. It's almost five, I get up and go out to make the morning coffee. Big day today, we'll have lots of company by this afternoon. Arthur joins me in the kitchen moments later, "Hey good morning! How are you? Sleep well?" he asks very enthusiastically for so early in the morning. I nod. "You? You're up early." I say. He smiles, "I've missed Ryan. Best night's sleep I've had in weeks.". I start to get organized, I need to make breakfast, put up the decorations, set out the food. "You go get dressed. Take a hot bath, relax, I've got the rest." Arthur insists. I do as I am told, I could use a hot shower anyway. I let the hot water wash over me, it almost makes me tired again. I put on my towel and go into the bedroom quietly as to not disturb Jimmie, but he's already up and out of the room. I wear a cute plain blue sundress I found on sale at the mall the other day with Deb. I braid my into one long loose braid and go out to the kitchen.

The house is already full of excitement. Arthur and Ryan are decorating with lights and flowers, laying a white cloth over our dining room table and Heather starts piling gifts onto it. Jimmie is outside mowing the lawn with Tyler on his lap. Ashley has the babies in the living room feeding them their breakfast. I assist her and then Jessie explodes barking loudly. She doesn't usually bark like that so I jump startled. Loretta and Wayne have pulled into the driveway. Jimmie gets off the mower to help them with their luggage. Jessie continues to bark until Jimmie snaps at her, "Down!" and she obeys. Wayne and Loretta enter the house and greet us all with hugs and kisses. Loretta fusses over the babies and Wayne and Jimmie head upstairs. Loretta, Heather, and I visit over coffee while Jimmie takes Wayne around the house and then the two of them head outside. Ryan and Arthur's decorating is finished and Arthur continues setting out some of the food I had prepared. Ryan leaves, I wonder where he's running off to. Liz, Donna, and Shawn arrive with their children in tow. They are followed by John and Deb, Jeff, and Jimmie's Aunt. We all eat, chat, and drink. Ryan returns with several sandwich trays made from the local deli and a cake. The party continues until Heather taps her glass with her spoon. "It's time for gifts!" she announces. Jimmie and I take our seats and begin opening the seemingly endless pile of gifts. We receive a crock pot, a new set of dishes, a very nice family Bible from Liz, a bunch of household stuff, towels, etc. Then the embarrassing gifts a set of flavored massage oils from Shawn and Donna, Jimmie rolls his eyes at this and Shawn laughs. Heather of course has bombed me with lingerie, some of it makes me red to even look at. Lacy bits of fabric and strings.... Jimmie also rolls his eyes at this too, but seems intrigued as I pull each one from its tiny box. I am embarrassed, my face is hot and everyone is staring at me. Heather is going to get it for this one. Each piece of lingerie brings "Ooh's" and whistles from our guests. Finally, Arthur hands Jimmie a large envelope.

He opens it pulling out its contents, plane tickets, and a brochure. "Peru?" Jimmie asks. Arthur nods "Think of it, swimming in the Amazon with pink dolphins, exploring Machu Picchu, touring the jungle. It's all arranged. You'll be staying in my family's guest house." He explains. That does sound pretty exciting. Jimmie nor I have ever traveled out of the country, and I've always wanted to see the Incan ruins. Perhaps Ryan told Arthur that I used to be very interested in the subject matter. "Thanks Arthur and Ryan" Jimmie says humbly. "Yes, thanks very much." I say excitedly. "You change your mind now? Actually looking forward to it maybe?" Ryan asks. I nod. I look over the brochure of Machu Picchu. "Plus you'll have a night layover in Cancun, you two can walk the beach and stay at my parents private beach house." Arthur continues. "Jealous!" Donna says playfully. Shawn nods and comes over looking at the brochure from behind me. "That is so cool. Man, you're marrying well." He jokes to Jimmie. The gifts all opened, I thank everyone and they continue to eat while I take my clothing gifts to the bedroom. Jimmie helps me carry things in, once in our room he shuts and locks the door. He walks to me quickly throwing his load on the floor. "You know. I can't wait to get you alone. Maybe convince you to try on some of that lingerie." He whispers as he holds me tightly against him. I snuff "Please, that stuff wouldn't last two seconds.". He smiles and kisses my neck, "You're right, it'd look better on the floor. But hey it's our honeymoon right?" he says. I nod "I've always wanted to see Machu Picchu, I studied the Incas in school, weird how they just disappeared. I can't wait to see it." I admit. He smiles again, I know I have been less than enthusiastic about the honeymoon and the wedding. "Come on, you better change, almost time

179

to get going." He says as he playfully pats my butt. He leaves and I put on some jeans and a little tank top, with a plaid button up shirt over it. I return to our guests moments later. Heather has disappeared probably to get ready. Loretta says "Oh no, not tonight girl, your sister's got your outfit in the bathroom for you. You are the bride. You can't wear that.". Great I stomp into the bathroom to find Heather and her choice of outfits for me. I change putting on the jeans that are so tight I can't breathe, but they do look good, and the little t shirt that barely fits me. Really? I have to wear this? "It's too small" I say. She shakes her head "No, it's supposed to be like that, it's just a little skin. You've got a great body you should show it off!" Heather jokes and then starts putting makeup on me. That's when I notice we are wearing the same outfit. "There. All done. You ready." She says pulling my hair out of it's braid. I nod and follow her out of the bathroom to find Deb and Donna are dressed in the same jeans and white tight t shirts. The guys are all wearing jeans and black t shirts. They must have had this all planned. Oliver pulls in with the tractor and wagon. I quickly go over my list of routines with Liz and Ashley. "Come on!". Heather whines. I kiss the boys and Ashley quickly before heading out to the wagon.

Oliver's tractor is an International 886. He's pulling a large hay wagon with side rails on it. The men have loaded up coolers full of beer and are all siting on bales drinking. I have to laugh as Heather climbs on taking Ryan's hand, she's wearing heeled cowboy boots. She is so out of her element, but she's trying. "Here, I got these for you gals. Nothing says sexy like a cowboy hat." Dad jokes as he tosses Heather a bag full of hats. Deb and Donna put there's on. Donna is positively beaming. I know she's been looking forward to this for sometime. Heather puts on her hat and Arthur gives her a thumbs up, I put mine on and laugh before opening a beer. If anyone sees the load of us, they will think we are escaped from a mental hospital! Jimmie and Jeff sit at the front of the wagon, Loretta steals Deb's hat causing Wayne and my Dad to roar with laughter. "I'm gonna get my freak on tonight boys!" Loretta jokes to the two older men. They roll their eyes at her, I bet she was a lot of fun when she was young. Me, I feel so stupid. There isn't enough beer in all these coolers to make me let loose. Donna and Deb are gabbing and really enjoying themselves. Heather just sits next to me, drinking her mixed drink from a large coffee cup.

It doesn't take us long to pull into Mel's. The parking lot looks really full, upon the wagon pulling in, a bunch of people probably twelve or more join our group. We all go inside and have our drinks, Ronnie has taken the night off to join us. A young girl is tending the bar tonight. Mel is already half in the bag, and he sort of leans on me and hugs me at the same time. Our group goes back out to the wagon and we continue drinking and riding onto our next destination. At the Waterfront bar, a band is playing on the deck. We all disburse and go inside. Loretta makes Wayne dance with her on the patio. Jimmie is whisked away by his friends from work. I stick with Heather, everyone seems to be enjoying this evening out. She sits next to me at the bar, Tony Jr. and his group of cronies are here. Tony waves a greeting. I wave to be polite. Then the bartender sets two shot glasses in front of Heather and me. "What'll it be ladies? They're on Tony." She asks. Heather responds "Fireball and keep em coming." The bartender pours our shots and we shoot them down in one quick gulp. Heather waves to Tony Jr. to thank him. He starts walking toward us as the bartender pours two more shots into our glasses. "Big Bachelor party tonight huh?" Tony Jr. says as Heather and I shoot down our shots. I pull out my money and set it on the bar, "They're on him, right Tony?" Heather asks flirtatiously. He nods, and I put my money away. Hey what the Hell? If he's buying, I'm drinking. "So, haven't seen you around lately, Jimmie keeping you locked in the cellar or what?" Tony asks me. "No, just been busy." I say in defense. Heather waves the bartender down for two more shots and motions for her to pour one for Tony as well. "To not being busy" Heather says and we all toast our shots. I know Jimmie has noticed Tony talking to me, and the last thing I want tonight is a fight, so I pull Heather away from the bar and out to the patio. I sit at a table near where Jimmie, Jeff, and the guys from the farm have gathered. I have to laugh at Loretta and Wayne, she's really a great dancer and he obviously isn't. Those shots have made me catch a bit of a buzz. Heather gets up and drags me to dance with her. Before I know it, Donna, Deb, Shawn and John are dancing in our little group. The band stops playing and we head to the hay wagon to find our next destination. We ride into the evening. It really is a nice night. Jimmie sits next to me this time and Arthur mixes Heather another drink in her coffee cup. "Do you got another one of those?" I ask.

I hate mixing beer and liquor, the effect is never good. I will stick with the liquor because I've had more of that, I didn't even finish my first beer. Arthur hands me another cup with a lid, it isn't as big as Heather's but it'll do. "Looking to get drunk tonight?" Jimmie asks me jokingly. "Oh, I don't know. Are you going to take advantage of me?" I joke back. He nods "Yes definitely!". Mel is enjoying this ride. He is so full of stories. He loves people and people love to listen to his adventures. Our next stop is a rough looking bar, I know I've never been to it before. The building itself looks more like a garage than a bar, the only clue it is a bar is the neon sign in the window. Heather and I look to each other questioningly, but follow the group inside. It sure is a small place, standing room only now that our group has come inside. A few of the bar's regulars sit and watch us carefully, strangers. Bar people don't like strangers. It isn't long before I feel we have overstayed our welcome and urge Jimmie to get the group going. One of the men at the far end of the bar is making obnoxious remarks to one of Jimmie's friends wives. I am sure this is going to turn into a brawl, so Jimmie agrees for us to leave. Once back on the wagon, heading to our next destination, we pass a patrol car on a side road. The policeman immediately pulls out and starts to follow us. He approaches the rear of the trailer and turns on his lights. Oliver does his best to pull to the side of the road without putting us in the ditch. The guys all hide their beer cans in the cooler quickly.

The officer exits his car, and walks beside the wagon. I recognize that it's Officer Reynolds. I wave and say "Hi there! How are you this evening?" Jimmie elbows me hard. "Well, what have we here? A little early for Christmas Caroling isn't it?" he asks to which Mel starts signing "Jingle Bells." Oh boy, looks like our party is over. "We're just having a little pre-wedding party. Our driver's sober." Jimmie says respectfully. Office Reynolds waves to Oliver, "How you doing tonight?" he asks. Oliver nods and replies "Pretty good." I am a nervous wreck, we've got to be breaking some law, I'm sure. "Well, I'm not one to rain on anyone's parade, but you've got at least twenty open containers, not to mention the trailer only has agricultural plates and it doesn't look to me like you are baling hay. But." Officer Reynolds pauses, "Because it's you guys and you really aren't hurting anything, I'm willing to let it go, I'm just finishing up my shift. I'm sure you guys are heading to Mel's. Tell you what, fair trade. No ticket for a dance." He bargains looking to Jimmie. Jimmie shrugs "Well, you're really not my type, but I guess if that's what will get us out of a ticket.". Ryan can't help but laugh. "Not you beefcake, maybe next time. I was hoping I could get a dance with the bride to be." Officer Reynolds jokes. Before Jimmie can even protest I say "Sure, it's a party right? Why not? We'll be at Mel's for a while. Thanks for turning the other cheek.". He slaps the side of the trailer and waves Oliver to carry on "See you guys later, and Congratulations on the wedding.". He walks back to his car and passes us before we start moving again. "Way to go Sara!", Heather says toasting her coffee cup to mine. "See, told you that cop was sweet on you." Jimmie says playfully squeezing my leg. "Oh, don't worry about it, it's just one dance." Arthur says. We ride and drink into the night on our way to Mel's. Everyone is buzzed and Mel starts a chorus of Christmas Carols. "It's Christmas in July!" he yells as we pass houses where people are outside. The onlookers looking at us like we are insane. This is going to be a night we will all remember.

Once at Mel's we go inside and Heather and I find some tunes on the jute box. Everyone is drinking, dancing, and laughing. Heather, Deb, Donna, Loretta, and I tear up the dance floor. We are having so much fun. Ronnie and some of Jimmie's friends wives join us and before long Arthur and Ryan have joined in too. A couple of slower songs play and it allows us to take a rest and refill our drinks. "Having fun Momma?" Jimmie asks as I stand at the bar sipping my drink. I nod, "Yeah you?" I ask. He smiles, "I never saw you dance like that before. You look damn good out there.". I roll my eyes, "Seriously, I didn't think someone could move like that to country. It's hot." He says and kisses my neck. I remove my hat and put it on his head and pull him out to dance with me. He obeys, smiling. We move in slow circles to the slower song and he holds me tightly to him. "I am having a really good time" I say, "Good" he replies smiling. I hope he isn't too upset about earlier with Officer Reynolds. The song over he puts my hat back on my head and we go back to the bar. A plain clothed officer Reynolds is sitting across the bar. He waves and the bartender puts two drink chips in front of Jimmie and me. "They're on that guy." She says pointing to him. Jimmie nods to thank him and I sip on my drink. Officer Reynolds gets his beer and walks over to us. He offers his hand for Jimmie to shake, after an awkward moment Jimmie does take his hand. "Congrats! Best wishes to the both of you." Officer Reynolds says. Jimmie responds with a "Thank you.". "So, how about a dance with the bride?" I glance quickly to Jimmie who seems to be all right with it, and then rise. Officer Reynolds sets his beer on the bar and I follow him to the dance floor to join the other couples. I am very careful to set my hands on his shoulders and he puts his on my waist. He seems to be leading me around, which is fine with me, because I hate slow dancing. "So, thanks for the cookies. Any trouble at the house?" he asks. I shake my head, "No, I just wish I knew where Tom was so I didn't have to worry about it any more." I admit. He nods "Well you know we're just up the road if you have any trouble. Any trouble with Mr. Personality?" he asks. I must give him a confused look because he says "Your boyfriend. I've seen and heard his temper.". I shake my head "No. We're great actually." He nods and we continue moving in our circle "Looks like he gets a lot of attention from the ladies." He says and motions so I can see Amy Pitcher, an old girlfriend of Jimmie's, hugging him at the bar. I do not want Officer Reynolds or anyone to see that this upsets me so I shrug and push the jealousy away. Our song finishes and I step back. "Well, goodnight Sara, congratulations again. Hope you two have a wonderful life together." Officer Reynolds says. "Thank you" I reply and then he walks out the door without even finishing his beer that still sits on the bar. I walk up to the bar and push between Amy and Jimmie retrieving my drink. I shoot Jimmie a look of disapproval and take my drink to sit by Heather. Seems she has struck up a conversation with a patron of the bar. I've never seen him before, I just know he isn't with our group. I see Jeff across the room talking to Dad and some of Jimmie's friends from work, I know he keeps looking over watching Heather talking to this guy. Every thing out this guy's mouth is a sexual innuendo. He's a jerk. Why does she always like the jerks? I push on her arm a little, "Hey let's get some better music playing so we can dance." I say and she nods in agreement. We stand and the guy says "Can't wait to watch you two back out on the dance floor.". I roll my eyes at him and pull Heather to the other side of the barroom. "Thanks, that guy was starting to creep me out a little." Heather whispers. "Well, don't just sit there and keep talking to him then!" I scold her. We stand looking at the list of songs and pick a couple. Deb and Donna scream as a new song comes on, they drag us out to the floor. We all start dancing again, Arthur and Ryan joining us. The creep Heather was talking to comes up behind her and starts dancing too. I keep pulling her away from him and he keeps following.

I really didn't see what happened, I just saw Heather pulling back down her shirt and then she turned around and punched the guy in the face. He stood there for a second and then burst out laughing. "Don't tell me your modest, I know better." He blurts at her. She is obviously upset and embarrassed. Ryan grabs the guy's arm and says "Why don't you get the Hell out of here?". The room falls silent, except for the blaring music. Everyone at the bar watching, Jeff, my Dad, and Jimmie come walking down to us. "Are you alright?" Jimmie asks me concerned. I nod, "Yeah, but this idiot thinks he can put his hands all over Heather." My father puts a hand gently on Ryan's shoulder, "I got this one son." Ryan releases the guys arm and Dad grabs him by the nape of his neck. The poor guy looks like he might cry. I would too if I had Jeff, Jimmie, Ryan and Dad looking at me like they are looking at him. Dad pushes the guy to the door and opens it for him with his free hand. The men go outside and Heather retreats to the bathroom. Not wanting this to be a night that everyone remembers because of getting arrested I follow the men outside. I hear my father saying to the guy "Now son, listen here. I come to this bar and I come here often. I don't want to see you around here again. I'm going to let you off easy tonight, because we're having a family celebration. But rest assured, I don't take kindly to men putting their hands on my daughters and next time I see you, well. You're likely to end up on a milk carton." The guy tries to defend himself "I'm...s s sorry sir. I was just k k kiddin around." He says stuttering. Dad towering over him, Jimmie, Jeff, and Ryan waiting for him to say or do anything to give them an excuse to rip him apart. "Get out of here." Dad says putting him into his car. The guy nods and starts his engine. "Shows over, back inside." Dad says to the guys and me. Ryan, Jeff and Dad go back in, Jimmie tugs on my arm for me to wait. I pause. "That is exactly why I didn't want us to have separate parties. You girls....." he says and pauses "Let's go have some fun." and then smiles at me. We go back inside. Heather seems fine, drinking at the bar. Jeff sitting beside her. He seems to be lecturing her a bit. I take my seat beside Jimmie sipping my drink. "Where did your friend go?" I ask him, he looks confused for a moment then shrugs "Don't know, guess she was hoping it was a bachelor party." He winks at smiles at me. "Ha, Ha, well just so you know, I was watching." I narrow my eyes at him. He rolls his eyes "I kinda think you're cute when you're jealous.". I punch his arm and go sit next to Heather to see if she's all right. She's fine just a bit shook up. We quickly recover and rejoin our friends on the dance floor.

The party seems to be winding down. It's almost midnight. Oliver motions for everyone to load up and head back to the house. We bid our friends good night and load onto the hay wagon. Jeff assists Heather up the side. We are all really drunk. Deb and John took off a while ago, Shawn and Donna left with them to go back to the house. Our wagon looks strangely empty with just Loretta, Wayne, Dad, Ryan, Arthur, Jeff, Heather, Jimmie, and I. The night seems silent compared to the loud music we have been hearing all night. We ride in the cool air. I snuggle into Jimmie, soon we are at the house and every gets off. We thank Oliver once again and then we head inside to turn in for the night.

25

Cold Feet

After the party our guests in their rooms, children sleeping, and the house quiet, Jimmie and I retreat to our bedroom. I am exhausted, and pretty well intoxicated. I undress and fall into the bed. Jimmie comes into the bed as well. He sighs deeply, "I really wanted to take advantage of you tonight, but I am too tired." He says and snuggles up to me. "Me too." I say. We lie there holding each other, "You're not getting bored of me are you?" I ask foolishly. He squeezes me "Not a chance.". After a long dark silence he whispers "You're not going to leave me waiting at the altar are you?" I shake my head. "Why would you ask me that? You're a goof!" I whisper back half laughing. He squeezes me and we fall fast asleep.

I wake before dawn, knowing we have guests and I can't go out into the living room I start going through our gifts from yesterday's party. I am not hung over to my surprise. I look through the brochure from Arthur and Ryan. I really have always wanted to travel. I am excited about the trip. I still have my anxiety about leaving the kids, and Heather. I feel conflicted, not sure what to do with myself I take a long hot shower. The sunlight barely peeking through the blinds, I dress quickly to not wake Jimmie. I tiptoe into the kitchen to make coffee and retreat to the garden to see how things are doing. I am startled when I open the door and find Dad sleeping on the deck. I go back inside and get him a blanket. I put it over him and he rouses as I do. "Hey kiddo." He mumbles trying to wake. "Hey Dad, why didn't you sleep on the couch? You must have been freezing out here." I say concerned. He shakes his head, I take the blanket back from him and put it in the house. I fix him a cup of coffee and take it out to him. "Couldn't sleep in there. Sounds foolish, but I kept staring at that picture of your mother and me...." he pauses and sips his coffee "I loved her very much despite what you might think.". I nod and sip my own cup "I know more than you think I do." I say and his eyes search mine. His face saddens, "Then you know too much." He reaches his hand out and takes mine. I feel like a child again, he pulls on my hand and brings me in to hug him. He is crying but I pretend not to notice, I pull away and change the subject. "Got lots of cucumbers. I'm going to make dill pickles." I say walking across the deck toward the garden. He follows me, "Sara" Dad says stopping me. "How much do you know?" he asks. I turn to face him "I know everything, everything that happened. I know what happened to Mom, what happened to me, what she did, what you did. I know everything. Mom told me, she told me everything before she died." I explain quietly my words barely a whisper. He nods acknowledging he heard me. "I am so..." he swallows hard. I take his hand again. "Dad, listen it's over. I am fine. She did what she had to do, as for you not understanding or not being able to handle it, well no one should have to understand those things or have to handle it. No one blames you, especially Mom." I say. He's staring at his feet, "It wasn't that I couldn't understand it, or handle it. I just HATED myself for not being able to protect her! Protect you! I was so glad that you didn't remember it, I wish you still didn't." He rants then continues quieter "I drank myself into believing you were all better off without me. I missed so much. I don't know how you kids could ever forgive that. I couldn't. You've all got more of your mother in you than me. All of you strong, smart, and damn good looking...." he laughs a bit "Maybe you get a little bit of that from me." I laugh at this comment. "I'm pretty sure we've all got your temper." I joke back. He laughs and messes up my already crazy hair and we walk through the garden picking cucumbers. When we go to the deck I see that Loretta is up, and she's starting to make breakfast. I go inside to help her leaving my father to sit alone on the deck with his coffee.

The house is up and full of people by the time Loretta and I finish making the bacon and sausage. We set up a buffet line for the breakfast. I make three pots of coffee before everyone has their fill. Jeff and Heather are acting strangely avoiding each other like the plague but exchanging quick glances at one another before anyone else can notice. My own mind reeling still from my conversation with my father. I know talking about what happened with him has upset him as well. His demeanor is different, it's opened an old wound and talking about it made it fresh. He is attempting conversation with Ryan, Heather, even Arthur. I know he genuinely feels that he needs to make up for lost time. I wish he could see that his presence in our lives is enough. It is for me at least. Jimmie is quiet this morning, must be hung over. After our breakfast, I clean up and the kids beg me to go swimming. I allow it, Shawn, Jimmie, Dad, Jeff, Ryan, and Arthur sit on the deck watching them. Loretta and Wayne come downstairs packed up and ready to get going on their trip back home. She comes out to the deck and whispers to my father who gets up and heads to his truck. He returns with a small wrapped package. He hands it to her, who in turn hands it to me. "This was your mother's, it's something old and blue." Loretta smiles as I unwrap the package it's a small white garter with a strip of blue silk around it and tied into a simple bow. Heather gasps at the sight of it. "I wore that in my wedding!" she says. "It was my borrowed, from Mom." She continues. "Well it's your borrowed too. I want it back." Dad states almost laughing. I hug Loretta and then Dad. "See you in a couple of weeks, take care of this girl Jimmie. Don't let her get cold feet!" Loretta says her finger pointing to Jimmie, I hug her and Uncle Wayne and then they make the rounds hugging everyone goodbye. "Well, that covers your something old, something blue, and something borrowed." Heather smiles at me. "All in one tiny little package" Ryan jokes. I smile at the little garter. I retreat to put it away in my bedroom. Having something of my mother's to wear at the wedding means more to me than I could possibly put into words. Loretta must have known it would. I miss my mother dearly and wish she could be here for everything. I wish she could see the boys, know that I finally found happiness with Jimmie. I know she is smiling down from heaven. Jimmie startles me when I am about to open the door. "Jumpy today?" he jokes. He moves closer to me, I lean into him, putting my head on his chest. He hugs me, it feels good. After this morning with my Dad, I needed a hug. "You alright?" he asks concerned. I nod, I am fine really, just a bit off today. "Your feet cold?" he asks, I smile and giggle a bit shaking my head. "Good. I'm going to buy you heated slippers." He kids. I roll my eyes at him "I'd be crazy NOT to marry you." I say. He smiles and takes my hand we go back out to our guests.

26

An Unexpected Surprise

The party over, our house settles back into a routine. I like the routine. Arthur is staying until the wedding, I don't mind Arthur being here. He's a part of the family. Dad spends every evening with us. Jimmie and all the men in the wedding spend the Saturday after the party fishing in his boat and then cooking them at the cabin. The guys bring their party back to the house. Dad and Jimmie make a bonfire in the yard. Heather and I join them after we get the kids settled in. She had made a joke earlier that our weekends are starting to resemble beer commercials.

Earlier in the week Heather had shared that she and Jeff talked a lot the night of the party. She told me that he came to her door soon after we all settled in. She opened it and he came in, sat on her bed and told her that the incident with the creep at the bar had upset him. He didn't like that anyone would dare treat her like that. She had tried to pass it off like it was no big deal and according to her that upset him even more. He told her that she was special and smart, beautiful and kind. She told him he didn't know her very well and then they spent hours talking about her. She spilled all her gory details to him, told him every lurid awful thing that she had done. She said she cried, and he just sat there and held her hand.

After she was done with her confession she said that she had tried to make a move on him, but he just hugged her and told her that it wasn't a good night for that. She is completely embarrassed by her actions and everything she told him, and has been avoiding him. Tonight though, she doesn't seem to care as she follows me out to the fire with her drink. Perhaps she took my advice, "let him see you for who you are, if he still comes around then he's worth it."

I sit in my chair watching the flames listening to the guys tell of their fishing adventures from earlier. I wish I could have gone. I am really nervous about the honeymoon, but I will enjoy being able to fish. I sit silently with my fears going through my mind. What if Tom comes to the house? What if Tom is hiding out right now in the woods waiting for his opportunity? What if he is watching and waiting for us to let our guard down? Jimmie must sense my distress. "You alright?" he whispers taking my hand. I nod. "Just thinking about stuff." I reply. I sit and watch the fire again, just holding his hand. It is hard to fear anyone or anything with him beside me. Before too long I am feeling tired so I excuse from the fire to go in the house to bed. I know sleep will not come for me. Instead the restless anxiety and violent dreams take up most of my night, denying me of much needed and wanted sleep. I wake several times before I find Jimmie in bed beside me. Just as the dawn is peeking through the blinds of our bedroom window I decide to get up.

Jessie and I go out into the garden and I begin my morning ritual of picking vegetables that are ready. I think I will make some pickles today. Once in the house I go into the basement and retrieve my mother's canning jars and her canner. I am washing jars in the sink when I hear a door upstairs open and see Jeff emerging from Heather's room. He comes down the stairs and sort of nods to me before using the bathroom. I smile to myself and start a pot of coffee. Heather comes downstairs smiling from ear to ear and blushes a bit before nodding to me. "Good morning" she sings. I smile back at her and continue with my jars. Jeff and she take their coffee and head to the back deck. I see him kiss her before getting into his truck. She comes back inside and instead of sitting at the counter and spilling out the details of their evening to my disappointment she goes back upstairs into her room.

I can't say that I am shocked, but I am surprised. I am happy for her. With a big day of canning pickles ahead of me, I busy myself with my own tasks. Trying very hard to forget about Tom, even if only for a little while. Heather eventually emerges from her room and although she does share a few details of what happened she insists nothing happened with her and Jeff other than conversation and cuddling. I think that's sweet. I am canning for hours, washing jars, prepping the brine, and making pickles. After lunch Jimmie says "No more pickles for a while, we've got to go into town for a bit.". I nod and finish up the batch I am working on.

Once in his truck I ask "Where are we going?". He smiles and replies "We've got to go pick up our rings.". We head into town to the jewelery store. The same woman is behind the glass display when we enter. She smiles and nods to Jimmie acknowledging that she knows why we are there. She retrieves two small boxes, she asks him "Do you want her to try it on?" and he nods. I offer my hand to her and she opens the box, to my surprise the ring inside isn't the plain simple band I had been fitted for. It is the gorgeous wrapping band with the two small diamonds on it. My eyes instantly start to tear up. Why would he do that? After everything that's going on with Heather and the finances. I feel almost shameful. I look to him confused and thankful at the same time. "You shouldn't have." I whisper my voice breaking. The woman puts the ring on my finger. It fits perfectly. "Now, don't get used to it. I'm only buying one ring so I figured it ought to be a good one." Jimmie jokes. I smile and push him with my hip taking the ring off and handing it to the clerk. "Thank you" I say staring into his eyes. How did I get so lucky? I don't deserve him. All he wants if for me to be happy. He smiles back and takes the rings from the clerk. "Let's go Momma.". He leads me out to the truck. Next week at this time we'll be in Mexico. We'll be married. I am still trying to wrap my head around that. Jimmie says I am the one who is full of surprises, well this was an unexpected surprise.

27

Guests

The Thursday prior to the wedding, our guests begin to arrive. Loretta, Wayne, their two children Lyle and Marissa, their spouses Anna and Brent, and their four children. Lyle and Marissa were my idols as a kid. I really looked up to them, they were much older than I was. Marissa was always very talented. Loretta had her involved in everything dance, band, chorus, soccer, gymnastics, cheerleading, and drama club. She was amazingly talented and intelligent. Both she and Lyle were very active in school and made the honor roll every time. I remember it being an expectation to live up to when I was in school. Heather and Ryan of course met that expectation, but I was mediocre at best. Lyle, Marissa, their spouses and children are going to be staying at the hotel in Jefferson, with Wayne, but Loretta intends on staying here with us. They also make it their plan to join us for meals and all the preparations that need to be done before the wedding. Anna is an interior decorator and is really looking forward to helping Heather with the decorating of the reception hall.

The house full of people, noise and chaos I find it very difficult to wallow in my apprehension of the wedding, the reception, and most menacing having to leave my family while they are still clearly in danger. I haven't slept in over a week. I know that the nightmares that plague my nights are a direct result from my anxiety about Tom. The fear, the unnerving unknown about his whereabouts taking all the progress, I had made in the previous months and throwing it out the window. I feel like I could pop out of my skin. My attitude, my demeanor leaves much to be desired. I am not playing the role of the excited bride to be. I am acting more like an inmate who is awaiting death row. Jimmie has tried to cheer me up, he brought me flowers earlier this week. He runs me a bath nightly. He holds me when I wake screaming, fighting, or crying in the middle of the night. Today we have too much to do for me to worry about anything. I am forced to smile and play hostess to our guests. Heather, Anna, Marissa, and I head into town to buy the shoes for my dress. Heather finds a pair that fit me fine, small heeled white satin shoes with tiny embroidered flowers on the top. Anna suggests getting lunch so we eat in the mall food court. I barely pick at my pizza. Heather is leading all the conversation talking about the flower arrangements and the gossamer and lights she plans to decorate the hall with. "You don't seem too excited about the wedding, everything alright?" Marissa asks me while we peruse one of the shops in the mall. Her words out of earshot to everyone but me. I shrug "I'm fine, I just don't get into it like Heather does.". She sighs deeply and asks "Are you sure he's the one?". I nod, of course Jimmie is the one. I love him very much, all my reservations are because he's making me go on this trip. Under different circumstances I would love to travel. "Yes, Jimmie's wonderful. I'm just really nervous is all.". I say hoping she is satisfied by this answer. She seems to be and proceeds with looking at the clothes on the racks. Heather finds me more outfits for my trip. She offers to pack for me, I allow it as long as I can pick out a few things for her to pack for me. She agrees to this compromise.

Later that night as we sit and visit around the picnic table Lyle retells an old funny tale from one of our early family trips to Pennsylvania. "Sara was like I don't know, seven or eight, she had a bed-wetting problem. She wanted to sleep in Dad's bed with Mom, and Dad was picking on her saying she better not pee the bed because he knows Santa Claus. She looked him straight in the eye and said "Oh Yeah well I know big foot!" Dad tried so hard not to laugh, he says "Well I got lots of big guns, I'll shoot big foot, and little Sara was such a fireball she sat straight up and put her finger right in his face "Oh yeah? Well my Dad's bigger and he's got bigger guns and he's the tooth fairy!". Everyone roared laughing, I don't remember that, but I don't remember much from my childhood. Jimmie loves hearing stories about me when I was a kid. Dad laughs along with Loretta and Wayne, "I am bigger, but you're older." He laughs patting Wayne on the shoulder. "You'd look good in a fairy costume.",Wayne teases. The evening continues with exchanging of childhood stories. All this nostalgia makes me miss my mother all the more. Her absence at this monumental moment in my life is devastating. The babies are teething and cranky thankfully, so I can excuse myself to the house away from everyone to have a quiet moment to myself. I give them each a dose of Tylenol, they each are running a fever and are really cranky.

Lyle and Marissa and their families leave heading back to the hotel. Aunt Loretta checks on me in the nursery before she heads upstairs to bed. "Hey there half pint. How are they feeling?" she whispers across the dimly lit room. "Just about asleep. They are cutting teeth, terrible timing for a wedding." I say meaning it to be funny, but she doesn't laugh. Instead she comes next to the crib and stands next to me rubbing little Shawn's back. "What's really bothering you baby?" she asks. My eyes well up with tears "Where do you want me to start?" I ask. "Well in my experience, the beginning is usually a good place to start." She says. "Tom" I say it's only one word, and it needs no further explanation. Loretta's blue eyes shine, "There are Tom Richards' every where in this world darlin. Some you can see coming, others you can't. That's part of living in a cruel world full of evil. I understand you're scared, and that's all right, but you can't live your life looking over your shoulder." I nod. "What else?" she asks. "I don't know, I guess I'm worried about Heather, I know I can't control what she does in her life, and she's starting to come around. I feel like I've lost myself. I know Jimmie has noticed that I have too. I don't want him to get bored of me. What if all of this is just him trying to do the right thing? I know he loves me, and I love him, but this wedding, I don't know it's just a lot to digest and now the boys are teething and I'm just tired." I say the words all very quickly. They just spewed from my mouth like rain from a cloud. "Children grow up, they'll be teething, then potty training, then they'll have school and activities, then college. You've got to have a life between all of that. They'll learn that it's OK for Mom to have a bit of a life and you will too. Because after a while, they'll need you less and less, and pretty soon you'll need them more than they need you. If you and your beau don't maintain that spark that you have, you'll lose it." Loretta's words always seem like a lecture. I nod acknowledging that I heard her. "I'm glad you're here." I tell her gratefully. She rubs my back with her palm. "I wouldn't miss it!" and bends in to kiss me on the cheek.

28

The Rehearsal Dinner

The rehearsal ceremony at the church is tonight at 5pm, followed by a dinner provided by Liz and Shawn at the same Italian place that Jimmie and I had our date at. Shawn insisted that the dinner be organized and payed for by their family since traditionally it is payed for by the groom's parents. I think all this tradition is silly and frivolous. I could have easily cooked a meal for everyone at the house for less than half the cost of a meal out. Loretta says that Jimmie wants everything with the wedding to be picture perfect, I know he does, but again I think it's all just a bit too showy for me. I don't even know half the people on the guest list, and I am sure if he was honest he doesn't either. I would have been happy with a simple wedding at our house and a nice barbecue afterward. Before we have the rehearsal, we need to decorate over at the Lakeshore Golf Course. Anna and Marissa plan to meet us there around noon today. I better make more coffee I didn't even attempt to sleep last night. I just lie in bed snuggling up to Jimmie hoping he would wake up and tell me everything was going to be okay, but he snored all night long.

Ryan and Jimmie are going to keep an eye on the boys while Ashley, Arthur, Heather and I head to the reception hall. I shower and prepare breakfast for everyone before waking Ashley. With all the guests in and out of the house, I feel like a cook, maid, and servant instead of a bride. I know my poor attitude is a direct result from not sleeping. I am hoping to get some sleep tonight. I would like my wedding picture to show a smiling bride instead of a half asleep zombie. There feels like there is so much to do, but honestly everything is all set. We just have to decorate the hall, have the rehearsal at the church, and go to the dinner. In the morning Arthur needs to meet the florist, I should pack Jimmie's bag for the trip, and my own as well. Again my nerves are getting the best of me. I quickly finish my cup of coffee and rinse my cup, I certainly do not need the caffeine. Ashley assists me with feeding the boys' breakfast and then she and I head out to the garden. I give up any prospect of doing any weeding today, or canning. I hope Ryan and Arthur at least keep up on picking the vegetables while Jimmie and I are away. "You alright Mom?" Ashley asks. I turn to her smiling trying hard to assure her as I nod. She shrugs "You just seem so....I don't know. I guess you're nervous. You shouldn't be, nothing is going to change. Everything's going to be great. You'll see." My daughter's words bring me little comfort. I know she and the boys' will be safe with Shawn and Donna. They won't let anything happen to them. I exhale slowly trying to breathe out all my negative energy. It helps a bit.   Just before noon Heather, Arthur, Ashley and I leave to pick up Donna and meet Anna and Marissa at the reception hall. Heather and Arthur have really out done themselves. They have every thing planned down to the slightest detail. Ashley and I assist a bit by putting some table clothes down and trying to arrange the crystal candle holders the way that Heather showed us. I have to giggle to myself because every time I think Ashley and I have finished a table Heather or Arthur come behind us and "fix" it. Finally realizing that our assistance is actually more hindering than helping I suggest "You want to go for a walk out on the pier? Pick out some spots to take pictures tomorrow?" to Ashley. She nods excitedly. Once we are outside we both giggle to one another "I think you read my mind Mom." she jests. I nod and take her hand. We walk along the pier and spot a few nice spots along the waterfront to take photos. Ashley finds a nice rock wall on the golf course. I think I might want to get a photo in front of that as well. Feeling we have spent enough time out of Heather's way we slowly begin walking back as they are just finishing up. The room is transformed. Gossamer with white lights drapes beautifully from the ceiling, all the tables covered with white cloths and crystal heart-shaped candle holders, and I can only imagine how wonderful it will look tomorrow once everything is lit and the floral arrangements are in place. "Thanks guys. You did a great job!" I say enthusiastically. The hour approaching four we head back to the house to get ready for the rehearsal at the church.

Jimmie seems anxious as we load the boys into the truck. Ashley jumps in and our family rides to the church in almost a nervous silence. Once at the church we exit the truck and go inside to greet the pastor. He explains each detail to us carefully. Jimmie and Shawn will wait in the room adjacent to the sanctuary. All of us girls will be in one of the rooms used for meetings downstairs. Our guests will arrive. Ryan, Arthur, and Jeff will seat our guests while the pianist plays soft music. Once everyone seems to have arrived Shawn and Jimmie will come out of the room, Shawn will escort Liz to the podium where Heather has arranged two smaller candles and a larger candle along with all the floral arrangements. Liz will light one candle. Loretta has offered to light the candle representing our family, Ryan will escort Loretta down, she'll light her candle. Then Liz and Loretta will join their candles to light the larger center candle. The bridesmaids will walk down and then little Britney will enter and throw rose pedals down. That's Dad's cue to bring me to the doors of the sanctuary. We have to stand there for a second or two then the pianist will play "Here Come's the Bride" and Dad will bring me down the aisle. He can shake hands with Jimmie or give me a hug or whatever he feels comfortable with. Then the ceremony is very traditional, and then quick as a wink we'll be done.... according to the pastor. It sounds like a lot to remember, so I'll just try my best not to trip over my dress or knock down any burning candles or anything. Jimmie has been holding my hand while the pastor explained everything to all of us. He squeezes it now just a bit and winks at me. I smile, I know he wants me to be excited and I am. I'm just nervous and tired. I hope he knows that.

We do one quick walkthrough of what we are supposed to do, and then we thank the pastor. Jimmie and our family follow Shawn to the restaurant. Once inside I see many familiar faces. Shawn and Donna have invited some of the people Jimmie works with and even my coworker Nellie from when I worked in the office at Appleton. The restaurant has arranged for us to have a separate room and a buffet. I actually am very excited about this because there were many items on the menu that I saw the night of our date that I would love to try. We take our seats and wait for everyone to arrive. Jimmie orders a few pitchers of beer but asks for a vodka ginger-ale for me. Must be he sees that I need a drink. While our family arrives and are getting situated he whispers "Don't worry it'll all be over real soon.". I squeeze his hand "I'm fine, I just hope everything goes as planned.". He smiles his little crooked grin "It will, and hey if it doesn't at least it'll give us a good story to tell later.". I sip on my drink and wait for someone to go up and start eating. Shawn and Liz do and Jimmie and I follow them. I am starving. I fill my plate and head back to my seat quickly. Once everyone has gone through the buffet, Shawn taps his glass with his knife. "Hey everyone. I just wanted to make a toast" he holds up his beer glass "To the beautiful couple. You took the fast and furious road. Here's to a lifetime of slowing down and enjoying life." Everyone toasts and begins eating.

The food is delicious. I haven't found one thing that I didn't like. Jimmie notices this and says "I think we've found your favorite restaurant." Jokingly. I nod as I stuff more of my garlic bread stick into my mouth. Finally feeling full, I start regretting eating so much. The thought hit me like a hammer between the eyes. Jimmie and all the guys are staying at Shawn's tonight, more tradition. It's bad luck to see the bride before the wedding. I'm going to have to sleep alone tonight and not only that but he won't even be in the house. My anxiety level begins to soar. Everyone else has finished and Heather looks like she's getting ready to leave. "You riding with me?" She asks. I look to Jimmie and he nods, "Go on home, rest, relax, I'm sure Heather will help you get the boys to bed. Try to get some sleep. I'll see you tomorrow right?" he says and then jokes at the question. "Yup, I'll be the one in white." I kid nervously. He holds my hand just a moment longer and then assists Heather and I with the boys out to her van. I thank Shawn and Donna once again for a lovely dinner. It was really nice of them to put that on for all of us. Donna hugs me tightly "Tomorrow, we'll be sisters," she says affectionately. I smile and nod. I wonder if becoming a Goodwin will make me be more outwardly affectionate over time. It must become less awkward at some point right?

Before shutting the door to Heather's van I hug Jimmie very tightly. I step up on my toes and kiss him. "Okay you two save it for the honeymoon!" Heather yells from the driver's seat. I stand there holding him, as if I would never see him again. As if some unseen force was going to suck him up into the atmosphere and he'd be lost forever. He kisses the top of my head "You going to be all right without me?" he asks. I nod and smile up at him "Good night" I say and get into the van. I see him standing in the parking lot kicking the invisible rock with his foot.

29

Our Night Apart

At the house, Heather and Loretta settle the kids down while I soak in the tub. I know I will not get any sleep tonight and I know Loretta understands the anxiety I have been feeling. I soak in the tub. My muscles still tense. My mind reeling in a thousand different scenarios as to the horrific things my imagination is telling me can happen. I know relaxing in the tub isn't going to work so I get out and dress in my sweats. I check on the boys who are sleeping soundly in their cribs. I walk to Ashley's door. She has fallen asleep with her ear phones in and the lamp on. I carefully remove them from her ears and brush her hair from her face. I turn off her light and am startled by a shadowy figure in the hall way. I gasp! "Hey kiddo, just me. Didn't mean to scare you." My father's voice says in the darkness. I walk to the hallway and follow him into the living room. "Jimmie mentioned you hadn't been sleeping. I thought maybe you would be up. Especially because he isn't here. Thought I'd stay here. Give you some peace of mind." He explains. I hug him, and he squeezes me tightly. It does bring me comfort to have him here. We sit silently for a long time on the couch. I begin to dose off, and I believe he is too. I rise to go into my room. "Going in?" he asks. I nod "Yeah, I'm going to attempt to get some sleep, big day tomorrow."

I reply. He nods "So do you mind me asking what's got you all worked up? Hopefully you're not having trouble with Jimmie. Are you?' Dad asks concerned. I shake my head "No, I'm just nervous, especially about leaving the kids and Heather. You never know when Tom might show up and try to kill us all.", I say almost sarcastically. Dad shakes his head and rises. He hugs me tightly again "Don't you worry your pretty little head about that piece of garbage no more. He's gone, I promise. Besides I'll be around, I'll keep an eye on the kids and Heather. You go in and get some sleep now.". He says very reassuringly. How can he be so sure that Tom is gone? "Besides, I've always wanted to go to the jungle. You'll have to come back and tell me all about it." he smiles and I head into my bedroom to attempt to get some sleep. Of course and not surprisingly sleep evades me once again, so I pack Jimmie's carry on and start packing some of my things as well. I leave the bags on the floor, I know Heather will want to finish packing for me. I walk down the hall once again and check on Ashley. I double check that the doors are locked and go upstairs to check on Trysten and Tyler. Everyone is asleep, except me and maybe Dad. He was lying on the couch, but I thought I saw him stir as I walked by. I walk back around to my bedroom and lay in my bed. I snuggle with Jimmie's pillow and finally the darkness takes me in.

My dreams are not my usual haunted violent visions. This time it's a jungle. An impassable cluster of trees and vines with large snakes and venomous frogs. Insects the size of Jessie chase me through the jungle and I keep tripping and falling. I am wearing my wedding dress and the vines catch and rip it as I struggle to become untangled. I wake with a gasp and sit straight up in bed.

I exhale slowly and try to calm my racing heart. The first light of dawn is creeping in through the window and my wedding day has arrived.

Dad is up when I go into the kitchen. He's already made a pot of coffee and he hands me a cup as I sit at the counter. "Cream and sugar right?" he asks. I nod and stir my coffee with the spoon. "Big day, you get any sleep last night?" he asks. I shake my head "I did sleep, but I had stupid nightmares about gigantic spiders and insects chasing me through the jungle. It was crazy." I explain. Dad shrugs "Better than psychopaths trying to burn you alive or worse." He says. I nod in agreement. "Seriously though, don't you worry about Tom Richards. I don't want you to even think about it! I will stay right here if makes you feel better, but I can assure you he ain't coming back.". Dad says lecturing me. I nod again. He seems very secure that we have nothing to worry about. Perhaps he's right. "You want breakfast?" he asks his tone much less agitated. Loretta pipes from the stairs "I'll make her breakfast, breakfast is the most important meal of the day.". Dad smiles "Well, we all know how much you love your breakfast.". He sort of chuckles to himself. "Yeah, Yeah Bill, I know. I'm fat. You're no stick figure there yourself." Loretta jests back at my father. Then she begins cracking eggs and frying potatoes. She sets my plate in front of me and I pick at it before I hear the boys crying from the nursery. I hurry to go and retrieve them.

"Let me get them for you. You go take your bath, I'm sure Heather will be up soon, You two have to get to the hair dresser's by eight." Loretta lectures taking Ryan from my arms. I had already prepared their bag for Shawn and Donna's house. I pull it from the closet and set two large jars of formula and several extra bottles inside. I have a huge box of diapers and an extra just in case package as well, along with several packages of baby wipes, baby shampoo, their chew toys, and all their clothes. I set everything together next to the door to be sure not to forget it. Then I head into take a hot bath.

Everything feels so strange. I'm not used to letting other people take care of my boys. I am sure Loretta is more than capable. I soak in the tub allowing the jets to massage my back. Heather knocks on the door from my bedroom. "When you're finished we'll get going." She says gently. I get out and dress in the bathroom. I can hear Heather packing my bag in my room. I wear my regular shorts and tank top. I might as well have a little normalcy today. Heather has laid my dress bag and shoes on the bed. The luggage is packed for our honeymoon, and all the dresses are loaded into Heather's van. "Do you think you packed enough clothes?" I ask Ashley as she sets her backpack on the seat beside her. She raises her eyebrows at me and says "Really Mom? They know where we live. If I run out of clothes, I'll just come home and get some. Relax.". I quickly kiss each one of the boys before getting into the van. Leaving Dad and Loretta on the porch holding my infants smiling and waving. I'll see them in a couple hours I tell myself. Dad is going to get Heather's boys ready he promised Heather he'd make sure their teeth were brushed, faces washed, and their hair combed.   We pull into the salon right on time. Heather is running the show today, so I allow her to explain how my hair should be. Donna and Deb arrive moments later. Everyone gets busy. Heather dominates the conversation telling the women working on us all the details of the wedding. "Sounds like a fairy tale" the woman working on Ashley says. My hair is rolled up into big rollers and the woman starts on my hands. She sculpts my nails into perfect looking fingers, and applies a bit of white to the tips. She tops it off with a clear gloss and then sets my chair back. She starts rubbing my eyebrows with hot sticky wax and then applies the tape. A quick yank and I feel like she's ripped my skin off. I must wince because she apologizes but continues doing the other brow. Then she applies cream to my entire face. She massages it in and then wipes it off with a hot towel, then she puts on a gritty feeling one, she called it exfoliation, she wipes that off too. Finally she puts on the final cream and sets my chair back into an upright position. She unrolls my huge rollers and starts arranging my hair so that it appears to be in long sculpted loose rings. It does look really nice. She puts enough spray in it I don't think it would move if I stood next to a helicopter. Heather comes over looking gorgeous, her hair in a fancy braid that starts behind her left ear and brings the entire braid to fall down the right side of her back. It looks great! Ashley looks so grown up with her hair into an up do. Heather nods to the woman that my hair looks good and then she retrieves my veil. The woman sets it where it should be, and then removes it again. She swivels my chair and starts applying my make up. Finally she attaches the veil into place with some bobby pins and swivels my chair to face the mirror.

I blink at first not even recognizing my own reflection. Funny what a little hair and make up can do. "Wow! You look amazing Mom." Ashley says from the chair beside me. I smile. I do look very nice. My eyes are highlighted making them pop. I don't appear tired, thankfully. "Thanks so much, you did a fantastic job." I say to the woman. She smiles "It's your day. Enjoy it!". Deb and Donna look equally as transformed. Little Britney's hair is done up in a pony tail with long ringlets she looks adorable. Deb loves being a part of the wedding, I can tell. She's super hyper and gabbing away. I love that girl. Donna looks so refreshed and happy. "We better get going" Heather says looking at her watch. "Do you want to get dressed here?" she asks sarcastically. We hurriedly get into our vehicles and head to the church. I see my father's truck, but I don't see Jimmie's. I hope he didn't go out last night. I exhale. He'll be here. Relax.

I go into the small room that the pastor had assigned for us. I put on the fancy white lace lingerie Heather had gotten me for the wedding shower. Heather helps me into my dress and then we open the door allowing Deb, Donna, and Ashley to come in. Loretta has already arrived with my babies. She joins us in the room while we finish getting ready. Heather looks amazing in her dress, her hair style accentuating the off the shoulder styles. Marissa and Anna arrive and come in. "Oh my God Sara!" Marissa says putting her hand over her mouth, and her eyes tearing up. "You look so beautiful." She says hugging me. Arthur comes in with our flowers. I really like the coral lily bouquets that the bridesmaids are holding, mine is bigger and has white roses around the outside. It's absolutely perfect. Heather hands me Mom's garter I place it on my thigh, above the cheap one we will use at the reception. Liz comes into the room, eyes teary. She hugs me, but doesn't say anything. Dad comes in and smiles proudly. He looks awkward in his tux, but very handsome. "Well" he says. "You got me in a monkey suit." He laughs. "You look great Dad." I tell him, my own eyes starting to tear. "Now don't start that." He says. "No, no bride has ever cried at a wedding before." Loretta says sarcastically. "Is Jimmie here?" I ask my father almost nervously. He huffs "Yeah? Of course he is. Been here since about seven I'd say. He and Arthur got all the flowers set. Looks real nice.". I exhale deeply again. Heather glances at the clock. "We'd better head up. It's show time." She directs everyone in her chipper tone. Liz, Marissa, Anna, and Loretta head out followed by Ashley, Donna, Deb, and Heather. Dad and I sit in the small quiet room waiting for the minute hand to tick.

30

The Wedding

My father takes my arm, and we walk out of the little room where we have been waiting. We walk up the stairs of the church to the foyer and down the hall to the sanctuary. Heather, Donna, Deb, Ashley, and Britney are waiting in line. Dad takes my hand "You don't know how much this means to me....." he says pausing to swallow hard "I love you, ya know.". My eyes begin to tear and I blink them back. Ryan nods to me and walks Loretta down the aisle to light the candle. Everything seems to be happening in slow motion. Donna, Deb, and Ashley walk down slowly. Heather enters the sanctuary, little Britney smiles at me and she begins walking down the aisle dropping the rose petals. Then Dad takes my arm again and we go to the doorway.

The sanctuary looks beautiful, tall lily and rose arrangements topped with tall lit candles line the aisle. Jimmie is standing at the front of the room, kicking the invisible rock with his foot, looking very handsome and nervous in his tuxedo. The pianist starts to play that familiar song, everyone stands, and time stops. Jimmie looks up his eyes locking on mine and I am almost floating down the aisle. My father must be holding me up because I don't even feel my feet moving. I just keep staring into Jimmie's eyes. They are the only thing in this room. Everyone has melted away. It's just he and I. All the things that we have been through leading up to this moment. My mind flashes through our best memories together, it seems to take forever for my father and me to get to the end of the aisle. My eyes still locked on his, Dad leans down to kiss my cheek and then give my hand to Jimmie.

I know the pastor is speaking, but I don't hear him. Jimmie's eyes locked on my own, we are lost in this moment. Finally the pastor asks me to repeat after him and I do. Vowing to love, honor, and cherish Jimmie to the end of my life. I take the ring from Shawn and place it on Jimmie's finger. Then he repeats his vows and places my ring onto my finger. No two people in the world have ever been more in love than we are right now. The pastor closes his Bible, and pronounces us man and wife. Jimmie leans down and kisses me deeply. Everyone applauds and I am pulled back to reality. There are at least two hundred people here. Jimmie and I make our way down the aisle followed by our wedding party.

We stand in a long line, shaking everyone's hands and receiving hugs as our guests exit the sanctuary. It takes forever, everyone congratulating us and telling us how beautiful the ceremony was. I see many relatives I haven't seen since my mother's funeral. Uncle Job and his children with their spouses and kids, Aunt Lydia, her daughter and grandson, and several more. I meet and shake hands with Jimmie's extended family. The line seems endless. Once everyone has exited, our wedding party goes out to the limousine Arthur had arranged and we head over to the Lakeshore Golf course.

Our wedding party stands and poses for several pictures in front of the water. We also get to take a few of just Jimmie and I. I can't seem to stop smiling, the wedding is everything a girl could dream of.

The DJ announces our wedding party and then James and Sara Goodwin. Our guest rise and applaud shouting and whistling wildly as Jimmie and I enter and our song starts playing. He and I take the dance floor and as I listen to the words, my head on his chest I think how true the words to the song are to us and our relationship. There is absolutely nothing in this world I wouldn't do for him nor him for me. No matter what obstacles stood in our way we would be there for each other. Our dance is not our awkward circling motion we almost seem graceful as we circle the floor and guests join us. It is a magical moment.

Our dance over we are seated and then quickly the caterer signals to us that it's time to eat. We start the line and soon everyone in the wedding party is seated again. Shawn taps his glass "To the best looking couple I know" everyone toasts and then Ryan stands "Sara, Jimmie I just wanted to say. I hope you have a wonderful life together. Best wishes to you.".

Our guests eat and drink and we all dance into the afternoon. Officer Reynolds and Kayla stop in and enjoy a meal and a dance or two. We do all the usual reception rituals, the tossing of the bouquet which Heather catches to my surprise, the tossing of the garter which Jeff catches, maybe it's fate? We do the dollar dance and there are more men in Jimmie's line than mine. Perhaps they all feel that it's demasculating to him, most of them seem to be getting a good laugh out of it. I dance with Uncle Job, Mel from the bar, and several other people. Finally my father asks if he can cut in while Jimmie and I are dancing. He looks at me thoughtfully and then asks "Are you happy?". In nod and smile at him, his face grows serious and he takes

Jimmie by the shoulder "You better be good to her. I'm getting pretty good at hiding bodies." Jimmie nods and laughs almost nervously. Bodies?? While we dance, I feel want to ask him so badly what he meant by his comment, I don't have to because as our song finishes he hugs me close and whispers into my head "I told you not to worry about him any more.". I look at him gratefully, he shakes his head and squeezes my hand before releases it and he leaves the reception. He didn't need to say anymore. I know he did what he felt he had to do. I don't know how I feel about the fact that both my parents are murderers...but Loretta's words ring in my head "Some secrets shouldn't be kept, but this one should.". I hear her voice over and over, and then Arthur whisks Jimmie and I away to collect our luggage and change in order to catch our flight.

I change into a little dress Heather got for me, it's very cute, a little blue sundress with white embroidered roses on it and flat sandals. I put my wedding dress into its bag along with the head piece then go help Jimmie who is trying helplessly to get out of his tuxedo. He's obviously intoxicated and keeps trying to maul me as I undress him. "We don't have time right now. We've got a plane to catch." I tell him anxiously. I find Loretta and my boys. I kiss and hug them over and over again. Then find Ashley and hug her tightly and kiss her on top of her head. "I'll see you real soon." I tell her. She smiles up at me "Have a great time Mom. I love you both of you. Enjoy yourselves.". Jimmie and I hug and wave goodbye to everyone and head out to the limo that takes us off to the airport.

31

The Honeymoon

We make it to the airport with ample time to go through the security check and board our plane to New York City. We have to fly to an international airport so we can get our flight to Cancun, Mexico. Jimmie has never flown before and I can see that he is nervous. He is sweating and his face shows distress. When we begin to take off he triple checks his seat belt and mine. We fly through to New York without a problem, thankfully, I think his head would have popped off if we hit any turbulence. We find our next gate and wait patiently for them to announce that our flight needs to board. "Here we go again." Jimmie jokes nervously. "It's just like riding in a car." I tell him reassuringly. He rolls his eyes at me and takes my hand as we enter the long hallway to board our flight.

I'm not used to being the strong assuring one with Jimmie. He's usually so composed and secure. The flight is really putting him out of his element. As we are thirty thousand feet above the Atlantic Ocean, we run into a bit of weather and the plane starts bouncing around a bit. It's really nothing to worry about, but Jimmie starts to panic. "What's going on?" he asks the flight attendant as she passes. "It's nothing to worry about sir. It's just a bit of a bumpy ride.". He will not allow me to unbuckle my seat belt and I know he needs a distraction. "So, it was a beautiful wedding, wasn't it?" I tell him more than ask. He nods and continues looking apprehensively out the window. The plane ride smooths out a bit and he relaxes a little.

We land safely in Cancun and as promised a man was waiting for us with a sign that read "Mr. and Mrs. James Goodwin." Arthur has arranged everything for us. The man directs us through the baggage claim and then out to his car. He drives us through the dark and busy streets, until the area looks much more prominent. Finally he pulls in front of a large iron gate. He stops and pushes a button on an intercom. "Mr. and Mrs. Goodwin." He stays. The gate opens and he drives into what at first I think is a resort. A huge fountain with three sculpted angels spouting water sits in the center of a u-shaped drive. A mansion like none I have ever seen is before us.

The driver stops and opens our door. Another man takes our bags from the car and we follow him to the door. It opens from within, another man says "Welcome, and congratulations on your wedding. I'll show you to your room." I look to Jimmie who seems to be in as much shock as I am. This place is unbelievable. Gigantic windows, gorgeous marble floors, a huge marble staircase that leads upstairs to where a balcony is. It would take days to explore this house and we just have tonight. We follow the man upstairs to two large oak doors which open to a suite. A large four poster bed with white curtains and blankets, a small couch, two overstuffed chairs, all plush red velvet, at the other side of the room is a glass door leading to a balcony. There is a hot tub on the small deck and I can hear the ocean. The warm breeze brings the smell of the salt. I breathe it in deeply. There also is a large bathroom off the bedroom as well. "If you need anything at all, just call downstairs and someone will bring it to you shortly." the man says and exits. Jimmie raises his brow at me eyes wide "This is their vacation house?" I laugh "I know for real? This place is insane. Good thing we decided to come. You and I better suck this up, we're probably never going to see it again." I say in disbelief of the luxury before me. Jimmie flops onto the bed and sits up on his elbow. "So Mama? How about we start our honeymoon?" he says. I look to the bedside table where a bottle of champagne is sitting in a small bucket of ice, with two flutes beside it. I open it and pour a glass for each of us. "How about we try out that hot tub?" I say coyly and Jimmie smiles undressing as he heads out to the deck. I join him and we make love for the first time as man and wife.

Jimmie and I spend a wonderful night in Cancun before enjoying breakfast on the balcony of our room overlooking the ocean. We really don't have much time to look around the city but do catch a few sights before we head back to the airport. We board our plane heading to Lima, Peru.

Landing safely in Peru, we are greeted again at the airport terminal. This time a man and woman, are holding a sign that reads "Welcome Mr. & Mrs. James Goodwin.". We approach the couple and the woman hugs me very excitedly and says "Oh Sara! It's so nice to finally meet you! I feel like I've known you forever. Arthur has told us so much about you, well really both of you!". The man shakes Jimmie's hand "I'm Miguel. I'm Arthur's father, and this is Rita his mother. We would like to congratulate you on your wedding. Come. We must collect your luggage.". Miguel seems friendly but very proper. Rita is much more like Arthur very energetic and animated. We follow them to the baggage claim, and collect our bags. Then Miguel signals another man who takes the bags from us and we follow them out of the airport to their car that is waiting.

We get into the back of the car, and Rita joins us. Miguel rides up front with the driver. Rita asks Jimmie and me about the wedding and how we liked Cancun. I thank her over and over for allowing us to stay in their home, remarking more than once how gorgeous it was. She tells us all about the things they have planned to show us. We will go today to our guest bungalow on their property. She and Miguel are archeologists, but have made their fortune buying property and renting it to tourists and making arrangements for them to tour the surrounding areas. Tonight we will take a boat up the Amazon River, we will enjoy an authentic jungle meal and return to the bungalow. Then tomorrow Miguel will fly us over the Nazca lines, a must see. We will also tour Galapagos Islands and fish in the Amazon. Then we will head to Machu Picchu where we will stay in a hotel for the evening. The following day we will tour the Incan ruins. The last day we are left to do anything we wish to do on our own or with their guidance, it is up to us. Now that I don't have to worry about Tom, I am actually excited about this trip!

Jimmie and I spend most of our days exploring everything that Rita and Miguel have planned for us. We see exotic plants, birds, and fish I've never even seen in books. Both of us are in complete awe of this place. It is strange, beautiful, and exotic. Jimmie becomes fond of the local cuisine, he tries every strange dish he can get his hands on. I am not a huge fan of most of it. I couldn't get the grasshoppers down! I tried, but it wasn't happening. I stick to a straight fish-based diet. I call Shawn each night to check on the kids, of course they are fine.

The highlight of the trip for me, has to be the night. Jimmie and I enjoy several evenings where Heather's lingerie and lotions really come in handy. We are enjoying our alone time. We never really had any, and it's fun to get back to us. Before either of us know it we head out to Machu Picchu. We stay at a nearby hotel and head into the Inca Empire with a tour group. We explore the ruins all day and into the evening. We decide our final day will be spent seeing all the things we didn't get to see the first time.

Thanking Miguel and Rita once again we shake their hands and give hugs when they drop us off at the airport. We begin our long journey home. I feel refreshed and ready to go home. Jimmie does as well. I miss my babies and Ash. I loved this trip, it was a wonderful experience that Jimmie and I will treasure forever.

32

Back to Reality

Our plane lands in Jackson, I am anxious to get home to the kids. The trip was a lot of fun, but on the plane ride back my mind was drifting back to reality. What happened with Dad and Tom? Should I even ask? Should I mention it to Jimmie? What about Ryan, does he know? What about Heather and the boys? What would they think? Perhaps Dad thought since I knew my mother's secret I could be trusted with his. The problem with knowing things is once you know them, you can't unknow them. I push the thoughts out of my mind and back into their locked safe place. Jimmie and I collect our luggage and meet Shawn in the lobby. Ashley runs to me and tackles me hugging me.

"Mom! I've missed you so much! How was it? Did you have fun? Did you bring me back anything? Tell me all about it!" Ashley shouts excitedly. I hug her tightly "I missed you too. Yes, we got you guys all some souvenirs. I'll show you when we get home.", I assure her. Taking our boys from Donna, who I swear have grown since I saw them last week, Jimmie, Ashley, and I get into his truck. Shawn and Donna wave goodbye and we thank them again for keeping the kids.

"You ready to get home Momma?" Jimmie asks me. I am, the trip was great, but I miss my kids, my bed, my garden, and my routine. He knows this, he must have heard me say it a thousand times since yesterday. I don't answer him I just smile and take his hand. We pull into the driveway and I feel instantly relieved. Heather and the boys did fine while we were gone. The house is in a bit of disarray, but nothing I can't handle once we get back into our routine.

Married life is really no different from before, the only thing that is different is my name. My daily routine of taking care of the kids, seeing Jimmie off to work, everything is the same. Ryan returns to his home in Pennsylvania. Heather and Jeff are together every evening. Our life seems to be settling down. Without the nagging fear over Tom, my anxiety has vanished. Heather's disposition has improved also. Jeff is a good influence on her. She has started on line school, taking classes on business and accounting. She's also being more accountable for her children and contributing to household expenses.

The children return to school in September allowing me much more time to spend with my boys. I really enjoy being home with them. I make it a point to see Deb, Donna, or Liz on a weekly basis. I also continue to take the boys to the library for socialization, theirs or mine. Harvest season sets upon us and the men all become busier at work. One evening in late October Heather comes into my room "Hey, you awake?" she whispers. I sit up and pat the side of my bed "What's up?" I ask her. "Well... I don't want you to be upset." She begins and swallows hard. Whatever it is it can't be good, but I nod assuring her to continue. "Jeff, wants us to move in with him. He just bought a house just outside of Greenville, it's only about three miles from here. What do you think?

Am I rushing it?" she asks. Even though I know Jeff is a good guy, they've only been together a few months. But I also know that no matter what I say she's going to do what she wants anyway, I shake my head. "No, you two are great together. He's good for you. He's good to the boys. And hey if it doesn't work, well...", I say. "This is always your home.". Heather radiates a smile and hugs me. I can't imagine her living anywhere but in this house, who will wake her up for work? Who will remind her of upcoming events the kids have or homework assignments? I breathe deeply and exhale slowly. She's a big girl, I remind myself. She survived twelve years while I was in California. Her life is hers to live and mine is mine.

The house feels empty without Heather and the boys. I guess I hadn't realized how much of my time I spent caring for them. The hours while Ashley is at school and Jimmie's at work are filled with playful fun with my boys and cleaning. Sometimes I feel like I am forgetting to do something, only to realize that the house is just emptier. It's not at all lonely, I love being here with my babies. I do miss Heather. Jimmie doesn't miss her, or Ryan, I think he enjoys having the house to ourselves. One thing is for sure, there isn't as much laundry.

While the house is silent, the boys taking their afternoon nap, I am startled by the "beep" of the alarm. Heather enters the living room looking a bit ruffled. "Hey! I was just thinking about you.", I tell her hugging her. She hugs me and then pulls my arm to sit me down at the counter. "I just left the doctor." she explains. Concerned I ask "Are you alright?". She nods "Yeah, wasn't expecting this, but Jeff and I are pregnant." My heart sinks, but I try very hard not to let Heather see the concern in my eyes. "It'll be fine, Jeff and I were planning a spring wedding anyway. We'll just have a small service a bit sooner." Heather explains. I had known they had discussed getting married, but adding a baby into the mix complicates things. "Jeff is really happy about it, he couldn't wait to tell Jimmie, I had to practically beg him to wait until I told you first." she continues. Well, that makes me feel a little bit better about it, but I am still concerned. "Honey, you've been through so much" I say and pause "I'm happy for you, if you're happy.". Heather jumps up excitedly "I can't wait to tell Dad!", she says grabbing her purse. She hugs me quickly and then goes out the door.

The months that follow are filled with weddings and holidays. A quick October wedding, the boys first Halloween, Thanksgiving, and Christmas all hosted at our home with lots of friends and relatives. And while I can't say we all lived happily ever after, at least we did for a while.